Love's Wicked Wager

When the elegant and arrogant Earl of
Chievely wagered that he could persuade Miss
Constance Osborne to be his bride, he was
foxed with drink. Still, he had no reason to
fear that he would fail.

After all, no female had ever been able to
withstand his dazzling good looks, glittering
title, and lavish resources.

But as he soon found out, Miss Constance
Osborne was quite unlike any other young
lady he had ever sought to conquer.

And now it seemed the jest was on the Earl.
Not only did he stand in imminent danger of
losing his bet—he also for the first time
had lost his heart to a maddenly stubborn
creature too proud to yield to him, and too
enchanting for him to give up. . . .

"**Even better than Georgette Heyer . . .
splendidly vivid . . . like a breath of fresh air.**"
—Mollie Hardwick, author of *Beauty's Daughter*
and *The Duchess of Duke Street*

"**Milne knows her period, her dialogue is sharp
and sprightly, the plot quite lively . . . an
entertaining tale.**" —*Publishers Weekly*

Big Bestsellers from SIGNET

If you wish to order these titles,
please see the coupon in
the back of this book.

Borrowed Plumes

by
Roseleen Milne

A SIGNET BOOK
NEW AMERICAN LIBRARY
TIMES MIRROR

Copyright © 1977 by Roseleen Milne

Library of Congress Catalog Card Number: 77-5761

This is an authorized reprint of a hardcover edition published
by Coward, McCann & Geoghegan, Inc.

 SIGNET TRADEMARK REG. U.S. PAT. OFF. AND FOREIGN COUNTRIES
REGISTERED TRADEMARK—MARCA REGISTRADA
HECHO EN CHICAGO, U.S.A.

SIGNET, SIGNET CLASSICS, MENTOR, PLUME AND MERIDIAN BOOKS
are published by The New American Library, Inc.,
1301 Avenue of the Americas, New York, New York 10019

First Signet Printing, July, 1978

    1 2 3 4 5 6 7 8 9

PRINTED IN THE UNITED STATES OF AMERICA

One

~~~~~~~~~~~~~~~~~~~~~~~~~~~~

IN THE FADING light of an evening in late September, a job-chaise bowled through Salisbury and followed the silver ribbon of the Avon along leafy Hampshire lanes. Mid-way between Ringwood and the sleepy hamlet of Pipers Ash, it passed through iron gates and down a winding avenue of copper beeches to a stone-weathered Elizabethan mansion.

It did not require a keen eye to detect the flaking paintwork or the sweeping lawns and ragged flower borders revealing the head gardener's unhappy battle with Nature. The downfall of Monksford, as any local worthy would testify, was due to the straightened circumstances of the Osborne family, and not, as one might suppose, from wilful neglect.

In the oak-panelled hall, Miss Constance Osborne consigned her travelling cloak to the waiting hands of her footman, who also served as odd job man when occasion demanded, and struggled with the strings of her best bonnet, which had knotted themselves tiresomely under her chin. She was a tall brunette, with a neat figure that somehow contrived to show to advantage despite the unfashionable travelling dress. No one would rate Miss Osborne a head-turning beauty; indeed, she was resigned to hearing herself dismissed as 'a well-enough looking creature for five and twenty'; which plainly implied that Constance was not only on the shelf, but unlikely even to be taken down and dusted.

Connie knew this only too well, and although she tried hard not to mind, her pillow was frequently a silent witness to the bitter tears that would come, in the small hours, when she dwelt on the dreams she had been foolish enough to cherish, of a husband to love her and children of her own. What use Uncle Maurie making encouraging noises about her fine, dark-lashed grey eyes (which, could she have but realised, gave her looks a character and sweetness far superior to mere beauty). What use, when only by contracting a wealthy match could she hope to save Monksford from the bailiffs?

Gathering her skirts, Connie ran lightly up the broad staircase to be confronted at the top by her housekeeper, Mrs Reed, who had emerged from the drawing-room, bearing an ice-pail at arm's length and wearing a belligerent expression on her thin, sharp features.

"It's simply not good enough, Miss Connie, ma'am!" she burst out. "Servant I may be, but—" She dabbed affectedly at her eyes with a corner of white apron, and gave an injured sniff.

Connie groaned aloud. "Whatever is amiss now, Mrs Reed?"

The housekeeper's sniff became more pronounced and her cheeks purpled with indignation. "He pinched me! 'See to the fire' he says—and when I stoops to get at the logs, he—he attacks my person!" Her small eyes rounded balefully on the closed door behind her. "There's no respectable female as has any guarantee of safety with him in the house! How you manages, Miss Connie, I never shall understand. If he were a kinsman of mine, I'd—"

Connie took the ice-pail from the older woman's trembling grasp and set it down. "Sir Maurice is a trial," she agreed, sighing, "but I shall ensure that he makes an apology." She glanced apprehensively at the housekeeper. "Is he sober?"

"Is he ever?" rasped Mrs Reed, with a derisive toss of the head, causing the lace streamers of her cap to fly wildly in all directions. "Been soaking in it since his jaunterings at Doncaster. St. Leger! What manner of saint was he, I'd like to know, turning gentlemen into instruments of their own damnation!" She stopped, perceiving the fatigue in the girl's eyes. "Hark at my going on so, Miss Connie, when you looks fit to drop from your journey! Let me attend to those bonnet-strings what you be fangling, afore you break them proper."

She removed the offending headwear and rubbed Connie's cold hands briskly. "Dinner'll be served in two shakes. There were some as desired it early, but I says he got to wait till your return from Bath, an' like it!" She hesitated. "Pardon my enquiring, ma'am, but does little Miss Fanny take to the school?"

Connie smiled ruefully. "She does not! St Ursula's Seminary has not the most eager pupil in my young sister. She threatens to fling herself into the river, set fire to her bed-hangings—oh, every conceivable pet, you would not believe!"

The mild grey eyes clouded suddenly, remembering the pathetic, tear-stained face that she had left behind in Queen Square. And yet, what else was I to do, thought Connie miserably. Monksford offered no proper companions for a child rising ten, and what governess would remain to be treated to Uncle Maurie's determined philandering? It must be hoped that Fanny, with her capacity for making friends, would quickly recover her youthful exuberance and settle down happily in Bath. Better that she be there, if it should come to the worst, and Monksford had to be sold . . .

"We shall dine in fifteen minutes, Mrs Reed," declared Connie, resolutely, and, bonnet in hand, she turned towards the drawing-room, to seek out the second and more troublesome of her responsibilities.

Sir Maurice Pinchbeck was a squat, bottle-nosed bachelor, with protruding light eyes and an abrupt manner of speaking not unlike that of his hapless monarch, the mad and enfeebled 'Farmer George', whose temporal powers were now entrusted to his eldest son, the Prince Regent. In the sixty-odd years since being spawned, Sir Maurice had run the gamut of excesses, and now, in the year of grace Eighteen Hundred and Sixteen, was an acknowledged authority on wenching, gaming and the grape. Despite asthma and a bad leg, the Pinchbeck enthusiasm for a lightskirt waxed dangerously strong, presenting a formidable anxiety, which his elder niece could well have done without.

His gaming debts were astronomical and largely through endeavouring to settle her uncle's creditors, Connie had been forced to the brink of her slim inheritance. Since the death of their parents, young Fanny and she had been under the care of this amiable but exasperating being, who was the first to admit his demerits, and who periodically donned the hair-shirt, during which he would strenuously avoid the temptations of flesh and dice, imbibe a punishing quantity of soda-water and generally become so wretched-looking that Connie's heart would be smitten with self-reproach.

Hearing his niece's step approaching, Sir Maurice Pinchbeck shot out of the button-back chair by the fire and with practised agility, pushed an incriminating wine decanter behind the flap of the sofa table. Breathing heavily, he resumed his seat, planted an ice-bag on his throbbing head and affected uncommon interest in a newspaper advertisement for Mr Speediman's stomach pills, one box of which, it was claimed, would 'disperse the wind in a very surprising manner'.

Connie dropped a kiss on her uncle's brow and perched on the arm of his chair. "Now, Uncle," she began, trying hard to sound disapproving. "What is this Mrs Reed tells me about your being rude to her?"

Sir Maurice removed the ice-bag gingerly and snorted.

"Old cat! Bullies me, Conn—poker-faced creature! No sense of humour. Starves me—oh yes, she does! D'ye know, she actually refused—"

"To serve you dinner early. Yes, she told me." Connie twined an arm consolingly about his shoulder and uttered a sigh of contentment. "How glad I am to be home! Bath is the most exhausting city! To begin with, it was mizzling when we arrived and of course Fanny had left my umbrella behind in the Mail coach and—" She broke off, catching sight of the unfortunate decanter at her feet. "Oh, Uncle Maurie! And after what the doctor advised about port being bad for your gout!"

The renegade shifted guiltily, knowing the game was up.

"Feller's a charlatan—can't tell his phiz from his fundamentals." He poked a stubby forefinger between the space separating his two chins from the black stock at his throat and wheezed coaxingly. "Been celebratin', Conn. Stroke o' fortune—met at the race—nice feller. One of the Prince's party, don't ye know." His eyes, which reminded one instinctively of boiled gooseberries, brightened with suppressed excitement. "I tell you, Conn, things are lookin' up. That's why I had a little—*hic!*—cel'bration. The '92, you know," he added, regarding the ruby liquid hopefully.

His niece's eyebrows arched in unfeigned amazement.

"The '92? He must have been some personage to warrant your prime vintage!" She removed the port to the safety of the console table under the window, and sat opposite him, with an enquiring smile. "I should guess Tom Cribb at the very least."

Ignoring this saucy dig directed against his passion for the prize-ring, Sir Maurice sank farther into the button-back armchair, linked his hands over the bulging brocaded waistcoat and with the air of one about to impart stupendous news, announced, "Earl of Chievely—plain as me snout—stroke of fortune, eh, Conn?"

"The Earl of Chievely?" Connie paled. "What has he to do with us? I—I understood him to be in Paris . . ."

"That was last year, after Waterloo." Sir Maurice produced his snuff-box and extracted a pinch of Kings Martinique.

"Ought to read the *Gazette* more, Conn. Feller's the buzz of London—well blunted—hot for the women, they say." He shot his niece a furtive glance. "Agreeable to stakin' forty thousand—estate to be negotiated separately. Good offer, Conn. Can't hope for a better."

Connie eyed him fixedly, unable to trust her ears.

"Uncle—are you saying that he wishes to— to buy Monksford?" Her voice tailed off in a stunned whisper. "But . . . how could he know that such a circumstance was in the wind?" Sudden suspicion caused her brow to furrow. "Oh, no—you would not—Uncle, you surely gave him no reason to suppose that . . ."

Sir Maurice squirmed farther into the black stock.

"No secret," he muttered, defensively, staring into the fire, watching the logs crackle angrily in the old-fashioned basket grate.

"Confound it, Conn, he was heir to Monksford! Only natural."

"It is twenty years since Papa purchased this estate from the Chievelys!" There was a break in Connie's voice as she faced her uncle. "Their fortunes were at an ebb then, as—as ours are now. I appreciate the present Earl's desire to regain Monksford—his forebears dwelt here for generations! As you say, it—is rather his birthright, but . . ." She made a despairing little gesture with her hands. "Monksford is our home now, Uncle Maurice! With a few resources, we can restore it to the beautiful property it once was! I . . . I would do anything rather than sell . . ."

Her gaze wandered round the lofty, faded drawing-room, a wave of heartache engulfing her as she beheld the moulded ceiling, chased with foliage and anthemion relief, now flaking and cracked; the bright patches on the damask walls where several fine paintings had gone under the hammer at Christie's auction rooms in Pall Mall, to stay the mounting flood of debt.

And this, she thought wryly, is the most presentable room in the house. Yet who could tell how long before this ceiling, too, caved in? The closing of the north and west wings for safety's sake, three years ago, had proved only a sop to economy, and Connie knew that unless the building structures were massively strengthened, the long-term effect would prove disastrous.

Each week, the housekeeping budget was eaten away, despite her ingenious efforts at pruning. Providence, it seemed, took an unprincipled delight in cataloguing a chain of misfortune on Monksford. Dry rot in the fine oak screen of the Great Hall, leaking roofs everywhere and a range to be installed in the new kitchen in the south wing, all necessitating relentless inroads into her dwindling capital.

The closing of so many country banks in the disastrous aftermath of the long war with France had mercifully spared her, but the torrential rains of that summer had spelled Monksford's death blow just as surely, bringing widespread flooding and total crop ruin on the estate.

There were still the jewels Papa had left her. A diamond set, which, Connie surmised, must hopefully fetch a thousand pounds at the least. And Mama's rubies, winking brightly in their old-fashioned setting.

Sir Maurice's peevish voice interrupted these reflections. "Thought you'd be in whoops! Handsome feller—favourite with the petticoats. Brought a bit to the races—coquettish redhead, with big . . ." He moulded his podgy hands expressively.

"Ahem—deep-bosomed, y'know. Set me in mind of Maudie Spettigue—dashed fine gel, Maudie!" Catching his niece's quelling eye, he continued hurriedly, "About Chievely. Desires to drop by, Conn. You know the sort of thing."

"I know precisely the sort of thing!" Connie's fine eyes flashed angrily. "I daresay he has a notion to measure the windows and—and mentally place his effects! And you are mistaken, Uncle! I do read the Society columns—I am fully aware of the measure of my Lord Chievely! Why, every salon from here to Milan knows of his—his scandalous reputation!" Barely pausing for breath, she continued, with an accusing glare, "I warn you, Uncle, no amount of persuasion will induce me to receive a—a worthless libertine, who considers women as being created for his own sinful purpose!"

"Now, Conn, flyin' in a wax don't mend matters. Entertainin' feller, y'know—once swam the Hellespont in the buff! Fact!" He cackled to

himself. "Like meself at four an' thirty—fond of
his greens."

"*Uncle!*"

Sir Maurice had the grace to flush. "Beg pardon, Conn. Keep forgettin' you're not a feller.
Gut-foundered, that's your complaint! Have a
bite dinner and forget Chievely. Returned to
town. Meet him in a sennight."

Connie spun round. "Meet him? Who is to
meet him, pray?"

Sir Maurice got himself to his feet. "Why,
me. Did I not say?—Deucedly remiss—fogged in
the bean. Meet him Tuesday twentieth. Ac-
quaint him with your decision."

Miss Osborne's bosom heaved noticeably.
"There will be no decision to give, Uncle! Lord
Chievely has the grossest impertinence to con-
template any such transaction without having
the—the politeness to consult me!" Angry tears
welled in her eyes. "I—I cannot imagine what
possessed you, Uncle Maurie, to agree to such a
charade."

Sir Maurice did not consider it prudent to reveal that he had been gloriously spiced at the
time. He merely shrugged, declaring, in matter
of fact tones, "Chievely don't discuss business
matters with females—said so. Bed warmin'—
that's their stretch, he maintains. Best I tackle
him, Conn. Give him snuff for you!"

The odium of the Earl's machinations remained with Connie all that week. Her vexation increased tenfold to find, upon opening a
copy of *The Ladies' Magazine* over breakfast
one morning, an article devoted exclusively to
my Lord Chievely's sartorial preferences, with

detailed reference to his eligible qualities (thirty thousand a year) . With mounting irritation, Connie forced herself to read of his having *twice* partnered the Honourable Miss Sophia FitzWalter at Almack's and of how he had come dressed as Apollo at a costume ball given by the Countess of Jersey.

"Only attend to this, Uncle Maurie!" she exclaimed, in disgust. "It reads—'No personage commanded more lively interest than his lordship, whose God-like countenance and bearing established him a worthy counterpart to the Divinity of the Castalian spring'!"

Tossing aside the journal, she attacked a piece of ham viciously.

"Did ever you read such toadying flummary? Here are we, with any number of diverting subjects to command, yet women are considered capable of digesting nothing more profound than the comeliness of my Lord Chievely and—and the sum of his conquests to date! Divinity of the Castalian spring, indeed!"

Her uncle, who was nursing a morning head, inched open one heavily lidded eye, muttered, "Spring—ah—um," and extended a limp hand towards the chocolate pot. Miss Osborne left him floundering in egg yolk and departed to don bonnet and gloves. Ten minutes later, she was bowling towards Pipers Ash, in a pony and trap.

The hamlet, nestling on the doorstep of the New Forest, consisted of one straggling main street of thatched, stone cottages, with the blacksmith's forge at one end and the parish church and Crown Inn (known irreverently as Salvation and Damnation) at the other.

Miss Hepzibah Smith kept the one and only store in Pipers Ash and here Connie stopped first, to leave an order for aprons and black worsted stockings, which Miss Smith would pass on to the Manchester man when next he called with his samples of goods and pack-horses. Servants' clothing ready-made came less dear this way and Connie was not too proud to own the fact.

As Miss Smith copied the order into a thick ledger, Connie looked about her with an indulgent smile, at the chaotic jumble of merchandise on display. Not only was Miss Smith the local grocer, dry-salter and haberdasher, she could always be relied upon to stock rush dips and candles, brooms and beeswax, besides firkins of rosy apples and a delectable array of peppermints and black liquorice sticks, over which hovered swarms of flies in a state of frantic enjoyment.

At the Crown, which served as receiving-office for the district, Connie collected a batch of letters, scanning each suspiciously for signs of an unfamiliar hand. There was one, in Fanny's childish scrawl, with a great blot in one corner. Connie smiled, and whilst she fished in her reticule for the acceptance fees, she listened to the amiable chatter of Mrs Cole, the landlord's boxom wife. Mrs Cole was a great one for gossip, but it came, nevertheless, as an unpalatable shock to learn that the good lady was already versed in the details of Lord Chievely's negotiations with Sir Maurice, and so, presumably, was everyone else in the neighbourhood. Connie fought back her annoyance with difficulty, wishing she might box her garrulous uncle about the ears for his indiscreet bonhomie with the landlord.

"'T'will be a grand day when his lordship comes again to the Hall, Miss Osborne, ma'am. I recalls his Pa, God rest his soul, astandin' at this very door when I wur a slip o' a wench. An' young Master—Lord Chievely what is—settin' his nurse the dandy of a chase, an' him not hardly breeched!"

Mrs Cole shook her head and eyed Connie with approval.

"My, how we does grow up an' change! There be yourself, Miss Osborne, ma'am, grown tall and taking. An' there be himself, what's bin stirring all London in a tizz, by accounts!" Her round face turned pink with satisfaction. "A fine gen'l'man, ma'am, though I's warrant you don' need the like o' me to tell you so, him what's makin' plans for the Hall." She winked slyly at Connie, and repeated, with a pleased nod, "'T'will be a grand day for Monksford when the Master comes home."

Connie's fingers clenched in a rush of frustration and anger. It was not Mrs Cole's presumptuous match-making which needled. It was the natural ease in which the Chievely creature was referred to as the Master. No hurt had been intended, Connie knew, but the fact that it had been stated, and with such undisguised relish, brought a lump to her throat. They do not think of me as owner of Monksford, she brooded, forcing back a suspicion of tears. For Mrs Cole and everyone else from here to Ringwood, Monksford will always be associated with the Chievelys. *I* may not even command their loyalty.

Within minutes of her return, Miss Osborne

settled herself determinedly at her tambour writing desk in the panelled library and began scribbling for all she was worth at what appeared to be a highly enjoyable communication. The neat, flowing script covered the single sheet swiftly and when, from necessity, she was obliged to trim the tip of her quill with a penknife, a sigh of impatience escaped her lips. Finally, she laid aside her pen, read the letter through with a smile of satisfaction, then, sprinkling fine sand over it, she carefully folded and sealed the paper with wax.

Two

TWO DAYS LATER this same communication was placed on a silver salver and conveyed, with the breakfast coffee, to the bed-chamber of my Lord Chievely, within his bachelor apartments in Albany, off Piccadilly.

The valet hesitated before entering, being well aware of the presence of a certain young lady whom he had personally shown in the previous evening, and who, to his knowledge, had not been seen to depart. He permitted himself a knowing smirk. His Nibs could certainly pick 'em.

This one was the latest comfort, a piece by the name of Désirée D'Erlon, who was currently packing the boxes of the King's Theatre with her nubile charms as an opera-dancer, and who, according to the domestic grapevine, had already done wonders for the entente cordiale between the sheets of Mayfair. A talented piece, Mademoiselle D'Erlon. The manservant coughed discreetly and tapped lightly on the door.

The chamber was in some confusion. The bed bore visible signs of the previous night's threshing but it was clear by the books, brushes and other missiles scattered about that a blazing row had taken place. His lordship, wrapped in a black silk dressing robe, with an equally thunderous expression on his handsome countenance, was standing with folded arms regarding the bed's occupant, a dazzlingly pretty redhead, who was propped on one elbow, with the sheet clutched to her naked shoulders and whose green eyes smouldered with rage and resentment.

The Earl took the letter, dismissed the manservant and, somewhat mystified, pondered over the hand-writing before breaking the seal. Adrian Noel Musgrave Vernon, Eleventh Earl of Chievely, was tall and slimly built, with fair hair brushed into a fashionable Brutus, and despite Miss Osborne's hopes to the contrary, was possessed of humorous blue eyes, remarkable for their clarity, set in a face altogether too wickedly good-looking for its owner's benefit.

He read the letter through, then read it again, because he could not believe his eyes the first time, after which he burst out laughing and sat down heavily upon the chaise-longue.

"*Que t'amuse?*" demanded Mademoiselle D'Erlon, pettishly. "'Oo writes to you?"

"A lady," retorted the Earl, glancing up momentarily. "A species, *ma chérie*, with which you are not acquainted." He slapped his knee, then his mouth quivered uncontrollably and he dissolved into another gale of laughter. "Oh, my stars!" he choked. "It's priceless! The gall of the chit! How dare she?"

Still chuckling, he poured himself a cup of coffee from the Meissen pot on the bed-table and returned with it to the chaise-longue, where he read the letter once more. This time, however, a tinge of annoyance flickered on his face.

"Impudent hussy!" he murmured, softly.

"*Tu n'as pas répondu à ma question!*" declared his mistress, eyes sparkling jealously. She allowed the sheet to fall aside, exposing her supple, perfectly moulded body and stretched an arm invitingly towards him, but he merely glanced up coldly, the strong, firm mouth tightening.

"I requested you to be out of here ten minutes ago!" he remarked, evenly. "You really are the most tiresome creature, Désirée." Striding to a dressing screen he tossed out some articles of female clothing. "If you consider your prospects better with Lord Barrymore, I suggest we end our association here and now! In any event, have the goodness to be dressed before I lose my temper completely!"

The girl launched herself at him in a fury, her nails clawing to get at his face. "*Vipère!*" she breathed, struggling in his firm grasp. "You English! You are all alike! I—I am not to be used like—"

"Like the baggage you are!" finished his lordship, prizing her talons effortlessly from him with an exasperated groan. "I've given you a carriage and matched pair, have I not? And baubles enough to please a Turk! What more is one to do in order to express appreciation?"

"You tell me zat you wish for to marry me," said the girl sullenly, pulling a comb through her tangled curls.

"I said that?" ejaculated the Earl, genuinely astonished. "Lord, I must have been foxed!

Look, put your clothes on, Désirée, for the Lord's sake."

"*Non!*" screamed Désirée, stamping with rage.

Lord Chievely immediately strode to the wash-stand, caught up a pitcher of cold water and emptied its contents over her nakedness. Impervious to her hysterical screams he threw her a towel, saying firmly, "I am not the marrying sort, and neither are you. We are both too fond of our pleasures to turn them into duty, for that, my love, is what it boils down to."

A well-aimed shoe almost shaved his right ear. The Earl's blue eyes gleamed appreciatively. In one swift movement, he caught the girl close, his mouth seeking her lips with savage intensity. She fell back against the bed, and he followed her down, laughing softly. Désirée raised a hand to his cheek, her eyes no longer aflame but heavy with passion.

"*Tu me pardonnes?*" she whispered, against his shoulder.

The Earl gazed down at her, then his face darkened and he crushed her to him, their quarrel, and all thoughts of Miss Osborne's letter, temporarily forgotten.

A little over a week later Sir Maurice Pinchbeck, sirloin fed and hiccuping, found himself seated opposite my Lord Chievely in a comfortable niche of White's Club in St James's Street, following, with a rheumy eye, the replenishment of his glass.

"Your niece pens a confoundly direct hand, sir," commented his host, at length. "How old did you say she was?"

"Five an' twen—*hic!*—five an' twen'y."

His lordship's eyebrows rose fractionally. "You don't say? What's the matter with her? Don't she like men?"

Sir Maurice hastened to set him straight. The Earl grinned, dismissed the subject of Miss Osborne's letter with an air of amused tolerance and thoughtfully flicked a speck from the lapel of his superbly cut dark morning coat.

"You understand, Sir Maurice, that unless repairs are set in hand immediately at Monksford, it's all Chelsea College to a sentry box there will be precious little to salvage. You yourself estimate the masonwork alone at not less than ten thousand." He fixed his guest with a grim smile. "Your niece has not that sort of capital. I have." His jaw tightened and a hint of anger entered his voice.

"My attachment to Monksford is not the 'mere whim of a dissipated London smart', as she so freely labels me! There have always been Vernons at Monksford, sir, and well Miss Osborne knows it. But for that damnable reversal of fortune suffered by my late father, such would yet be the case!"

He rose abruptly and stood for some minutes at the bow window, looking out reflectively at the Corinthian pilasters of Brooks', opposite.

"It's simply that—I desire my children to know and love Monksford as I did—as I still do," he said, softly.

"Good God, Chively, not contemplating a netting? Dashed bad move, old fellow."

This interruption hailed from the lips of a languid-looking gentleman who had strolled over from a group at the far end of the Members' room. Everything about him proclaimed the bored aristocrat, from his heavily lidded eyes to the flick of his jewel-top cane. He was the perfect man-milliner; shirt-points, cravat were faultless and the shoulders of his blue cut-away were padded to an incredible degree, giving added exaggeration to his cultivated mincing gait.

"Hankering after your own stud, Chievely?"

The newcomer lowered himself into a leather armchair with meticulous care, and stuck a quizzing glass to his face. Lord Chievely called for another glass and introduced the gentleman as Mr Lucian Frome, pillar of Watier's gaming rooms and fellow-degenerate.

"My dear Frome, what is so objectionable about matrimony? For some, it is a highly proven remedy against sin."

"Dr Johnson called in unnatural," sniffed Mr Frome, inspecting Sir Maurice with cold distaste.

"On the other hand, savages swear by polygamy," mused the Earl, perfectly grave. "In my opinion, for a man to marry at all is an act of extreme courage."

This careless utterance, delivered with facetious candour, roused Sir Maurice from intoxicated limbo. Staring fixedly at his host, he belched majestically and at length, and stabbed the ornate wine-table with an authoritative forefinger.

"Thash your answer—ma'rimony!" Fishing in his pockets he produced a gold snuff-box, with a miniature painted on the lid. "Thash Connie—thash my Conn. Doshile filly."

"Docile?" echoed his lordship with feeling,

studying the miniature critically. "Hardly my description, after that scorcher of a trimming! I allow her eyes to be tolerable, otherwise . . ." Shrugging, he passed the box to Mr Frome, for inspection.

"I may command any woman I choose, Sir Maurice. I'm damned if I'll go on the catch for a vixen! And yet . . ." A smile dawned slowly upon his handsome features. "It *is* feasible, by Jupiter!"

Naturally, Mr Frome must be initiated into the tale of Miss Osborne's stubbornness. Sir Maurice, torn between loyalty to Connie and a heaven-sent solution to his financial problems, wrestled with his conscience and said nothing.

"Dashed if ever I was dealt such a scold," mused the Earl, eyes agleam. "But a touch of spirit in a bride is no bad thing. I am half persuaded to post back with you, sir, to look the lady over."

"Waste of time," grunted Sir Maurice, whose scheme, upon reflection, bristled with obstacles. "Conn won't bite. As lief bed down with Lucifer."

"The devil she would!" expostulated the Earl, incensed. "There are precious few women, sir, would dare thumb their noses at the title of Countess of Chievely!"

Mr Frome's air of ennui evaporated magically. Sir Maurice, unaware of Mr Frome's reputation for betting on anything, almost expected to hear him pant.

"Wager you eight hundred on her refusal, Chievely!"

"Done, Lucian!" The Earl called for the club

betting book, a determined sparkle firing his glance.

"Time limit to be Derby day, at the off!"

"Haven't a snowflake's," muttered Sir Maurice, dejectedly. He knew Connie. Lord Chievely, however, merely smiled.

"The French thought the same of Wellington's chances, my dear sir, but he trounced 'em at Waterloo."

Calmly, he refilled the glasses, remarking, as he did so, "The hunt is up, gentlemen. Let us drink to the Chase."

Before leaving town, Sir Maurice did his best to probe the Earl's proposed strategy but other than declining, upon reflection, to accompany him there and then to Monksford, Lord Chievely remained politely enigmatic. He let it be understood, however, that he raised no objection to Miss Osborne being informed of his designs.

Connie immediately declared that nothing, but nothing, would induce her to accept his lordship.

"To look me over?" she choked, furiously, nails digging into her palms. "Does he suppose me to be a horse? My heaven, but the creature has a monstrous nerve! To seek me in marriage as the means to securing a—a wager! How dare he insult me so!"

Half blinded by angry tears, she rushed upstairs and changed determinedly into her riding habit, a rather worn affair of dark green velvet frogged with gold. Her one thought was to mount her chestnut Firebrand and ride and ride, with no considered destination.

So Lord Chievely believed she might relinquish Monksford in favour of his hand? Connie gritted her teeth and set Firebrand's head in the direction of the river. As if she cared two straws for a title! The conceit of the creature bereft her of speech. Let him dare to make his approaches, she seethed. Only let him dare!

It was a blustery October afternoon of pale, fitful sunshine and scudding clouds. Connie reined her mount at the crown of a rise, her anger cooling a little as she drank in the beauty about her. Hampshire, that most beautiful of counties, was especially so in autumn. Below, meadows, hedgerows and winding lanes stretched in a giant panorama to the protecting gold and brown of the New Forest; to her left, the slow-moving Avon twisted silver-flecked almost to the gates of Monksford, its banks overhung with willow; and in the near distance the rooftops of Pipers Ash basked in the late afternoon sunlight.

Sighing, Connie urged Firebrand down the grassy bank, a dull ache at her heart. How long before circumstances forced her to leave this haven of peace and beauty? A year? Less, even . . .

No, she vowed, resolutely. I mean to continue fighting. Not merely for myself but for little Fanny, for all the individual families to whom Monksford gives a living.

Fresh indignation at Lord Chievely's high-handedness strengthened this resolve. Settling her deep-crowned black riding hat, she spurred the animal to a cracking pace over hedge and meadowland, encouraging him with soft words. Firebrand caught her enthusiasm and streaked like a thunder-bolt for Monksford, long tail flying, nostrils distended exultantly.

Crouched low in the saddle, Connie thrilled to the speed, finding relief for her pent-up emotions in the exhilarating gallop. They were approaching the house by the old north gate, once the carriage road, but now rutted and overgrown from disuse. Just as Firebrand sailed effortlessly over the high surrounding wall, a gentleman tooling a light curricle and pair appeared without warning round a bend in the drive.

There was no time for Connie to ask herself how or why he was there, for she was almost upon him. With split second timing, the gentleman swerved hard into the verge, but Firebrand's electrifying appearance in their path caused his greys to rear up, terror-stricken and even as Connie stared in horror, he was flung violently from the box to land heavily in the ditch, with one leg crushed unnaturally beneath him.

Three

~~~~~~~~~~~~~~~~

FOR ONE INTERMINABLE minute, Connie sat paralysed in the saddle, then she pulled herself together. She must calm the panic-crazed carriage horses, before they trampled the unconscious figure in the ditch.

Urging Firebrand forward, she grasped the bridle-rein of the nearmost animal and pulled with all her strength. The grey lashed out, wild-eyed, and the curricle plunged forwards, careering down the drive towards the open road. Willing Firebrand to keep pace, Connie felt her arms being dragged almost from their sockets but she held on grimly, though the leather was biting into her hands and she could barely see for dust.

After what seemed an eternity, she felt the straining horses slacken pace and come to a head-tossing, sweating halt. With a sob, Connie slid from the saddle and soothed the greys, feeding them the remains of the lump sugar which she always kept for Firebrand. When she was certain that they had accepted her, she coaxed them back along the drive to where the injured stranger lay, face upwards, on the muddy bank.

There was blood trickling from one side of

his forehead but it was his leg which most worried Connie. She was almost certain of its being broken. Kneeling beside him, she wiped the blood gently from his face. He was younger than she had at first supposed, in his early thirties perhaps, but what with the dirt and matted blood it was difficult to tell what he looked like.

At her touch, he stirred, his eyes flickering open. He made as if to sit up, then his face contorted in agony, and he lay back heavily on the grassy verge, with a stifled moan.

"I beg you will not attempt to move!" implored Connie, rubbing desperately at his limp wrist. "I—I greatly fear your leg is broken. You must have a doctor at once."

The gentleman's eyes focused on her half-wonderingly, and she could not help but notice how remarkably blue they were. The ghost of a smile hovered on his pain-racked countenance.

"Was it you who was riding that great brute of a horse which dropped from the heavens?" he murmured, but the effort of talking was clearly a strain.

"Yes, and I am most dreadfully sorry," whispered Connie, biting her lips. "You see, I—I did not expect anyone to be using the old drive. Oh, please keep still, sir!" she cried, as he made another attempt to drag himself on to one elbow.

"The gardener's lodge is only a little way from here. I shall have him fetch the doctor from Ringwood immediately."

The blue eyes lingered questioningly on her face. She saw the beads of perspiration on his brow. He was obviously in great pain but all he

said was, "I think you had better. This confounded leg's giving me Old Harry. It's—"

His eyelids closed and Connie saw, to her
consternation, that he had lost consciousness
again. Scrambling to her feet, she covered him
with a thick rug taken from the curricle, and
mounting Firebrand, she galloped frenziedly to
fetch help.

Grundle, the head gardener, was not available but his eldest boy set off at once on horse-
back to fetch the doctor. Connie pressed Mrs
Grundle into finding some strips of clean linen
and rode on towards the house to have a bed
prepared for the stranger.

When the doctor arrived on the scene, he
found Connie awaiting him. She had bound the
broken limb securely to the sound one in a
make-shift splint and was now engaged in
sponging the gentleman's gashed forehead.

"Well, Miss Osborne, reckon you've done as
efficient a job as ever I could," observed the
doctor cheerfully, after he had examined the injured limb. "We'll leave your splint just as it is,
until I may set it properly."

"Be gentle with him!" cried Connie in anxiety, as the patient was lifted carefully into the
doctor's cart.

"I—I never can forgive myself, doctor. It was
entirely my fault, you see."

"But what were gen'l'man about, ma'am,
makin' use of the owd carriage track, when the
main gates be at west side of house?" queried
young Grundle, scratching his shock of carroty
hair.

"I considered that odd, too," admitted Connie.

Lord Chievely opened his eyes on a room which was alien and yet vaguely familiar. It took him some minutes to recollect the events of the previous day, or was it the day before? All he knew for certain was that his left leg throbbed like the devil.

He was lying on a comfortable couch, before a crackling fire, and propped up by a mountain of pillows. His limb, splinted and heavily bandaged, protruded grotesquely from under the counterpane.

A cautious hand beneath the sheets produced the interesting fact that he was naked as Adam from the waist downwards. They had not given him a night-cap, thank God, but the cambric sleeping-shirt he was now wearing was vast, and might have been all the crack some thirty years back, though he privately doubted it.

His eyes wandered round the room with interest. It was not a bed-chamber, as he had first supposed. A fine grand piano stood in one corner, near the lattice windows which overlooked the terrace. Near the couch, on a Pembroke table, a burnished copper vase held an arrangement of vibrant beech leaves and rowan berries, their beauty contrasting with the mundane companionship of a laudanum bottle and spoon.

All at once, his memory clicked. Of course! This had once been the south drawing-room. Gazing about him at the undeniable stamp of shabbiness which not even the homely touches could erase, the Earl remembered how once this room had reverberated to the murmur of intelligent conversation, the gracious chink of tea-cups. An elegant, cared-for room—it had never looked this way. So this, he thought grimly, is Monksford.

The door opened softly and a girl entered. She was tall, with dark brown hair caught up under a wispy morning cap and her bearing was quietly graceful. By the stark simplicity of her gown he took her to be a governess or the like, although no governess had the right to such magnificent eyes.

"You are awake, sir! I am glad." Her voice was low, faintly apologetic. She took a tray of lint and bandages from somewhere behind him and set it on a chair near the couch.

"I am come to change the dressing on your forehead and . . ." She stopped, diffidently. "And to tell you how grievously wicked I feel at having caused your fall. You see," she continued, in a rush, "I was vexedly upset, on account of that odious Lord Chiev—" Instantly, she blushed crimson and and put a hand to her mouth. "Does—does your limb pain you wretchedly?"

"A bit," admitted the Earl, ruefully. He cocked her an impish grin. "I am in hopes of learning your name, else I must call you Bright-Eyes."

She flushed becomingly, looking thoroughly confused. "How rude you must judge me, sir. I am Miss Osborne."

His lordship sat bolt upright, like a man who has just sat on a nail, and let out a strangled oath as an excruciating pain seared his injured leg. The girl pressed him back against the pillows, her eyes big with alarm.

"Is the pain worse?" she exclaimed, feeling

his brow. "You do appear uncommonly hot. I fear the shock is not yet worn off."

"It's only beginning," muttered the Earl, closing his eyes in disbelief. God's teeth, he thought, can this be the waspish man-hater I've come to seduce? Covertly he watched her as she set about bathing and dressing his brow. This was no coquette, no Désirée D'Erlon, but there was frankness and intelligence in the fine eyes. It seemed hardly conceivable that this same piece had torn him to shreds in that sizzling letter.

He had come prepared to take the citadel by storm, to overcome her hostility with his usual, practised technique. Now, by an evil chance, this plan was exploded. With a leg in splints, he could not hope to deflower so much as a dandelion.

Nothing of these strategical headaches showed in his smile. "I have a faint recollection of your bending over me, Miss Osborne, like the Angel over St Mark." He extended a hand. "Musgrave. Noel Musgrave." No untoward reaction. Sir Maurice Pinchbeck had obviously elected to divulge nothing, praise be. The Earl's smile lingered. "Tell me, do you always ride in that neck or nothing fashion?"

An apologetic flush heightened her colour. "Did I give you a turn?"

"My good girl, I almost died the death of Alexander!" He cocked a wicked eyebrow. "Er—might I presume to enquire after my nether-garments? They were not much, but one becomes deucedly attached."

He saw her lips twitch, try as she might to remain grave.

"Well, you see, we had to cut your breeches off. That is, *Uncle Maurie and the doctor* cut them off," she added hastily, "together with your riding boot. You have a fractured tibia— quite a bad break, the doctor fears." She looked up earnestly. "If you care, I shall fetch a pair of Uncle Maurie's drawers—"

"Thank you, no!" put in his lordship, hurriedly. "I have given you a deal of inconvenience as it is. There is something, however. Might I prevail upon you to send for my valet? I left him with my baggage at the Monmouth Arms, in Ringwood, and I greatly fear the landlord will have him clapped in irons unless the reckoning is settled."

"Grundle's boy shall go this very hour," reassured Connie. Instinctively she liked this light-haired stranger with the humorous, quizzing eyes and not, she told herself severely, merely because he happened to be uncommonly good-looking. He seemed to bear her no grudge for breaking what had been a prefectly sound leg, and he could hardly be blamed for desiring to rid himself of Uncle Maurie's spare night-shirt.

She caught him regarding her with frank interest, and promptly set about busying herself with the contents of the tray.

"Is—is there anyone else whom you wish to contact, sir?" she stammered, feeling herself blush like a school-room miss.

"As a matter of fact, there is," murmured the Earl, smiling faintly. "I was on my way to Berkshire. My friend owns a hunting box there, and he will be expecting me."

Another black lie, but there was no help for it. She had accepted him as Noel Musgrave,

gentleman, which after all, was no great deception, for it was his name, if only half. He was
not certain that he enjoyed abusing her gener-
osity so blatantly, now that he had met her.
Damn, thought his lordship, irritably. Why
must she look at him so—so trustfully, with
those great eyes?

Connie fetched a pen and some sheets of hot-
pressed paper from the library and placed them
before him on the tray, drawing up a chair by
the couch for the ink-pot. The Earl wrote somewhat laboriously, for his arm had been bruised
in the fall, but his mind was racing towards the
possibility of another prime move. He decided
to try her out.

"There, Miss Osborne," he declared, sealing
the letter with a wafer and stopping himself
just in time from franking his initials on the
outside, as he would normally do. "If you will
arrange to despatch this scribble, I shall be
vastly indebted. Why—is something amiss?" he
queried, feigning surprise, and wishing, as he
observed her face whiten, that he need not feel
such a rat.

"Y—Your letter! It—it is directed to . . . to
the Earl of Chievely!"

Her eyes flew to his, registering something
like fear. The Earl noticed the swift rise and
fall of her breast, the immediate hostility in her
manner. Devil take her, he thought resentfully.
Am I some barbarian, that she starches up so
fiercely at the mention of my name?

"I perceive you move in exalted circles, Mr
Musgrave." Connie strove to regain her composure. "Have—have you been long acquainted
with Lord Chievely?"

"All my life," admitted the Earl truthfully, studying her tense features keenly. "We happen to be cousins. Flung to the miseries of Eton and Cambridge together. I've spent no end of amazingly carefree vacations with him, here at Monksford."

Ignoring her start of surprise, he pressed on brazenly. "That is actually why I came to be in your drive. Being in the neighbourhood I— well, I suddenly was possessed of an urge to visit here again. You are fortunate, Miss Osborne, to own such a beautiful old manor house." He looked directly at her. "Although I must say I find it disturbingly in need of attention."

Connie could not bring herself to reply. Mechanically she removed the tray and ink-pot but her eyes were misted and she could scarcely see what she was about. She felt a hand touch her wrist.

"Forgive me," he said, gently, making her sit down. Then, "I had no right to make criticism. It must be astonishingly hard to keep such a property in shape."

"Your cousin does not believe so," returned Connie, trying to keep the break from her voice. "Did he send you here, Mr Musgrave?"

The Earl hesitated. Ought he to cease this confounded play-acting and come clean? What was it about this girl that caused him to feel like a worm with every fresh half-truth? He, who normally had no scruples where women were concerned, was now actually searching his conscience—and all on account of a pair of expressive grey eyes. Chievely, he told himself, you are becoming soft.

He met her direct gaze with the faintest arch

of his eyebrows, a trick generally accompanied by a roguish smile. This time he was deadly serious.

"No one sends Noel Musgrave anywhere, ma'am! However, I shall not feign ignorance. It has ever been Chievely's dream to regain Monksford and I am party to the hopes he cherishes with regard to yourself."

"I imagine you are not alone in *that* respect, sir!" retorted Connie, coolly. "They tell me this mischief is the jest of every gentlemen's club in London." Her voice sank to a bare whisper. "Oh, why does he humiliate me so?"

"Miss Osborne, Chievely enjoys the reputation of a rake, but I know him more intimately than most." He regarded her steadily. "He has integrity and, I am persuaded, regrets this ill-advised wager as fervently as you do. But surely you realise how impossible it must be for him to retract now?"

He stopped, fearing her suspicions must be aroused by this emotional outburst but she remained perfectly still, the dark head bowed slightly, as untouched by his words as though he had not spoken.

The Earl found himself possessed by a strong desire to tip back that defiant chin, until he realised she was fighting to conquer the agitated trembling of her lower lip. In an altered voice, he asked, "Would it be so evil a circumstance to accept Chievely's hand?"

Connie looked up quickly. "Could I but respect him, no. But he is a—a bed-hopper! A womanising dissolute!"

She blushed hotly under his thunderstruck expression but determined to continue. "Much as I love Monksford, I had rather sell to that man, and go—than remain here as his wife!"

"Why, for the Lord's sake?"

Connie's lips trembled in the ghost of a smile.

"It is given to few, sir, to marry for love. I had liefer remain a spinster than accept the hand of one I so heartily despise."

"You are unconscionably prejudiced, my girl!"

Sheer outrage prompted the Earl's ejaculation, an anger charged more profoundly by her devastating honesty.

"Chievely is no monk! But you are wide of the mark to believe all you may hear or read concerning him! He loves this house more passionately than you can envisage!" His eyes flashed. "How the deuce you contrive to judge a man you've not even met is beyond my understanding! At least allow Chievely the means to prove himself. You owe it to Monksford, if naught else!"

Connie sat rigid, shaken by this unexpected reproof. There was a striking truth in his words, whether she liked it or not. Yes, she *was* prejudiced but never had she been made to appreciate the fact so bluntly. She cast him a cautious glance from under lowered lashes and found him doing the same, so that they were both obliged to laugh.

"Pope said most women have no characters at all," declared the Earl, ruefully. "If only he had encountered you first, Miss Osborne, I declare he would not have *dared*!"

He grinned approvingly at her. "You ought to laugh more, you know. It becomes you."

Under the disconcerting appraisal of those wickedly blue eyes, Connie's heart was executing the oddest skips. No gentleman had ever before regarded her in that impudently caressing manner. He ought, she knew, to be given a proper set-down, but she could only marvel at how deliciously pleasant it was to have those same eyes smiling at her.

She became aware of his voice breaking in upon her reverie and started guiltily, praying that these foolish emotions might not register in her face.

"I merely begged to enquire if your maid might find leisure to stitch a button on my shirt," he said, smiling apologetically.

She coloured, saying, in a flustered tone, "Oh—give it here, pray. I shall attend to it myself." Seeing the surprise in his glance, she added, defiantly, "I—have no maid, you see."

"But, surely—"

"I daresay you find that inconceivable, sir. But truly, I manage vastly well without." And if, she thought wryly, you were to inspect my poor wardrobe, sir, you would speedily understand why. She laughed at his incredulous expression. "And when I confess that Rose, the parlour-maid, manages my hair cleverly on occasion, you will doubtless be infamously shocked and disapproving. Why—here is the doctor come already!" she broke off, as a carriage drew up in the drive outside. She hesitated, as if about to add something, then turned towards the door.

"Are any of the retainers from the old Earl's time still around, Miss Osborne?" queried his lordship, suddenly struck by a pertinent thought. He saw her brow wrinkle in surprise.

"Gracious, no, sir! They are for the most part with their Maker or grievously infirm. I believe the only one to be acquainted with the previous Lord Chievely is poor Thomas Buxton, who used to be pot-boy in the kitchens. He took the King's shilling in an Irish regiment, and was badly mauled at Salamanca." Her eyes saddened. "He is to be found any day outside the Crown, hopeful of employment. He only has one arm now, you see."

"There are a great many of his like, I fear," remarked the Earl, soberly. He was disturbed by her intelligence. As a boy, he had enjoyed many a rough and tumble with young Tom Buxton. He wished he might do something for the fellow, but it would be nothing short of madness to arouse speculation by a charitable hand-out. He realised, moreover, that Buxton would instantly recognise him, should their paths cross.

"Do not forget my letter to Chievely," he reminded, as Connie prepared to withdraw. For the moment, Buxton must wait. Time enough for such affairs once Monksford was secure.

"Of course." She accepted it from his outstretched hand. "'A faithful friend is the medicine of life.' One must remember that."

It was stated quietly but with resolution, and if the Earl had been longer acquainted with Miss Osborne, he might have wondered, but his limb was aching, which rather dismissed the matter from his mind.

Four

〜〜〜 〜〜〜 〜〜〜

LATER THAT DAY, however, his lordship received
a visitor, in the portly shape of Sir Maurice
Pinchbeck, who lumbered in with a face as red
as a turkey-cock and a glazed look in his watery
eye.

"Chievely—we're done for!" he croaked, flopping into a chair with the theatrical flair of a
Kemble. He was evidently in a high state of agitation, for his chins were quivering. "Flush
hit—straight to the muzzler—Conn!" A dejected
groan escaped him. "No right. Constipates me
bowels."

The Earl's face was a study, try as he might
to remain solemn. Sir Maurice, perceiving that
the urgency of his message was not registering
as it ought, tried again.

"Shock. Goes for me privates," he confided,
mopping his perspiring forehead with a large
handkerchief. "Now, see here, Chievely—we're
in a hobble. Christmastide—spend here—you—
that is, Chievely! Burn me, what a fangle, this
names business of yours is!" He goggled tragi-
cally at the Earl. "And we're out of calomel."

"Are you saying that an invitation has been
issued to Lord Chievely—to me?" gasped his
lordship, appalled.

Sir Maurice swivelled a pale eyeball in his direction.

"Conn got some bee in her bonnet—dull for you here—no fittin' company." His expression assumed the intent, accusing glare of a stuffed frog. "Says *you* told her—bigotry-blindin' her to what's right!"

"My sweet heaven, so I did—in a way!" muttered the Earl, scarcely hearing, so aghast was he at this turn of events. Here was a pretty mess! Lord Chievely was to be received, albeit with distaste—and on account of his very persuasion, no less. But how in blazes, pondered the Earl, do I hope to achieve anything for Monksford, unless I may continue to gain her confidence as Musgrave? And how is Musgrave to be sustained when Chievely is expected to turn up, in the outside of a month, on two sound pins?

He put the problem to his valet that evening, after having racked his brain unsuccessfully through the rigours of a blanket-bath and shave. Benson was a suave, rigidly correct specimen, the perfect gentleman's gentleman. He moreover possessed an astonishing aptitude for intelligent thought, when the need arose. The Earl's need was immediate.

"Do you realise, Benson," he groaned, struggling into a freshly laundered shirt. "I spend my entire life like a—a blasted razor, either in hot water or a scrape! As though I am not deeply enough involved with the little D'Erlon, I have to plunge headlong into a farce even more diabolical! Well, you must extricate me, Benson, and soon!"

"Very good, my lord." Methodically, Benson re-buttoned the silk shirt which his lordship, in the anxiety of the moment, had done up in the wrong buttonholes. "Is it to be the willow green cravat, m'lord, or the white?"

"The white, man. I am expecting Miss Osborne. And you are not to address me as my lord whilst we are under this roof! Servants have a reprehensible habit of eavesdropping at keyholes, Benson. We cannot afford to have suspicions aroused."

He forced his chin heavenwards while the valet perfected the starched muslin into an octagon fold and pinned a single diamond discreetly to the finished work.

Benson removed the towel and basin of water and handed the Earl his favourite cologne. Only then, did he condescend to turn his mind to lesser matters.

"Are we to understand—ahem—sir, that it is absolutely of the essence for this invitation to be accepted?"

The Earl pondered this aspect. "I do not see the means of avoiding it, Benson. Every salon in town is tattling with this confounded wager, to say nothing of the stews! Frome assures me that bets are being laid on its outcome at Watier's!"

"So publicly declared an intention of matrimony must naturally excite speculation—doubly so when your lordship's widely held views on the subject were known to be warmly against!"

Benson sniffed pointedly. His own opinions on holy wedlock were unsparing, and his lordship's proposed entry into that state smacked, to the valet, of deliberate treachery.

Lord Chievely glared. "There are times, Benson, when I marvel that we contrive to rub along so well as we do." He pursed his lips in vexation. "Miss Osborne will expect me to jump at this Christmastide business! She swallowed that damnable cousin stuff so beautifully that she's bound to be suspicious if I do not turn up! Besides, it must be the most abominable slight to refuse! I will not countenance it!"

"Have we considered, sir, the possibilities of Mr Sibbald?"

"Sibbie?" The Earl looked wholly astonished. "I do not altogether follow, Benson. Sibbie's pledged to saving rustic souls in Wivelsham. And he don't have any possibilities that I know of."

The valet coughed discreetly. "If I may point out, sir, Mr Sibbald may be our only—ahem—path to salvation. Naturally, he does not possess your lordship's grace of expression, but—"

"But of course! Benson, you are a genius!"

A beatific smile engulfed the Earl's countenance. "He's uncommonly abstemious and not over-bright in the upper works but . . . Lord, it'll not serve!" He groaned aloud. "Sibbie wants to be Archbishop one day, Benson. Against his principles."

"Mr Sibbald is your lordship's first cousin."

"Ties of blood are no guarantee—an ambitious curate is a sensitive animal." He pondered deeply, arms folded across his chest. "No, it must be the poor-box! Cousinly gratitude will fall like manna if I fork in the blunt. And after all, no one can call that an outright bribe." He began to look more cheerful.

"Is Miss Osborne's invitation despatched to Albany, do you know?"

"I understand, sir, it has been directed to the same destination as the letter which your lordship penned—ahem—to your lordship's self."

Benson's left eyebrow elevated, as only he knew how.

"That was merely for the look of the affair!" returned Lord Chievely, piqued by the valet's attitude. "You shall post to Wivelsham at first light, Benson. When you arrive, lay the ground well—compliment Sibbie on those sermons of his. Then weigh in with the facer. . . . Now, don't assume your undertaker's countenance, man!—I shall furnish a letter of explanation. And most importantly—not a word of this to anyone! Impress that fact into his skull, for Sibbie's such a gaby, he's liable to spill the juice!"

"And—ahem—should the possibility arise that Mr Sibbald feels unable to oblige your lordship?" Benson lifted both eyebrows, a sure sign of his vexation. He was exceedingly proud of his station in the Earl's household, and posting about the Somerset countryside was well beneath his ideas of the duties of a gentleman's gentleman. His master, however, was of a less discriminating disposition.

"I shall instruct Child's bank to release two hundred pounds," decided Lord Chievely, turning his attention to an old copy of the *Annual Register* which lay within stretching distance on the table. "That ought to brighten the eye of Sibbie's bishop. And you had best have Sir Maurice see me right away, Benson. He must be primed to play along with our masquerade."

When Connie revealed her plan of hospitality later that evening, the Earl was consequently able to express genuine satisfaction, visualising entertainment of no common order in the weeks ahead. He prevailed upon her to play a little on the piano and even persuaded her to sing for him. Connie's voice was not strong, but it had an appealing sweetness and he listened attentively as she bent over the instrument, accompanying herself to the simple ballads that she knew best.

"You must promise to sing for me another evening," he smiled, when she had slipped back to her retreat in the wingchair. "Now I hope you mean to tell me about yourself."

Under his gentle insistence, Connie found herself unburdening to him the crushing problem of running Monksford, the extent of its deterioration and the seeming hopelessness of ever being able to restore it. She told him frankly of Sir Maurice's debts and his weakness for wine but there was remarkably little bitterness in her tone.

Listening to her talking, the Earl felt a surge of anger and contempt for her whining, drink-fuddled relative, who was nothing but a parasite sponging on her resources and good nature.

He enquired the estate's annual income and was sobered by her reply. The problem, she explained, was poor drainage, due to the low-lying nature of the fields. Flooding had been a curse in his father's time also, he remembered, but the damage would hit her income harder. Something must be done, and soon.

She talked of the tenant farmers and her reluctance to ask for a higher rent.

"Times are hard enough for them. The scarcity of wheat has almost doubled the price of a quartern loaf. As for the cottagers, with their little ones to feed . . ." She sighed. "I encourage them to grow vegetables, and give what I am able, of course, in the way of fruit and meats from the larder, but bread and potatoes is the most any of them sit down to through the week." A worried frown creased her brow. "One feels responsible—especially towards the widows and elderly. Why, Mrs Beals tells me—"

"Good Lord! Is she still alive?" ejaculated the Earl, caught off-guard. "She must be edging ninety!"

"How in the world do you know of Mrs Beales?" exclaimed Connie, wide-eyed. It was incredible that he should be familiar with the name of the estate's most far-flung dependant.

"I—er—I have heard Chievely mention her," rejoined his lordship, floundering. "Her husband was head groom at one time, I understand?"

"You must be inordinately acquainted with Monksford, sir!" declared Connie, regarding him thoughtfully. "Why, only minutes ago, when we were discussing the origins of the house, I realised how deeply informed you were, in comparison to myself. I know that Monksford occupies the site of a Norman monastery, razed by King Henry the Eighth at the time of the Dissolution. But I had no idea that Queen Elizabeth had set foot here!"

"Supped in the Great Hall, in regal style!" he smiled. "Oh, I know it's the thing for every great house to claim Queen Bess among its residents, but she truly did come here—the first owner was one of her favourites. Can you not picture it? The richness of the costumes, the long table groaning with roast swan and stuffed boar, the gaiety, the minstrels strumming in the gallery above . . ."

"You describe it all so vividly!" breathed Connie, eyes shining. "How Papa would have enjoyed talking with you! He was deeply interested in Tudor culture. That is partly why he bought Monksford." Her eyes misted. "He loved it on sight."

"Tell me about him," prompted the Earl.

"He was the dearest Papa that ever was," she said, simply. "He was on the Bench, you know, but ill health forced him to retire prematurely. We moved here when I was four years old."

The Earl nodded, recalling to himself that bitter day when, as a young stripling down from Eton, he had glared through the branches of a sturdy elm and watched his father greet a tall gentleman and his lady who had arrived to view the property. That day, Monksford passed from his family.

"It has been a perpetual struggle, then, since your Papa's demise?" he asked, tentatively.

Connie nodded. "We lost him five years ago come Michaelmas and Mama two summers before that. I have raised Fanny, with Uncle Maurie's aid, since ever she learned to walk."

The Earl privately doubted her uncle's aptitude in this quarter but kept his thoughts to himself. He made her describe Fanny and she ruefully admitted her inner struggles over the child's schooling.

"I taught Fanny myself, at first. Reading and letters, and the use of the globes—elementary lessons, you understand, with a little music and embroidery. But such a screaming and sullens as we had over arithmetic!" She laughed at the recollection. "I decided to engage a governess— one of the vicar's girls, who has brought Fanny on wondrously! But—well, to be truthful, my sister is a graceless young torment, who has been not a little ruined by affection. I—I thought it best to enrol her in a properly run establishment, where she may be instructed as a gentleman's daughter ought."

"You have done well. Your sister will thank you for it one day." .

"Would that enlightenment may dawn with all speed!" dimpled Connie, grimacing. "Her letters seethe with grumpings over burnt porridge and an over-abundance of school-work! I enrolled her for French and Italian studies with additional tutoring in the harp, but now Fanny writes that *all* the girls take dancing and deportment twice weekly in Laura Place."

"Which presumably entails an additional fee?"

Connie nodded, biting her lip. "Twelve pounds extra per term. It is not such a sum but . . .

She fell silent, colouring for fear he should consider her cheese-paring. It came as something of a shock that she should be so ardent to secure his good opinion—and he a total stranger. Connie placed a fresh elm log on the fire, thankful for the excuse to occupy herself.

"Perhaps you had rather I fetched you some books from the library?" she ventured, turning up the lamp.

"I espy a capital chess-set yonder," smiled the

Earl, inclining his head towards an inlaid games-table. "Do you play?"

"Very indifferently," she dimpled, rising to fetch it. "I am so stupid at remembering the various moves."

"I do not judge you in any way stupid," he reproved, setting up the ivory pieces in their respective ranks. "I *shall* say, however, that you display a deplorable lack of self-confidence, which it must be my business to correct. Now Miss Osborne, shall we toss for possession of play?"

He watched her, dark head bent in rapt concentration over the game, the candlelight shining on her hair. He imagined the softness of it rippling through his fingers. She was so close that he could discern each separate dark lash, down-curved against her cheek. As though becoming aware of his gaze, she looked up, disconcerted.

"I beg your pardon," he smiled, penitently. "It was not my intention to be rude. It's simply that you are so—so refreshingly different to young ladies in general."

Connie regarded him shyly. "I expect you are a vast favourite in the smart set, Mr Musgrave."

"I bask in Chievely's glory," he admitted with truth, juggling a pawn thoughtfully. "But I have little patience with the Dandy element. I cannot see the justification for spending five hours at one's toilet, when savages get by wearing only a smile." His mouth tilted upwards in amusement. "Do you know, I itch to stroll into some dignified assemblage of an evening, sporting a loincloth! I doubt whether those empty-headed Mama's darlings on the catch for a husband would cling quite so prettily then!"

"Is it so irksome to be sought after, sir?" choked Connie, laughing.

"I cannot abide hen-wits!" he declared, bluntly. "However comely!"

At his aggrieved air, Connie smothered her amusement with difficulty. "Dear me! You condemn the majority of my sex on that count! I will not believe you so utterly lost to feminine wiles, Mr Musgrave."

He caught her eye, bright as a dove's, regarding him candidly, and a chuckle escaped him. "I've sown my wild oats, I admit. But should the right woman happen by, Miss Osborne, I'd have the vicar pronounce sentence like a shot!"

"I fear you will break many hearts along the way."

She was unaware of having voiced her thoughts until his amused grin confirmed it beyond hope. Connie would gladly have sunk through the floor, but he seemed to relish her discernment hugely, and dissolved any embarrassment by impudently capturing her Knight, which audacity so incensed her that she determined to put him in check, if it took all evening.

"You have been infamously untruthful with me, my girl!" he accused, with mock severity, when after a further hour's hard play, he discovered her Queen poised to attack.

"If you do not have a care, I *may* choose to wed *you*, which will be no more than you deserve, for having humbugged me so monstrously!"

In the ensuing weeks, Connie found herself turning increasingly to Mr Musgrave for advice. His judgment was sound and he was so easy to talk to that she felt no hesitation in approaching him.

Their evenings quickly became the highlight of her day. Sometimes they played chess or backgammon and when, as often happened, Uncle Maurie elected to enliven proceedings with his company, instead of whiling away the evening over a bottle at Westdean with his crony Colonel Drew, she was mortified to discover how fierce her resentment burned. Usually, however, her relative's snores signalled release and Mr Musgrave and she were permitted to talk contentedly far into the evening, until the clock struck ten and coffee was brought in, leaving Connie to wonder guiltily where the hours had flown.

He cheerfully admitted to having been sent down from Cambridge, and she rather suspected him of knowing quite as much of the world as his loose fish of a cousin, but for all that, he was undeniably well read and widely travelled. He talked enthusiastically of the antiquities of Greece and Albania, and his interest in art and architecture, his appreciation of which had been considerably heightened by ten years in India, where he had managed his uncle's tea plantation.

Despite her protests, he insisted upon Connie accepting a consideration to cover the expense of Benson and himself, and the sum caused her to gasp.

"Please take it." He regarded her earnestly, with that something in his expression which her heart found increasingly hard to ignore. "And purchase yourself some frippery with the remainder."

There was no dissuading him and the stack of bills, which had been Connie's secret worry for weeks past, were settled accordingly. In Southampton she chose some badly needed curtain material, having no desire to hear Lord Chievely echo Mrs Drinker's unfortunate observation that the steeple of Piper's Ash might be clearly viewed through the threadbare hangings in the upstairs drawing-room.

She had warned Mr Musgrave of this brash matron some days before, whilst measuring window-frames. Snow was falling outdoors, although it was only the third day of December.

"Mrs Drinker is a banker's widow from Louisiana, whom Uncle Maurie encountered in Brighton. She and her daughter are 'doing' Europe." Her eyes twinkled. "Have ever you met with any American ladies, Mr Musgrave?"

"Most assuredly! Lady Holland is American-born and her new-world forthrightness is terrifying! What is this Mrs Drinker like?"

Connie considered. "I do believe she means well, but . . . she is so profoundly talkative. Poor Uncle Maurie was quite wilted by the end of their visit here." Her mouth twitched at the recollection. "But Miss Drinker rhapsodised so over Monksford that when she hinted at a 'genuine English Yule-tide' . . . well, what else was one to do but agree?"

"Miss Drinker displays commendable taste, at any event," he declared, cheerfully. "How old is she?"

"Turned eighteen, and not one of your

bread-and-butter misses!" laughed Connie, wrestling with a yard-stick. "I am persuaded you and she will deal extremely."

"Oh, are you? What do you take me for, pray? A cradle-thief?"

"I allow you are old enough to be Lizzie-May's father," agreed Miss Osborne, crushingly. "But Mrs Drinker is willing to consider anything—and you did suggest you were in the market for a wife."

"I am minded to conduct my courting nearer home, Miss Sauce-Box!" he retorted, folding his arms over his chest. "From what you say, I suspect you mean to foist a fright upon me!"

"Indeed not!" cried Connie, indignantly. "Lizzie-May is an attractive girl! I—I should think you will take to her like anything."

She stared out at the snow-laden grounds, a curious sinking feeling at her heart. Christmas would herald the end of their comfortable times together. He had entered her life, turning it gloriously, sweetly upside-down; but his limb was healing splendidly, and by springtime he would be gone.

Five

~~~~~~~~~~~~~~~~~~~

ON THE MORNING following Connie's departure for Bath to collect young Fanny from school for the Christmas vacation, a chaise and four dashed up to the snow-wreathed gates of Monksford and halted at the front steps, where the housekeeper stood awaiting her first glimpse of a peer of the realm.

Lord Chievely was clad in a fashionable driving coat with nine capes and a beaver hat but for all his sartorial elegance, Mrs Reed could barely conceal a sniff of disapproval. A poor-looking creature was her opinion, though she supposed he could hardly help his gangling exterior and lack of chin. He appeared to have had the gall to bring along a friend, for she could glimpse a fur coat in the process of extricating itself from inside the carriage.

She screwed up her small eyes for a closer look, then took to her heels with a piercing scream. A huge English sheepdog, howling rapturously, was streaking towards her in a flurry of snow. The good lady plucked up her skirts and made an indecent gallop to the sanctuary of the south drawing-room where she prayed Mr Musgrave might offer some protection from those bared jaws.

She had scarcely succeeded in garbling out the salient knub when in bounded the hellhound, barking fit to burst, and launched itself, not at her, but into the astonished arms of Mr Musgrave, pinning him by the chest, whereupon it proceeded to lick enthusiastically at his face with a tongue like an ant-eater's, and gaze up at him like a long-lost brother.

"St George!" ordered the dumbfounded Mr Musgrave. "Get down this instant! *Down*, I say!"

The hairy mass obediently subsided to the floor and commenced a reconnoitering sniff of its new surroundings. The housekeeper backed warily to the door and almost collided with his lordship, who ambled in self-consciously, dropping his beaver hat and searching around for it at her feet with scarlet-faced apologies. When Mrs Reed had beaten retreat he closed the door firmly and immediately rounded on his handsome cousin, who was regarding him from the couch in unfeigned amusement.

"Now see here, Chievely, I don't know that I can go through with this charade! All very well for you to say it's only for a couple of months! If the bishop ever finds out, I—I'll be defrocked!"

"Sibbie, do cease behaving like a wet hen and remove your greatcoat," implored the Earl. "But first, tell me what in Heaven's name possessed you to bring along St George?"

Mr Sibbald glowered at the animal in question. "Wish I might recall," he responded morosely. "Have ever you been confined with that brute in a closed carriage for more than five hours, Chievely? It leaves a strong im-

pression on the mind—to say nothing of the nostrils."

The Earl chuckled, with a hearty disregard
for his cousin's sentiments. "Poor Sibbie! You
had best settle in, before we—er—get down to
business. Miss Osborne is gone to Bath, so you
may relax."

Some twenty minutes later Mr Sibbald returned, having exchanged his outer garments
for a waspish morning coat of olive superfine
with enormous brass buttons and a pair of yellow pantaloons which sprouted from his tas-
selled Hessians like bean shoots.

In looks, he bore little resemblance to his
dashing cousin. If anything, one was reminded
of an earnest halibut, for his eyes held a gog-
gling, faraway look and his lower jaw disappeared mysteriously into a collar with enormous
shirt-points which extended almost to his ears.
A cravat of eye-blinding violet completed this
ensemble and a clutch of fobs and seals dangled
from his striped waistcoat, as befitted a dandy of
the first stare.

"Decided I'd best attempt to dress the part,"
explained Mr Sibbald, defensively, not much
caring for the expression of appalled disbelief
in his cousin's eye. "Had 'em run up in Taun-
ton. The fellow swore I looked a perfect Tulip!"

The Earl reflected on his own tastefully elegant image. "I forgive you, Sibbie," he murmured, stilling his impatience to see Miss
Osborne's reaction to this magnificence. "Will
you not join me in a splash of Madeira? Settles
the nerves, old man."

Mr Sibbald normally refreshed himself with

nothing stronger than tea but on this occasion he downed a full glass outright and sank into a chair, with a wary eye turned on his cousin.

"The situation is this, Sibbie. I require time to win over Miss Osborne. You, my lad, must endeavour to set the scene convincingly. A woo here, a dally there. By the way, how is your technique in that line? I refuse to have my addresses paid simply any old how."

"Now see here, Chievely, this is the first mention of any fooling of that sort!" spluttered Mr Sibbald, looking more like a fish than ever. "Not my line! I shan't do it!"

"Really, Sibbie, there's gratitude! Have I not donated a substantial fistful to further your good works, out of cousinly benevolence?"

"No!" retorted Mr Sibbald, squaring what little jaw he possessed. "You're doing it so's I may get you out of a fix! Well, I—I absolutely refuse, Chievely! Never made up to a woman in my life."

"Then I suggest you seize this opportunity, old man," counselled his cousin, amiably. "Virtue is all very well, but it's not natural. A clergyman with the hint of honest sin is a winner by a head—why, you can bet your surplice that every female worth her garters will be scratching to set caps at you! Look, Sibbie—all that counts is for you to make a straightforward offer to Miss Osborne—for the look of the thing! Remember you are meant to be me, and matters will go smart as be damned."

"But, Chievely, the girl's bound to smell a rat! Dash it, everyone knows you for the devil of a fellow. I ain't got your finesse."

"Oh, we can soon fix that!" soothed the Earl,

kindly. "First, you must endeavour to look By-ronic. Scowl a little—no, Sibbie, not like that, you'll frighten her to death!"

"Chievely, old man," gritted Mr Sibbald, with saccharine undertones, "how would you care to be disembowelled with a blunt carving-knife?"

A throaty growl from somewhere about his ankles awakened him to the presence of the dog St George. Mr Sibbald hurriedly retrieved his leg, having lost more than one set of footwear to the animal's jaws, whereupon St George settled his rump contentedly on the reverend gentleman's other foot and promptly went to sleep.

"Now, Sibbie, don't be feudal," remonstrated the Earl, coaxingly. He cocked his head side-ways, regarding the prospective Romeo shrewd-ly. "How is your voice? The ladies will expect to have you sing."

"No!" croaked Mr Sibbald, paling. "Couldn't I do my farmyard impressions instead?"

"Not a chance, Sibbie. It must be a song. Something suitably romantic. Oh, and do re-member to look yearningly at Miss Osborne every so often. Let's see you yearn, Sibbie."

Mr Sibbald turned purple, but his cousin merely snapped an authoritative finger.

"Augustus Sibbald," murmured the Earl, manfully attempting to still his twitching lips. "What you are yearning after I dare not con-template, but your expression is positively lech-erous! Now don't look so liverish, old man," he added, encouragingly. "Things cannot go far wrong."

"No?" moaned his cousin. "What if she fancies me?"

The Earl sought refuge in a cough. "I consider it unlikely. You are here on sufferance, do not forget. If anything, relations will be on the—er—frosty side." He pricked his ears, suddenly alert. "Lord, that's surely not Miss Osborne's carriage already?"

Mr Sibbald stepped into the window embrasure for a better look, followed by an excited St George, barking furiously.

"It's a chaise, with a pair of females," he reported, craning forwards, suspiciously. "Never seen so many bandboxes in my life."

From the front steps, a shrill female observation smote their ears, exhorting Lizzie-May to hitch her drawers half-mast, on account of the snow. At this point, Mr Sibbald almost fell through the lattice windows, recovered himself, and goggled wordlessly at his cousin.

"Miss Drinker and her Mama, I believe," disclosed the Earl, smoothly. "My stars, Sibbie, only consider what a fortunate dog you are! Two eligible young ladies with whom to dally—it looks remarkably like Fate." He grinned at his relative's outraged countenance.

"It never ceases to amaze me how the mere dangle of a coronet will draw the female of the species like vultures to a rotting carcase! See if I'm not proved correct."

Mr Sibbald reached a nerveless hand for the Madeira, holy orders forgotten in the horror of his situation.

"Chievely, I could kill you!" he croaked, mournfully.

When Connie returned that evening, she

found her houseparty already complete. Mrs
Drinker, overpowering in striped cerise, with a
turban and feathers, had trapped Sir Maurice
in a corner and was lecturing him on the evils
of drink. Her daughter, a hefty young maiden
whose plump, hearty face seemed at odds with
the modishness of the upswept, honey-blonde
curls framing it, stood giggling infectiously before the fire in company with a loose-limbed
creature, a veritable Exquisite of fashion, who
must be none other than the unlovable Chievely.

Connie, observing him covertly from the doorway, almost laughed aloud from sheer disbelief. Where, in this lanky man-milliner, was the
devil-may-care rake with the infamous reputation?

His reaction to her entrance was no less star-
tling, for he jumped up like a scalded cat,
tripped over his feet and sprawled full length
at her skirts with a stifled ejaculation. Connie
hid her amusement in a cool curtsey. She was
no longer nervous; indeed, the mere thought of
this namby-pamby daring to insult her with his
designs forced her to bite fiercely on her lip, for
fear of delivering a tongue-lashing there and
then.

She waited until a quiet moment brought
them together, before stating, with dignified
reproof, "My lord, let there be no misunder-
standing. My sentiments remain unaltered, and
I trust you do not mean to embarrass us both
by pursuing the matter. I beg you—allow me
leave to finish!" she added, as he gurgled something about being most fearfully pipped. "Had
you approached me concerning Monksford in

an—an honourable manner, I might have been disposed to consider your offer. As it is, we have nothing to say to each other."

So saying, she discovered, to her chagrin, that she must now give him her hand into dinner. So beside herself was Connie with confusion, that it was several minutes before Mrs Drinker's drawl at her elbow recalled her to the fast-cooling white soup and her duties as hostess.

"Say, Miss Osborne, is he a genuine, out and out Earl?"

Connie assured her of his lordship's pedigree.

"My! Ain't this too dandy for words?" Mrs Drinker turned pink with excitement. "Only observe how attentive he is to my little girl! If only dearest Hubert had been spared to witness this!"

She dug Connie a conspiratorial nudge in the ribs. "The one downstairs—is he Quality, too?"

Connie blinked at this abrupt turn-around in conversation.

"Mr Musgrave is first cousin to Lord Chievely, ma'am. Having met him, you must perceive him to be a gentleman of the highest calibre." She spoke with quiet warmth, but a faint heightening of colour caused Mrs Drinker to regard her narrowly.

"To be sure—but ain't he a Duke, or somethin'?"

Understanding the drift of this persistent interest, Connie suppressed a smile. "I fear not, ma'am." She turned her head, eyes twinkling, as an uninhibited burst of laughter from Lizzie-May brought all conversation to a stand-still. Lord Chievely's quizzing glass was seen to be submerged in the contents of his soup bowl, to the acute misery of its owner, who was making pathetic work of rescuing it from its watery grave.

"His lordship appears bent upon making a memorable impression on Miss Drinker," murmured Connie, uncertain what to deduce from such eccentric behaviour.

"Oh, call me Lizzie-May!" implored Miss Drinker, emerging weakly from behind the table-napkin which she had found necessary to stuff in her mouth to preserve her countenance.

"You poor man, now see what has happened!" she broke off, examining his lordship's sleeve which he had managed to trail through the soup in pursuit of his quizzing glass. "I guess you ought to have those stains duded up right away."

She watched sympathetically as Mr Sibbald allowed himself to be led ignominiously from the room by the footman.

"Say, Miss Osborne, his Earlship surely is sweet, don't you think?" She dimpled wickedly. "I've been instructing him how to talk Yankee, you know. And guess what, Momma? He is the one with the fancy reputation! I told you so from the first, but you wouldn't have it!"

"Is he, now?" Mrs Drinker fixed his lordship's retreating back with renewed attention. That image of chinless idiocy must be nothing other than a subtle disguise. Impressive. Something to do with his blue blood, no doubt. She beamed benignly on him across the room.

As soon as she decently might, Connie excused herself and hastened downstairs to Mr Musgrave. At her entrance, an enormous white sheepdog bounded towards her, sending a footstool flying, and all but prostrating her in its excitement.

"St George! Come back here!" ordered Mr Musgrave, turning an apologetic face to hers. "This great lump belongs to me, I fear. Chievely brought him, thinking he'd cheer me up."

Affectionately, he rumpled the animal's coat, beckoning Connie to sit beside him with a warm smile. "Harmless as a baby actually, and the greatest coward imaginable. He'll jump on one's lap at the sight of a mouse."

Connie laughed and bent over the dog. St George obligingly licked her hand, decided she was a friend, and ensconced himself with his head on her knee, soulful eyes fixed upon her face. He was an irresistible handful, decided Connie, but he dribbled rather and his pedigree was open to doubt.

"Picked him up in Westmorland two years ago," he explained, reading her thoughts. "I did not dream he'd grow to this size."

"Fanny will love him," smiled Connie. "She is quite hagged with our journey so I have put her straight to bed, but you shall meet her tomorrow. I . . . I believe Mrs Drinker and her daughter have made themselves known to you," she added, diffidently.

He surveyed her with quizzing amusement.

"Oh, more than that! I have been pumped, squeezed and turned inside-out with questions." He grinned. "From which we may deduce that I am approved of. Although I did receive the impression that your excellent Mrs Drinker does not altogether condone your harbouring members of the opposite sex in your downstairs drawing-room. I told her it was an old English custom."

"Mrs Drinker had no right to vex you so!" whispered Connie, fiercely. She stared at him. "You—you told her *what?*"

He chuckled deeply. "As I recall, the lady displayed a distinct interest in my intentions toward yourself. I informed her they are strictly dishonourable and that, as soon as I may, I mean to abduct you for my own sinful purpose!" His hand closed feather-light on hers. "Would you mind awfully if I did, Bright-Eyes?"

"You are the most ridiculous creature!" protested Connie, although inwardly, his absurd teasing sparked a dull ache within her. There was no one, no one in the world by whom she had rather be abducted, and feel the world well lost, but such things did not happen to staid maidens of five and twenty. He was regarding her in that special way of his and for the life of her, Connie could not meet his eye.

"I—I have just offended your cousin Lord Chievely," she stuttered, grasping feverishly to change the subject. Haltingly, she related the unfortunate exchange, expecting him to be annoyed, but he merely said, with a brief smile, "I anticipated something of the sort. Perfectly natural. What—er—what is your impression of Chievely, now that you are met?"

"He is not the least as I imagined," confessed Connie, in an undertone. "I—well, I had hoped for someone more . . . more positively wicked!"

He burst out laughing. "You are wholly delightful!"

His eyes swept over her in the way which

never failed to disconcert her. "I cannot comprehend your having evaded the bridal snare! Was there someone, perhaps?"

Connie shook her head, wondering why it was she should answer so personal a question without reluctance. "No one who mattered. I ceased attending the Assemblies months ago, and there is little else where one may hope to meet—" She stopped, flashing him a defiant little smile. "Besides, I am very well content. I—I read, and there is my music, and Firebrand, and . . ."

"And Monksford for you to worry over, and Sir Maurice and your sister, and the Lord knows what else!" he finished, soberly.

Connie bit her lip. "You must find me amazingly dull."

"I find you—" he began, then stopped himself, saying instead, "I consider you charmingly unaffected. Did you secure the tooth-powder I wanted, in Bath?"

"I have it upstairs." Connie rose. "We met the doctor's cart coming through Ringwood. He tells me you hope to be on crutches soon. Is that really the case?"

"Indeed yes. My limb feels much stronger of late. Your excellent physician is confident I may not even be left with a limp."

"Oh, I am glad!" Her eyes glowed. "It will be so satisfying to have you among us at last."

"Thank you," he replied, gently. "I anticipate it with enormous pleasure." He paused. "Your friend Miss Drinker sat with me this afternoon. I must grant you she is as personable a romp as ever I met. One might take her for one and twenty, she has such assurance. I confess myself properly surprised."

That was all he said but the unmistakable admiration in his voice realised Connie's inmost expectations. No one could do other than warm to Lizzie-May, so why, she thought miserably, why should I feel so wretched?

It happened that Sir Maurice Pinchbeck had early observed the arrival of a pert young abigail in Mrs Drinker's entourage. Well fortified with a stimulating bottle or two, he settled to planning his strategy.

It was well after three, and the household long retired to bed, when he stumbled along the darkened gallery, his fuddled brain bent on locating the maid's sleeping quarters. More than once, his toe caught in the hem of his nightshirt, causing the dauntless lover to keel over on the cold floor. To add to his difficulties, there seemed to be fewer stairs than he remembered to the servants' quarters, and every door looked the same.

Hiccuping softly, Sir Maurice turned the knob of the most promising bed-chamber and stole in. The room was in darkness, but he succeeded in lurching to the window, where he drew the curtain a little, and there made out a large hump in the middle of the bedstead, from which proceeded a light snore.

Grunting with exertion, Sir Maurice turned back the sheets with a flourish, and crawled in beside the abigail. An exploratory hand assured him that the girl possessed a greater abundance of soft flesh than he had supposed, and removing the flannel nightcap from his head (for he was nothing if not polite) Sir Maurice embraced his prize with vigour.

His paramour's reaction was not what he expected. A frantic scream rent the night air, followed by hysterical accusations of murder and rape, which penetrated the entire house. The hump dealt him an almighty blow on the chest, leaving him gasping, and leaped from the bed, screaming for assistance.

It did not take Sir Maurice long to realise that he had stolen into the wrong bed. It took him even less to recognise his victim as being the harpy, Mrs Drinker. Dimly he could perceive her majestic shape, attired in a voluminous night-gown, with curl-papers sticking from under a muslin sleeping cap, groping frantically for the door knob and alarming the sleep of three counties with her cries.

Next instant, the door burst open and Mr Sibbald charged in, bringing down what he took to be the escaping intruder with a spirited tackle below the knees. Mrs Drinker's screams mounted to the heavens, summoning the rest of the household at the double but there was little she could do, for Mr Sibbald was sitting doggedly on her chest, grappling with her clawing fingers.

Perceiving his chance, Sir Maurice padded on all fours past the struggling couple, narrowly escaping being felled by the hairy St George, spoiling to launch his five stones into the fray. Thoroughly unnerved, Sir Maurice stumbled to a nearby linen-closet, where he collapsed, trembling, to listen to the confusion outside.

In vain did Mr Sibbald protest his innocence. Mrs Drinker, with a hartshorn bottle lodged

halfway up her nostril, and her bosom heaving
like a demented bellows, denounced him in
ringing tones as the lecher who had attempted
to unleash his bestiality on her person. Mr Sibbald could only stand with his mouth open,
clutching at his night-shirt, which St George
was doing his best to relieve him of, feeling the
accusing eyes of all and sundry trained upon
him.

"Oh, Chievely, it was terrible!" he quavered
next day, when his cousin demanded an inquest
on the night's events. "Old dame was shirty as
Lucifer! If B-Bishop Rumbelow should ever get
wind of this—"

"Really, Sibbie, however do you manage it?"
choked the Earl, weak from laughing. "As it
happens, I suspect you have strengthened our
deception no end. In one stroke, your vile reputation has been proved conclusively."

"*M-My* vile reputation?" echoed his cousin,
faintly.

"Well, mine, if you prefer," qualified the
Earl, cheerfully. He regarded the licentious
monster with approval. "I understand you are
making progress with Miss Drinker."

"That girl! She acts as though I were some
rare species of p-pond life! I do my utmost to
shake her off, but she sticks closer than a tick!"

"My dear fellow, there are but three places
where one is safe from women—the club, the
monastery and the grave. Depend upon it, old
man, you are doing splendidly!" He eyed the
hunched shoulders sympathetically. "I realise I
ask a vast deal, Sibbie," he said, quietly. "But
it's the only means I know of rescuing

Monksford from ruin. I'm relying upon you, cousin."

Mr Sibbald opened his mouth to make a suitable retort, but the undisguised wretchedness in the Earl's expression caused him to reply, with a brightness he did not feel, "I shan't chicken out, coz. 'England expects,' and all that, what?"

Six

~~~~~~~~

MRS DRINKER'S SENTIMENTS ran close to this
maxim but, in her case, her convictions were as-
sailed by doubt. On the one hand, she felt obli-
gated to exert her utmost talents in hunting
down Lord Chievely, whilst on the other,
maternal instinct questioned the wisdom of parcelling off her only daughter on a depraved
peer, however sought after.

Upon this blossom of American girlhood
were centred Mrs Drinker's cherished aspirations. From the cradle, Lizzie-May had been
drilled in the creed that woman's chief end was
to secure a husband and enjoy his riches for
ever.

To this end, her devoted Mama had dra-
gooned her into the recognized killing ground
of balls, soirées and Assemblies, adding a few
devious measures of her own, so that from an
early age Lizzie-May understood the advantage
of positioning oneself whenever possible under
the chandeliers' winking glow. She became adept
at painting her eyelids and darkening the lashes
to give them added fire, and meekly complied
when Mama advised dampening one's muslins to
to allow the filmy softness to cling seductively
where it would most show to advantage.

Despite these most strenuous efforts, however, Mrs Drinker was unable to disguise the
melancholy fact that Lizzie-May was a born hoy-
den. Although her daughter's natural exuberance drew any number of rackety young
Bloods, she despaired of the girl ever contracting a good match when Lizzie-May strode about
with her drawers conspicuous and ungratefully
deplored her Mama's efforts at husband-hunt-
ing on her behalf.

"You attend to your Momma, Lizzie-May!"
counselled Mrs Drinker, after her daughter ob-
stinately refused to be coaxed into a pair of
stays.

"If this Chievely is worth having, it would be
abominably provoking to have him slip through
our fingers for want of encouragement."

Critically, she studied her offspring's generous bosom.

"You got to make the most of what the Lord
blessed you with, child."

"But he blessed me with so much, Momma!"
wailed Lizzie-May, casting a disgusted eye to
the looking-glass. "It ain't fair!"

"Gentlemen judge womenfolks like they do
wine—and horses!" retorted her Mama, briskly.
"It's full-bodied, with a kick in their instep—or
goodbye! And if you aim to get a sight of the
Chievely tin, honey, I suggest you make a start
on this darned complexion goo."

She indicated a pot of Gowland's Lotion on
the flap of the enclosed dressing-table. "Womenfolks ain't meant for to go stridin' outdoors in
all weathers. Why, you'll end up with a face red
as a Cherokee!"

"Oh, Momma, cease beefing, do!" Lizzie-May

heaved a long-suffering sigh and held up the stays between finger and thumb with an air of revulsion. "I'll do all you ask—but I draw the line at this bust-improver!"

Her Mama hardly heard. "Languid apathy— that took a good deal when I was acourtin' your Pa," she mused. "They do say, however, that religion is much looked for by men of profligate habits..."

"But I got no desire to hook Lord Chievely!" protested Lizzie-May, fiercely. "Sure, he's reckoned the cream amongst these English girls but I had as lief do without!"

Snatching up a filigree hair-brush, she applied it vigorously through her blonde curls, continuing heatedly. "If I ain't to be permitted to wed Cousin Bertram, which you know very well is what Papa hoped for, then why may not I have someone like ..." She brightened optimistically. "Well—like that peachy Mr Musgrave, for example?"

"Musgrave has no title!" snapped Mrs Drinker, infuriated by this strain of wilfulness. "And he don't fetch enough to keep you in garters!"

"Momma—you didn't ask him outright?"

"Certainly I asked him! No point in his fingerin' the goods if they ain't for sale!" Mrs Drinker snatched up the stays and deposited them in a chest of drawers. "No miffs, Lizzie-May. You are marked down for Chievely!"

The week before Christmas arrived all too soon for Connie. There was so much to be done and so little time, it seemed, in which to accomplish it. She had planned what she hoped would be a pleasing festive table—succulent goose, garnished with apple rings and a sauce, and a crown roast of lamb with turnip and dumplings, followed by jellies and a quiddany.

Such was her proposed fare. But the goose, when it arrived, proved disastrously long in the tooth, and another must be got. Mrs Drinker declared herself averse to quinces and the quiddany was perforce abandoned in favour of a blancmanger. There were mince pies to make and punch to be prepared, besides the hundred and one other details of preparation which must not be neglected.

It was hardly surprising, therefore, that Connie, immersed in the supervision of these particulars, should find little leisure to share in the activities of her young sister.

For the present, however, Fanny's affections were wholly divided between St George and Mr Musgrave, with whom she had quickly established a firm friendship bordering on hero-worship.

Not a morning passed without finding her playing about the couch in the south drawing-room. Lord Chievely might be a willing participant in building snowmen; Miss Drinker (when away from her Mama's eagle supervision) was obliging in the exhibiting of cartwheels across a room; but no one, not even St George, could usurp Mr Musgrave in Fanny's estimation.

He was demonstrating the construction of a card-house for her one morning when through the window she espied Mr Grundle's boy bearing an armful of holly boughs towards the house.

"Oh!" she breathed, ecstatically, running to the window-seat. "We shall be decking the walls soon! Do not you rate Christmas the splendidest time of the year, Mr Musgrave?"

"No question of it," he smiled, allowing the cards to collapse in a heap on the counterpane. "I daresay you are hoping for some extra special treasures on Christmas morning?"

Fanny's face fell. "Connie says I am not to think of anything grand this year," she began, resuming her stance by his side. "I suspect she means to have a new stuff gown made up for me—I caught Mrs Reed measuring my old blue worsted the other day when she believed me gone out, and that surely means Miss Fisk from the village is to have the making of it!" The pert nose wrinkled expressively.

"Is that bad?" hazarded the Earl.

"Oh, it is ten times worse than bad! Miss Fisk only possesses one pattern, and she has no understanding of what is tonnish—why, she is only now converted to the idea of Mameluke sleeves—those with the ribbon and puffs, you know—and everyone recognises them as having been the crack for ever so long!"

"Oh, most assuredly." Affectionately, he ruffled her dark curls. "Do not be despondent, my chicken. I think you will find more than one present awaiting you when the time comes. Christmas is the season of giving, you know."

Fanny nodded importantly. "Honoria Price, who is in my form at school, maintains we exchange gifts at Christmas on account of the Duchess of York."

"No, do we? I really feel someone ought to have informed Saint Matthew!" The Earl strove to remain grave, having no wish to spoil the child's explanation.

Fanny perched herself cosily beside him with a confiding air.

"Well, you see, it is a German custom which the Duchess introduced upon her marriage to the Duke. The gifts, you know, are a token of those brought by the three Kings to the baby Jesus. I consider it a lovely idea!"

The Earl stroked his chin thoughtfully. "You have just reminded me of another German custom, Princess. Do you know how Queen Charlotte celebrates Christmas at Windsor?"

Fanny snuggled closer. "With a big cake and candles?" she hazarded, hopefully. The Earl smiled and pinched her cheek.

"Not precisely, little one. A yew tree is brought into the Castle on Christmas Eve and the Queen then banishes everyone from the room until it has been transformed."

"How do you mean—transformed?" breathed Fanny, wide-eyed.

"Oh, with tiny candles and spangles, and the most intricate glass ornaments that you can imagine! And on the topmost branch she places a glittering star, to remind everyone of the Christmas story."

"O-O-Oh!" Fanny's eyes sparkled. "What happens then?"

"Why, then she adds specially baked biscuits cut in all manner of pleasing shapes, and ends by piling presents around the base of the tree, for the Christkind or Christ Child to hand out to the young children."

Fanny flung her arms about his neck, wild with enthusiasm. "Oh, Mr Musgrave, may we try it? May we? Grundle will provide a tree—I know he will! We shall have to allow Connie into the secret, but no one else! And," she continued, excitedly, "I shall beg sugar from cook to sprinkle on my star, after I have it cut out! Oh—but we have no candles," she exclaimed, with a woebegone expression. "And no glass ornaments."

"We shall make our own decorations!" decided the Earl, tweaking her curls affectionately. "I shall make a list of the items we require this instant."

On Christmas Eve, the interior of Monksford was gay with holly and boughs of evergreen. A roaring fire of logs crackled in the upstairs drawing-room, casting its glow upon the burnished copper punchbowl, over which Sir Maurice hovered with the zeal of a fly round a honey pot. In one corner, resplendent with sugar frost and wax candles (the last provided post-haste from London upon the surprise arrangement of Mr Musgrave), Fanny's tree stood proudly decked, awaiting its crowning moment of glory when the candles would be lighted and their glow transform the room.

The new curtains looked well, concluded Connie, although they tended to show up the worn carpet even more than she had feared.

The door opened and in danced Fanny, dragging a laughing Lizzie-May by the hand. Miss Drinker was looking handsome, in a modish gown, low-cut and appliquéd with flowers. Connie sighed, trying not to mind Fanny's howl of disappointment on seeing her wearing the same old pearl grey silk from last year.

"Oh, Connie, why are you not dressed up?

Miss Drinker looks just like a princess, and I did so want you to be pretty, too!"

"Fanny, I simply cannot afford another gown meantime," replied Connie, with a brave attempt at gaiety. "Now run along and escort Mrs Drinker to a chair, like a good girl."

She turned apologetically to Lizzie-May. "Fanny does not understand. But it grieves me vexedly to have her suffer the disagreeableness of our situation."

"Why, Connie, honey, I assure you no one would suspect your gown to be above *two* years old!" declared Lizzie-May, with well-meaning tactlessness, slipping an arm about Connie's waist. "I do wish you might try a hint of rouge. I declare you look fearfully knocked up."

The sound of voices on the stair made them turn. Next moment, Mr Musgrave stood in the doorway, supported by Lord Chievely, with his other arm resting on a wooden crutch. He was immaculate in a dark tail-coat of superb cut, with a white cravat at his throat. A single fob hung from a waistcoat of white sarsnet. Connie was dimly conscious of black knee-breeches and clocked stockings but her eyes were blurred with threatened tears. He looked so tall and handsome—and he could walk!

Across the room they held each other's glance, then he winked irrepressibly at her and limped forwards. Connie hastened to greet him, unable to hide her happiness.

"I hope you mean to allow me the privilege of escorting you into dinner," he whispered, taking her hand warmly in his own.

"I wish you might," she ventured, "but I feel you had best take in Miss Drinker, before

Uncle Maurie offers. Old Colonel Drew from Westdean presented him with a magnum this morning, and now he is quite disguised." She looked up pleadingly. "If you were to remain with Miss Drinker, Uncle Maurie will not press his attentions."

The Earl glanced to the far side of the room, where his cousin was now seated on a striped sofa, with a Drinker on either side. Mr Sibbald wore an expression of dazed subservience, and his hand clutched at an open volume of verse held by Lizzie-May, whilst Mrs Drinker could be heard rhapsodising at length on Lord Byron and his poetry.

"I suspect my cousin Chievely to be more in need of rescue," murmured the Earl, wickedly. "But be at ease, Bright-Eyes. Miss Drinker shall command my undivided attention."

"Such a lovely girl—in a favourable light," commented Mrs Drinker, gesticulating towards Connie from behind her fan, after dinner was over, and the gentlemen had rejoined them. This observation was directed with pointed emphasis to Mr Musgrave, about whom Mrs Drinker could not quite decide, for although he evinced every pleasure in her daughter's society, his glance rested frequently upon Miss Osborne.

"I confess to feeling mighty sorry for her," she continued in an undertone, meeting Mr Musgrave's upraised eyebrows without discomposure. "Let us be plain, sir. Within five years of thirty and without an offer of any note! No good man will come askin' now, that's for

sure—" She fixed him with unflinching deliberation. "Or will he?"

"My dear lady," he responded, much amused.
"As I understand it, men become old—they
never become good! Pray excuse me. I am anxious to have Miss Osborne sing for us."

He took himself off to where Connie sat with
such courteousness of manner, that it was some
minutes before his inquisitive companion realised how firmly she had been countered.

Despite Mr Musgrave's coaxing, Connie
would not sing, so Lizzie-May was bidden by
her Mama to sit at the piano. Miss Drinker's
touch was spirited and her medley met with
warm applause, none more heartily than from
Mr Sibbald, who, fired with hot punch and the
prompting in his cousin's eye, actually got up to
deliver a chorus.

The generous lines of Miss Drinker's bosom,
however, competing with an unencouraging
snore from Sir Maurice, brought his efforts to a
bleating stand-still, and his moment of agony
was only saved when young Fanny, who having
long ago discovered his one and only talent,
begged for animal impressions such as he alone
could produce.

Gales of laughter and genuine praise followed, so that Mr Sibbald was able to meet his
cousin's eye with more than a hint of satisfaction. The Earl smiled but said nothing.

What with charades and fortune-telling and a
hilarious game devised by Mr Musgrave, in-
volving paper and pencil, in which everyone
joined, it was almost ten o'clock before they
knew, whereupon chestnuts must be roasted in
the grate, with punch to help them down. Then

Mr Musgrave lighted a taper, and Fanny, burst-ing with pride, lit the lower branches of her tree, amid the exclamations and cheers of the assembled company, with even the servants peeping round the door to admire the fairy-tale spectacle.

Connie completed the illuminations and one or two of the precious biscuits which the con-certed efforts of the two prime conspirators had won from the cook's hands were handed round and nibbled. Shortly after, carol-singers were heard in the drive, and everyone rushed to the deep oriel windows to hear them the better.

Gazing down on the cheerful, lantern-lit scene below, Connie felt a lump in her throat. How beautifully the voices blended on the frosty night air, the age-old story of God's love for mankind seeming more fresh and compell-ing than ever she remembered. She knew that this Christmas Eve would remain in her mem-ory when others were forgotten. She met Mr Musgrave's eye, and knew why.

Naturally the choristers must be rewarded with mince pies and spiced ale, and more carols were sung. At half past eleven the steeple bells of Pipers Ash began to peal for the midnight service and Mrs Drinker was marshalling the company into cloaks and bonnets with a resolu-tion which the Iron Duke would have envied.

"Must you go?" whispered Mr Musgrave, as Connie made to follow the others downstairs to the waiting carriage.

She hesitated, longing to remain, yet know-ing guiltily that she ought not to. Surely there would be a crush in the carriage, as it was, without her? They waited, not speaking, until the horses' clop had died away on the night air. With a rueful smile, Connie removed her bonnet and cloak, and accepted Mr Musgrave's invitation to share the window-seat.

"Thank you for remaining behind," he said softly. "You see, I have something for you, and I wish you to receive it now, whilst we are alone."

From his inside pocket he withdrew a letter and handed it to her. With trembling fingers, Connie broke the seal and scanned its contents, her eyes widening in disbelief.

"But—but this is a directive for shares in my name, to the value of . . . *five hundred pounds*!" she whispered, looking up bemusedly.

"They are an excellent risk," he smiled, stilling her shaking fingers with the warmth of his hand, "and should ensure sufficient means to institute repairs at once."

Mutely, Connie shook her head, barely able to reply.

"I cannot accept charity from you, sir," she whispered chokily. "Indeed I cannot."

"My dearest child, for once you will put that devilish pride behind you and consider the matter settled. I want to help—Heaven knows your unselfishness to me is greater than I may hope to repay!"

Connie hesitated, not knowing how to answer. To him, five hundred pounds might not constitute so vast a sum, but translated into practical terms it could mean a start on the badly decayed west wing, where new flooring and masonwork had been too long delayed.

"If . . . if you will treat this sum as a

loan," she stammered, "then I shall be happy to accept, Mr Musgrave."

"Of all the perverse, nonsensical females, you are without exception the most stubborn!" declared the Earl, in exasperated tones. "If I considered it might do the least good, I'd—I'd lay you over my knee and beat some sense into you!" He cupped her chin between his hands, despite her efforts to shy away. "Why are you weeping?"

"I . . . I am not w-weeping!" choked Connie, dissolving completely into tears.

The Earl gazed at her for a long moment, without speaking, then he opened his arms and drew her against him, rocking her securely against his shoulder until her sobs lessened. Then, still with his arm about her, he whispered gently, "Now, my girl, what was all that about?"

"B-because your leg is almost healed and—and s-soon you must be g-going away!" hiccuped Connie, against his shirt.

"I see. And will you miss me so greatly?"

She could not answer but the dumb misery in her eyes was more eloquent than any words. He raised her gently, and turning up her face, kissed her lightly on the brow, saying, in an unsteady whisper, "Constance—Connie . . . Will you come to London with me?"

"To—to London?" whispered Connie, bemusedly. Her senses were reeling and the closeness of him, with the feel of his lips still burning her forehead, left her with a curious sense of unreality. She found herself trembling.

"It's hardly the end of the earth." There was an amused tenderness in his smile, which caused her heart to thud so dreadfully that she felt he must hear. "You have never been there, I understand?"

Connie shook her head. "But—but I am acquainted with no one in London," she stammered. "I could not possibly—"

"You know me." His eyes held hers, eager, insistent. "Think of it, Bright-Eyes. All the places you have longed to see. St Paul's, Richmond, Rotten Row . . . and theatres and balls enough!" He possessed himself of her hand, turning it in his own. "It's time you had a little fun, my girl. The waterspouts come too easily to your eyes for no good reason, and Dr Musgrave prescribes a change of scene immediately, with all worries to be left behind!"

He saw the beginnings of a smile tug at her lips.

"That's the dandy! Now, you shall leave all arrangements to me and—"

"It is out of the question! And . . . and quite improper besides." She blushed hotly. "Surely you must see that."

"Improper? Good Lord, girl, I'm not asking you to be my mistress!" he expostulated angrily. "What the deuce do you take me for? One chaste kiss hardly constitutes unbridled lust!"

"I beg your pardon," whispered Connie, striving to keep her voice from breaking. "But I—I cannot go with you."

If he had slapped her face, she could not have felt more wretched. His last words had stung her to the quick; she had insulted him abominably and worse, his pride had been caught on the raw.

"God grant me strength! You do believe I'm

trying to compromise you!" he exploded, pushing the hair impatiently from his brow. "We have not been long acquainted, Miss Osborne, but I had hoped you might understand that my esteem for you is too deep *ever* to go beyond the line!"

"Oh—I beg you!" she moaned, her hand going out as if to ward off any further blow. "If I have offended, I am truly sorry!" Bright tears glistened in her eyes. "I had sooner lose all I hold dear than have you think ill of me."

His expression softened immediately. "Lord, what a brute I am. As if you could ever give me cause to—" He paused, awkwardly. "I have a rare temper, you know, although it does not often show. I wish you might reconsider—about coming to London, I mean. My grandmama would have you with pleasure, although at present she is at Bowood, with the Lansdownes." He grinned boyishly. "She will likely plague you with all manner of gossip—there are normally around ten separate anecdotes in circulation relating to the Princess of Wales at such house parties—each one more shocking than the last! And my maternal grandmama revels in a little character dissection by way of diversion."

"I never conceived you as having a grandmama," admitted Connie.

"We none of us blossom from the heart of a rose," he teased. "Look, Mrs Drinker means to be in town this spring. I am confident she and her daughter would wish to return your hospitality."

"Mrs Drinker is to be in—London? But—she has made no mention of this! I—I am persuaded she would have told me."

"It is the case, I assure you," he replied, earnestly. "They mean to take a house in Manchester Street. It was settled between us some days ago." He gestured helplessly. "I'm sorry. I thought you knew."

Connie made an inaudible rejoinder, determined not to show her hurt. Mr Musgrave's plans are none of your affair, she told herself. Why should you care whether or not he escorts Lizzie-May about town? But her heart was leaden within her. What a gull you have been, Connie Osborne, she reasoned bitterly. He thinks of you only as a benefactress.

Forcing a bright smile, she said. "It sounds a splendid arrangement. Miss Drinker must be vastly thrilled at the prospect. I—I know how greatly she admires you." She put up a hand, as the clock on the mantelpiece chimed the hour, and said quietly, "I believe it is Christmas morning. May I offer you the season's greetings, Mr Musgrave, and—and trust you may always regard me as . . . as your f-friend . . ."

Her voice died away in a choked whisper and without daring to look at him, she picked up her skirts and fled from the room, heedless of his entreaties.

Seven

~~~~~~~~~~~~~~~~~~~

THE STRAIN OF maintaining an outward gaiety
was harder to bear than Connie at first supposed. Before Lizzie-May, especially, it was impossible not to feel torn in two. The younger
girl's enthusiasm towards the impending trip
sorely tried her, yet Connie's generous spirit refused to allow her inmost feelings to dampen
the pleasure of her friend.

"Mr Musgrave has promised to take me to
Vauxhall," confided Lizzie-May, one afternoon
when they were alone. "The firework displays
there are really something, he says, and there
are booths where one may listen to the orchestra and eat cold collations!"

And exchange kisses in the Dark Walk,
thought Connie, dully. Uncle Maurie had told
her all about Vauxhall Gardens.

"And we are to inspect Madame Tussaud's
waxwork collection, in the Strand," continued
Lizzie-May, excitedly. "And guess what?" She
giggled coyly. "Should the exhibits prove over-
gruesome, Mr Musgrave gives me liberty to
turn my head into his coat! Oh, and Connie—
there is a huge old lion, named Nero, at Exeter

'Change, which he assures me I must not miss, though it does smell rather."

"It sounds altogether delightful," said Connie, looking up from the menu which she supposed herself compiling for the cook, but when opposite Tuesday's dinner, she saw that she had scribbled roast lion, she gave up with a sigh. "And what of Lord Chievely? Does he return to town also?"

Lizzie-May's gaiety vanished. "I guess so, if Momma has her way," she answered, flicking disconsolately through a fashion journal. "She has every detail planned, down to the nosegay in his wedding coat!" Her fists clenched mutinously. "It is downright hateful! And—and unfair! I don't want no Earl—I don't want no husband, neither, 'xcept I have the pickin' of him!" She cast the journal from her, regarding Connie in lively curiosity.

"Say, is it true that Chievely took a shine to you, honey, and you turned him down flat! Momma is adamant she recalls some gossip concerning a wager . . ."

"I—I had rather not discuss the matter," replied Connie, taken unawares. "There was some nonsense of the sort, I allow, but it is quite at an end. Lord Chievely's only reason for being here is—is on account of his cousin."

"Momma declares you to be real sweet on Mr Musgrave," persisted Lizzie-May, thoughtfully. "Or is it the other way around? I never can recall—Momma talks so. Why, Connie . . . say, have I spoke out of turn, honey?"

Connie put a hand to her scarlet cheeks, dropping the menu list in her confusion. "You must excuse me . . . the bed-linen. I—I have to consult Mrs Reed. I shall see you at dinner, Miss Drinker."

On the snow-covered terrace the Earl and his cousin stood deep in discussion before a weathered stone urn. Mr Sibbald's agitation was plain. His hair stuck up like the quills of a maddened porcupine and his profile had a waxy tint which owed nothing to the chill air.

"A precious line you have got me into, Chievely!" he quivered. "That Drinker woman means to centre-aisle me with her b-blasted offspring! What with her 'dear Lord Chievely-ing' me in that syrupy manner of hers, and—and hinting of 'romantic London'—and some poet or other's beastly guff about 'Hymen's sacred altar'." Feverishly, he plucked at the Earl's coat sleeve. "You must stop her, Chievely! Tell her I'm not available!"

"I underrated her partiality, I allow," mused his cousin, with knit brows. "I have, however, consulted with Benson who agrees that our only course is for you to propose directly to Miss Osborne."

"No!" croaked Mr Sibbald, grasping at the urn for support.

"This very hour!" returned the Earl, crisply. "There is no alternative, Sibbie."

On her way upstairs, Connie encountered Sir Maurice, hovering like a fugitive on the landing. He beckoned to her conspiratorially, saying, in a mournful undertone, "Conn—it's me snuff-box. Confiscated!" He glowered resentfully at the door leading to the morning-room. "Flumpity old parrot! Gloating in there with her chest over your work-table like—like Vulcan over his fire! S'not a filthy habit!"

"I'm sorry, Uncle, but I refuse to interfere. I have no doubt Mrs Drinker means to return your snuff later."

She regarded him in some exasperation. "Why must you persistently antagonise her so?"

"Woman's a ruffian! Shrivels the soul to the size of a lemon pip! Can't think why you chose to invite her, Conn."

"Had you refrained from the gaming tables at Brighton, Uncle, as you ought, there would be no occasion for fault-finding now!" Connie turned on her heel, in justifiable indignation.

Later, she felt badly at having been so sharp with him, but somehow of late her patience was stretched to its limits. Each day seemed longer than the last, and she could barely wait until the house was her own again. What she really meant, although she refused to own it, was that every waking moment her thoughts were tortured by Noel Musgrave. The coolness between them was an anguish scarcely bearable, yet she resolved he should not know it.

As luck would have it, the first person she encountered upon re-entering the drawing-room was Lord Chievely, looking more than usually nervous. His presence had ceased to be other than a thorn in her flesh, but today she found him more irritating than usual. He seemed to be hovering, as if there was something on his mind.

After he had circled three times from windows to chimneypiece, like a wolf on the prowl, Connie laid aside her needle, with which she had been attempting to mend a tear on Fanny's newest petticoat, saying, with a mixture of amusement and pleading, "My lord, if something troubles you, I beg you will speak and be done, for my poor Wilton is worn enough to shreds."

Mr Sibbald swallowed nervously, wishing he were anywhere but Monksford at that particular moment. He could not hope to understand the machinations of his cousin's mind, nor why Fate should choose him for its instrument. He only knew that the Earl was listening behind the door, and he had better have the beastly business over with.

"M-Miss Osborne," he stuttered, flopping down on one knee and feeling the greatest ass alive, "I . . . I insist you hear me out! I—oh, bless me—t-two ships on the sea of life, and all that stuff. No sense in putting off one's doom—I mean, *d-destiny*!" He poked weakly at the inside of his collar, and croaked bravely, "M-Miss Osborne, I am captivated! Your beautiful eyes, y-your shining hair, your—"

"Lord Chievely, is this a proposal—or are you taking an inventory?" murmured Connie, wondering how she was to keep a straight face.

His lordship mumbled something about making an honest woman of her. His left cheek had developed a twitch, and his mouth felt dry as a piece of bark.

"Why?"

Mr Sibbald gaped. He had not expected this. His mouth opened and closed helplessly. "B-Because of M-Monksford," he stammered. "And—and—oh, and the wager!" he added, with sudden inspiration.

"I see." Connie's tone was implacably calm.

"And what is the true reason, for I do not believe a word of what you have just told me."

Mr Sibbald let fall a groan, feeling his ground slip irretrievably from under him. He looked into her eyes, saw the air of studious enquiry, the faint elevation of her brows. It was too much. Mr Sibbald decided that self-preservation was the better part of valour.

"Made me do it," he moaned, pulling despairingly at his gaudy neckcloth. "Devilish jape. Not decent by half."

Connie froze. "Wh-what are you saying?" she breathed, staring. "Am I to understand that— that someone put you up to this mischief?"

"M-Musgrave," croaked Mr Sibbald, sitting down heavily on the carpet.

"Mr Musgrave?" whispered Connie, dazedly. "No! There must be some mist—" She looked wildly at his face, and knew there was none. That Mr Musgrave, of all people, could mock her so! There was no sense to it, no reason. She felt as if a knife had been plunged into her heart. The pain was agonising, remorselessly real. Trembling, she rose to her feet, scarcely able to think straight. She heard herself whisper, as though from a distance, "Why?"

"That is for myself to answer," said a firm voice from the doorway. He stood there, face taut. Connie stared back, unable to move a muscle. How long had he been outside, she wondered? A burning anger possessed her. Of course—the whole incident had been a prearranged sham! He must consider her an almighty fool!

He stood regarding her, his keen eyes fixed unwaveringly on her face. One arm leaned heavily on the crutch. With the other he motioned to his cousin.

"Leave us, old man. Miss Osborne and I have matters to discuss."

Mr Sibbald required no second bidding. With a sheepish apology to Connie, he slunk to the door. He entertained a private hope that the Earl might come clean with the girl. There was no sense in pushing one's luck, for one thing, and for another, his own constitution simply could not face another day as a bogus peer of the realm. He had the gnawing suspicion, however, that his cousin would not give in so easily.

"Well, sir?" Connie's voice sounded reedy, totally unlike her own. Her chin lifted proudly. She waited, willing him to speak, and all the time her heart cried out inside her, as if by some incalculable sorcery of its own the darkness might be lifted, the nightmare banished.

"What am I to say?" His eyes strove with hers, bleakly. "I did not mean this to happen—not this way."

He advanced nearer, until he was but a few feet from where she stood. "I would not hurt you for the world! Think of me what you will—I deserve your contempt, but let me say this! My motive in—in abetting Chievely was wholly with your interest at heart. Please, Constance, you must believe that!"

She stared at him unseeingly, with a throat so choked with threatened tears that she could barely bring herself to reply. He put out a hand towards her, then allowed it to fall helplessly to his side.

"I wonder you have the gall to face me, sir! I

see it all. A mere country nobody—an . . . an unsuspecting pea-goose with whom to amuse yourself!"

Angrily, she brushed the hot tears from her cheek with an unsteady hand. "Well, I do despise you, sir. I despise you more than anyone I can think of."

His eyes darkened. "Will you have the goodness to let me explain this—this wretched business. I beg you, Connie!"

"I am Miss Osborne! Not Connie, or your good girl, or—or your anything!" she choked. "I thought you a gentleman . . . I—I thought so many things. Oh, how I wish to God we had never met!"

"Look," he said, gently. "You're setting yourself in a monstrous pet over nothing. I never knew such a girl for dealing a scold! Now blow your nose this instant, else I shall slap your cheeks soundly."

"You have the most confounded nerve!" breathed Connie. "You will oblige me, sir, by releasing me from the indebtedness I owe you."

Sweeping to the mahogany escritoire, she unlocked its drawer, and withdrew the directive he had given her on Christmas Eve.

"I wish you to—to repossess what is yours at the earliest moment possible," she said, tightly.

"I have not the least intention of doing so," he retorted, waving away her outstretched hand. "So you may as well lock that document up again. It belongs to you."

"But I wish none of it!"

The blue eyes gleamed wickedly. "Then I suggest you come to London with me and straighten matters with Consols."

"I—I *hate* you!" breathed Connie, fighting for words, but knowing herself out-manoeuvred.

"That is what I find so refreshing about you, Miss Osborne," he replied, with a dry smile. "No lick-spittling, and truthful to a fault!" He examined a pedestal vase critically. "You have excellent taste. I wish you might show the same degree of sense now and again." Limping to the escritoire, he scribbled a couple of lines on a sheet of notepaper. "This address will find me, if ever you should require my help. Hold your tongue, girl, and let me finish!" he lectured, as she opened her mouth to ridicule his suggestion. "You think ill of me at this moment, and justly, perhaps, but I am not dismissed so easily, you know." He grinned at her outraged face.

"We leave next week, if you recall. Do not let us part on ill terms, I beg you."

He was looking down at her with the old, amused expression which had so captured her heart, and despite herself, despite everything, she knew that the bitter-sweet magic lingered still. But Connie's pride reasserted itself just in time. She was not such an easy conquest as he imagined. His fine words might work well enough with his light o' loves in town, but he would discover that such practised flirting miscarried dismally with one female, at least.

"Mr Musgrave," she sighed, hardening her heart, and throwing as much exaggerated forbearance into the words as she could muster. "I am heartily sick of this conversation. I think we have no more to say to each other."

A glint entered his eyes, which she found hard to interpret.

"I see. Then, as the tedium of my company is so patently world-wearying to you, ma'am, I can render you no greater service than to take my leave a week in advance."

He inclined himself politely over her hand, and before Connie had power to digest his meaning he had gone, leaving her transfixed, with a thousand emotions somersaulting inside her.

At ten the following morning a chaise was at the door, and he and Lord Chievely were gone, his lordship so patently distressed at the incivility of his conduct that she almost forgave him his ridiculous foibles there and then. Towards Mr Musgrave her manner was calm and coolly polite, but long after the chaise had disappeared from sight, Connie stood gazing at the deep tracks made by the vehicle wheels in the crisp snow.

She wanted to weep, but the tears refused to come. The idyll was over; now she must try to soothe little Fanny's sense of outrage that her new-found friends would no longer be there of an evening to tease her into paroxysms of mirth, that the fun of spillikins and charades, and snow-ball fights with Lord Chievely (which he inevitably lost) and the doggy companionship of St George, were all at an end.

There was Lizzie-May also to consider. Hard enough to account for Mr Musgrave's sudden departure, without making evident the distress she felt at every mention of his name. Lizzie-May was a warm-hearted girl but she was no fool. More than once Connie was aware of her

friend's glance of curiosity, but any tentative
questioning was politely side-stepped. Connie's
hurt was too real, too recent, for her to unbur-
den her wretchedness of heart.

Within the week Lizzie-May and Mrs Drinker
were also due to depart, the latter all too obviously satisfied with her campaigning to date. She
foresaw in the projected stay in town the culmi-
nation of the carefully sown hints and maternal
scheming which had worn down his lordship's
resistance to a satisfying pulp, and which, Mrs
Drinker was confident, would be moulded skilfully into a special licence by June.

What a fine thing it would be for Lizzie-May
to win the catch of the Season! Details such as
her daughter's idiotic notions about the importance of partiality, troubled her not at all.

Love might be all very well between the
pages of *Clarissa* or *Pride and Prejudice*, but
Mrs Drinker knew that what counted in a suc-
cessful partnership was not the depths of
ardour involved, but the acreage of an estate,
and whether the profits were sufficient to support a town house in London, the correct number of servants, with a carriage, horses, grooms,
coachmen and a couple of hunters.

A girl must needs calculate squarely the sta-
bility of whose money she was to marry. Mrs
Drinker was not precisely in penury herself, her
late lamented Hubert having left her comfortably off, but her Louisiana blood was instilled
with the immovable conviction that money
should marry money. To have a coronet thrown
in for good measure was a bonus to be sa-
voured.

During the next few weeks the weather worsened, preventing Fanny's return to school until the roads opened, a fact which young Miss Osborne hailed with undisguised glee. The circumstance did not make Connie's lot any less hard to bear, for her young sister must constantly be amused.

She was no bookworm, turned up her nose at any suggestion of working a sampler, and mooned about the house in Connie's wake, making disgruntled observations, until her sister was almost distracted.

Connie entered the library one afternoon, to find Fanny's dark head bent laboriously over pen and paper. There was a smudge of ink on her nose, but Connie was too much astonished to mention the fact.

"I am writing a letter," explained Fanny, importantly. "But you are not to see. It—it's a secret."

"I have no wish to read your correspondence, my little foozle-top," laughed Connie, delighted that the child was applying herself to some useful pursuit. "You are writing to one of your school-friends, I expect."

"No," replied Fanny, scribbling energetically.

Connie frowned. Fanny had always been a frank, open child, bursting to confide the event of the moment. However, she did not press the point, but merely sat herself on the low library steps and began browsing through a volume at random, confident that Fanny would divulge all in good time. Out of the corner of her eye she watched the bunched ringlets bob up to fetch down a dictionary from the shelf. Evidently a letter of some importance, to warrant such indecent care.

"Connie, does one spell languishing with a W?" frowned Fanny, looking up, after much thumbing of pages. "I cannot find it here."

"Fanny," declared her sister, suddenly suspicious. "I think you had best let me read that letter."

"No! I—I promised I would not. You cannot make me, Connie."

Thoroughly alert now, Connie held out her hand.

"Fanny! If you please." Seeing the mutinous set of the young mouth, she added, coaxingly, "I shall not be in a taking with you, dearest. Only tell me to whom you are writing."

Fanny's lower lip wobbled. "It was to be our secret," she wailed. "His and mine. Now it's quite spoiled!"

She threw down her quill in disgust and ran from the library, leaving Connie staring after her in bewilderment. Picking up the discarded letter, she glanced down the page.

'Dear Mr Musgrave,' it began. She read on, a slow anger kindling inside her. So he had gained Fanny's confidence for a purpose. Her young sister's bubbling pen would tell him all he required, whenever it suited him.

She found Fanny sitting disconsolately before the fire in the morning-room, scuffing at the fender with the toe of her slipper. Connie slipped an arm about the dejected shoulders, saying, with forced cheerfulness, "Why, my love, I did not dream that you should be corresponding with Mr Musgrave! Perhaps I shall include a note of my own."

Fanny glanced up quickly. "He will be vastly surprised if you do, Connie. He was blue as megrim because you do not like him any more."

"What nonsense is this, Fanny?" Connie's cheeks turned pink. "You know nothing of such things. Mr Musgrave left us early simply because—because . . ."

She stammered over the words, patently aware that her sister was regarding her with a candour all too disconcerting in a child of ten.

"I like Mr Musgrave most nearly as much as I love you," whispered Fanny, snuggling close. Her eyes, heavy with trouble, fixed upon Connie beseechingly. "Do please allow me to send my letter, Connie, You may read all of it—truly you may! It will be ever so lonesome for him in town, you see, without St George!"

"And where is St George to be, pray?" asked Connie, faintly. It struck her that Fanny knew far more of Mr Musgrave's domestic arrangements than she herself did. Not that Connie was the least interested. Noel Musgrave might go to—to China, for all she cared. As for Fanny's concern, there would be any number of fashionable pieces willing to console him in that line.

Fanny propped a hand under her chin and considered Connie's question.

"Mr Musgrave owns a hunting box near Reading. I truly think St George is looked after there during the Season."

"I fear you are mistaken, dearest. It is Lord Chievely who has the hunting box in Berkshire."

Fanny shook her dark ringlets emphatically. "No, for Mr Musgrave described it to me precisely! And his estate is ten miles from Cambridge, Connie, with a lake, and grotto, where one may observe all manner of wild fowl, and baby ducklings, and—oh, Connie, do you know, he breeds race-horses there! Why, he had a first in the St Leger only two years ago, and he means to run Oriol and Azor in the Derby this spring! They are his latest colts, you understand, and—oh, do not you find it ever so exciting?"

"I—I had no idea." Connie looked at the upturned, eager little face and smiled. "You had best complete your letter, Miss. Perhaps, if you ask Mr Grundle's boy very particularly, he may have the horse put to, so that you may catch the Mail."

"Connie, I love you ever so!" squeaked Fanny, throwing joyful arms about her sister's neck. "I shall go this instant!" and tearing off her pinafore she was gone, like a bird.

Connie picked up the garment with an indulgent grimace, and took the vacated seat, smoothing the muslin ruffles thoughtfully. At the back of her mind, Fanny's disclosures disturbed her, although she could not pin-point why.

She stared into the fire, watching the flickering spurts of flame dance blue-tongued through the fragrant pine logs. He had been gone almost six weeks, and the raw hurt within her was searing as ever.

She tried to assess his villainies, willing herself to recall the hurtful aloofness in which he had left, but all she could think of was the warm intimacy of his glance, and the feel of his lips as they had brushed her hair. The blue

flames laughed back at her from the grate, and
they were so much the colour of his eyes that
she could bear it no longer. Sobbing, she buried
her face in the muslin pinafore, great salt tears
slipping hotly through her fingers.

Thus Mrs Reed found her, with a face so
blotched and red-eyed from weeping that the
good lady was obliged to scold severely.

"This simply will not do, Miss Connie. A rest
is as timely a cure for the blue devils as I know,
and it's what you require this minute. Whatever will little Miss think, if she finds you in
such a state?"

Drawing the window-curtains with a disapproving swish, the housekeeper put a taper to
the candles, saying briskly, "I've packed Miss
Fanny's things in the big trunk but I cannot lay
my hands on her sprig percale, though I've
searched the house through!"

"She has hidden it, I shouldn't wonder," said
Connie, a wan smile lightening her countenance. "That young Miss is grown inordinately fashion-conscious since going to Bath.
Tucks, she informs me, are quite gone out, and
hem flounces must be all of four inches deep."
She uttered a sigh. "I must have some new day
dresses made up for her. She has shot up fa-
mously since September and those hems will
not unpick very much more."

"Connie!" Fanny burst into the room, cheeks
aglow from her ride into Pipers Ash. "Mrs Cole
gave me this letter for you! It came by the London Mail. Oh, Connie, is it from Mr Musgrave?
Do, please, open it quickly!"

Connie examined the direction, frowning
slightly, before breaking the wafer. She read

the single sheet through once, then sat down heavily with a dejected groan.

"It is from Granby and Fairbrother," she explained wryly, casting the letter from her. "You recall we had their man here in August to survey the house, and estimate repairs. This is his figure. It is quite impossible! I . . . I cannot meet half this sum. Unless . . ."

Mistily, her eyes rested on Fanny. Only one hope remained if she was to keep Monksford. With calm deliberation, Connie went upstairs to her bed-chamber, and unlocked the jewel casket which stood upon the dressing-table. The gems winked back at her from the velvet lining. Very gently, she drew out the magnificent diamond set and held the necklace against her throat.

They had belonged to her grandmother, and were an heirloom of priceless sentimental value, which nothing but dire necessity would cause her to relinquish. But I must, she told herself sadly, I must.

A slight noise from the doorway made her glance up. Fanny's face peered round, curiosity turning to horror as she recognised her sister's intention.

"Connie, no!" she cried, throwing herself against her sister's skirts. "You must not! They are too beautiful!" The young face crumpled suddenly. "Oh, not the rubies, *please*, Connie! P-Papa left them for me."

Connie stooped down, hugging the little body tightly to her, and whispered reassuringly, "The idea never once entered my head, little one." Tenderly, she wiped away the threatened tears with her forefinger. "No, dearest, my diamonds should be sufficient. As soon as you are back at school, I mean to have them valued."

"In Bath?"

Connie considered, then shook her head slowly. "No, Fanny," she replied, and there was a peculiar half-smile on her lips. "I fear, I truly fear, it must be London."

Eight

~~~~~~~~~~~~~~~~~~

BRAND'S HOTEL, IN Dover Street, enjoyed a considerable reputation, and deservedly so, as Connie early discovered. It was the only hotel in London that she knew by name, Papa having stopped there many years previously, and being utterly worn out by the arduous coach journey from Hampshire, she had not the energy to seek farther.

A comfortable sitting-room and bed-chamber on the first floor were subsequently hers, and after the chambermaid, with a condescending sniff at sight of Connie's unfashionable and sadly crushed travelling dress, had laid a fire and departed, she crossed to the window to take her first really good look at London.

Piccadilly, with its dash of carriages and elegant shops, might just be glimpsed if she craned her neck far enough. From the hackney coach she had espied Hatchard's bookshop, of which she had heard so much. Other half-formed impressions sprang to mind. Tall, splendidly proportioned buildings, glimpses of green squares overhung with bursting foliage, and people everywhere and endless streams of vehicles.

To Connie, used to the unhurried quiet of

rural life, it was unnerving, yet at the same
time she experienced a delicious tremor of anticipation. Not far from Brand's adjoining Piccadilly, was St James's Street, where the gentlemen's clubs were, but there was one gentleman
alone uppermost in Connie's thoughts. Too late,
she had discovered that Albany, the exclusive
bachelor chambers where he had rooms, was
hardly more than a street away from the hotel.
What if they should meet by chance? What
would she say to him? What was there to say?

Biting her lip she turned from the window.
Rose Fletcher, whom she had promoted from
parlour maid to accompany her on the trip, was
painstakingly smoothing the creases from the
contents of the trunk, in hopes, no doubt, of
being permanently engaged to attend upon her.

Sighing, Connie set out brush and comb on
the dressing-table. Perhaps he might not acknowledge her at all. Lizzie-May's breezy letters
indicated that she and Mama frequently called
at Albany. Being a kind-hearted girl, she took
especial pains to describe minutely the gay so-
cial whirl into which her parent was now
launching her, and would have been horrified
to learn the unwitting distress caused to Connie
by her carefree pen.

Every ball, every rout party, every visit to the
play or opera, every walk in the Park, every carriage drive—Connie saw them played out in
vivid detail, and with every letter the ache was
redoubled, for although Lizzie-May did not spe-
cifically include Mr Musgrave in her accounts
of these engagements, it took no great imagina-
tion to read between the lines.

Because of this situation, she had hesitated to

impart her projected visit to town, knowing full
well that a certain party must immediately get
wind of it. Not for the world should Noel Musgrave suspect how agonisingly she longed for
the sound of his deep, rich voice, the merest
glimpse of that handsome, athletic frame.

Time and again, she reminded herself not to
be a fool. It never worked. Why else should she
keep every one of Fanny's letters, when she had
never done so previously? Their spontaneous
confidences were her sole link with him—Fanny
related every scrap from Mr Musgrave's letters,
and Connie hung upon them unashamedly.

And yet, Connie knew, if they were to meet
by chance the wound would only be reopened,
more deeply than before. To guard against
such an event she gave Lizzie-May only an ap-
proximate date for her visit, adding that she
would certainly call, should circumstances per-
mit, yet knowing in her heart that she could
never bring herself to do so, while the slightest
chance remained of encountering him there.

She did, however, beg the Drinkers to furnish the name of a reputable jeweller with
whom she might do business, and the very day
following her arrival, Connie dressed with especial care in her best bonnet, which had been
freshly trimmed, and chose a complimenting
pelisse of fir-green serge, to seek out the
celebrated Strand premises of Messrs Rundell
and Bridge.

She had only Lizzie-May's scribbled directions to rely on, and was horribly afraid of losing her way in the maze of streets. Rundell and
Bridge's, when she finally found it, proved

dauntingly elegant, as befitted goldsmiths of royal appointment.

The interior recalled a fashionable drawing-room rather than a jewellers; dainty Hepple-white chairs were ranged invitingly for the customers' use, tall pier-glasses and soft lighting fostered the illusion, reflecting on to glass-topped cabinets housing magnificent gold and silver ware, and the finest jewels Connie had ever seen.

At her entrance, the senior salesman glanced up momentarily from his cataloguing of stock, made the private observation that Connie's business, whatever it might be, would not be worthy of his valuable time, and motioned to an underling to attend on her. This piece of rudeness was not lost on Connie, and it did nothing for her self-confidence.

The young salesman, an eager, fresh-faced lad, bade her a polite good morning and enquired if there was any particular line he might show to her. Nervously, Connie shook her head.

"I understand, sir, that you occasionally pur-chase gemstones. I—I have brought some dia-monds which I rather hoped . . ."

The counterhand regarded her sympatheti-cally.

"We don't go in for second-hand stuff, not 'xcept it's top notch, like." His voice dropped to a confidential undertone. "Look, ma'am, why don't you try Gray's, in Sackville Street? More their line, see."

"Oh, I beg of you!" whispered Connie, in des-peration. "Will you not even examine my stones?" While she spoke, her fingers fumbled at the neck-buttons of her pelisse, revealing the winking collar of diamonds at her slim throat. "It would mean so much to me. I—I have journeyed especially from Hampshire—"

"Having trouble, Simms?"

The senior salesman looked Connie over with suspicion, and decided he had better intervene. Upon seeing the diamonds his lower jaw dropped, but he recovered quickly, saying with his most ingratiating smile, "A chair for the lady, Simms! Now, ma'am, how may we assist you?"

Connie began her explanation over again, and undid the necklace for his inspection. The salesman screwed a strong magnifying lens into his right eye, examined the stones from every angle, pursed his lips, then straightened, regarding her narrowly. He was used to dealing with the very rich. When young women of the other sort approached him with business one resented their presumption. When they came dripping diamonds of the first quality, one sent for the Runners.

"What did you say your name was, ma'am?" he enquired, still smiling blandly. Connie told him. Taking the necklace, he excused himself and hurried upstairs to find Mr Rundell, convinced that Connie was a light-fingered ladies' maid who had made free with her mistress's jewels.

Thirty minutes later Miss Osborne departed, well satisfied, having enjoyed the personal attention of Mr Rundell, whose courtesy and understanding in this delicate transaction had been lavished as freely as though she were a duchess. No, he could not quote a ready figure, but the diamonds were inordinately fine. If

Miss Osborne cared to leave her address, he would make a detailed valuation and send his card in a day or two.

So it was agreed, and Mr Rundell watched her leave, well pleased with himself. Then, snapping his fingers at the chagrined head salesman, he motioned him into his private office.

"This!" he rasped, indicating the winking necklace in his hands, "is the piece of business we have been warned to look out for!"

Stumping to a drawer, he deposited the gems in a lined leather case, and labelled it securely before locking it in the safe.

"There! Now, sir, you will instruct young Simms to convey this note without delay to White's Club." He scribbled busily as he spoke. "Brand's Hotel, was it not? Excellent. Our patron should be vastly gratified to learn it."

Back at Brand's, Connie was about to change for luncheon when there came a tap at her sitting-room door. It was Mrs Stewart, a genial, middle-aged Scottish lady with whom she had become acquainted the previous evening. Mrs Stewart's husband had recently been elected to Parliament, and they were staying at Brand's until a suitable town house might be found.

"I just looked in, dearie," she declared, in the carefully nurtured accent of upper-class Edinburgh, "to see if you might care to join us at the Italian Opera House this evening. Mr Stewart has taken a box—for a two-month, mind you!"

She paused long enough for this information to impress, before adding, with a rueful chuckle, "Of course, you'll understand it's expected of a gentleman in his position, but och, I had as lief watch yon Vestris woman kick her legs in the pantomime—and I'll wager anything Mr Stewart would as well!"

Connie thanked her warmly, but hesitated to accept.

"It is bound to be exceeding grand," she said, quietly. "I should feel grievously out amongst those splendidly gowned ladies."

"Oh, away with ye!" scoffed Mrs Stewart, yet understanding the girl's reluctance. "Now see here, Miss Osborne, it's no' every day you come to London! So just you go pick out something smart from your wardrobe, dearie, and I'll lend you my black lace shawl with the fringe!"

The King's Theatre in Haymarket, home of the Italian Opera and the ballet, was London's most fashionable centre of entertainment, and Connie found it every bit as intimidating as she had feared. Every box in the five-tiered auditorium was filled to capacity with gorgeously gowned, bejewelled ladies of the highest rank, and their escorts.

Once the performance began, however, she relaxed. Her last year's white muslin did not show too badly under Mrs Stewart's beautiful shawl of Brussels lace. Whilst Catalani sang, Connie was obliged to lend an ear to her benefactress, who was more interested in pointing out the notables in the audience.

"See yon roly-poly with the head like a muckle pineapple?" hissed Mrs Stewart, stabbing a gloved finger at the royal box. "Yon's the King's third son, the Duke of Clarence—the one who's had ten bairns by that actress women Mrs Jordan! They do say his language would curl the tail from auld Nick—but what else is one to expect, when the puir man has spent half his life on the quarter-deck of a man o' war! Now, take a guid look yonder, dearie—with the bosom and feathers—that is the Countess of Cowper, the most amiable creature! One of the patronesses of Almack's club, you know. I do believe that it's easier to get an Aberdonian to open his purse than to obtain a voucher for yon place!"

"Who are those ladies in the second tier, wearing ostrich plumes in their hair?" whispered Connie, indicating a bevy of glittering beauties coquetting shamelessly in boxes nearmost to the stage. Mrs Stewart smartly informed her that those were the 'other sort'—kept doxies on the catch for wealthy patrons, for whom a box at the opera was their accredited soliciting ground.

The curtain rose again, and the corps de ballet came on stage, ethereal creatures in white floating gauze. The principal dancer in particular caught Connie's eye. Lithe and deep-bosomed, with auburn hair gleaming like living fire, she pirouetted light as thistledown, lifting exquisitely shaped arms into graceful attitudes of repose. Every so often, the girl would glance upwards as if searching for a face in the crowded tier of boxes. Connie followed her gaze with interest—only to freeze, transfixed.

He was there, light head slightly to one side, ranged well back in his seat with one arm resting carelessly against the velvet upholstery. The shock was so intense, Connie could not wrest her eyes from him. He was preoccupied in following the dancer, a half-smile playing at his mouth. Even as Connie watched, hypnotised, he inclined fractionally forward, and she caught the unspoken gesture, the girl's answering, perceptible nod. Connie's limbs turned to lead. If that girl was not already his mistress, she very soon would be.

Connie could barely suffer the remainder of the performance, so overwhelmed was she. In the press of people leaving the theatre she momentarily lost Mrs Stewart and made blindly for the exit, dropping her fan, not stopping even to pick it up. Someone called after her, but she did not look back. The cool night air hit her sharply as she leaned thankfully against a pillar at the Haymarket entrance, dimly conscious of the crush of carriages and shouting coachmen around her.

"Snap my garters, it *is* Miss Osborne!" exclaimed a voice, close by. Startled, Connie looked up. Mrs Drinker, over-dressed and elaborately coiffured, was regarding her in round astonishment.

"Well, I'll be darned! Lizzie-May!—Now where is that tiresome child gone?"

Clucking impatiently, she excused herself from the party of acquaintances in whose company she was, and raised herself to full height to see above the crowds in the foyer, fanning herself energetically the while in the manner of a high-born Chinese Mandarin.

"Lizzie-May!" she screeched, to Connie's intense embarrassment. "How often must your Momma remind you not to dawdle? Only see who is here!"

"Connie!" Lizzie-May let out a piercing whoop, to the great scandalisation of a clutch of vinegary dowagers standing near by, and disengaging herself from the circle of young friends about her, she launched herself into Connie's arms, embracing her warmly, and all but sabotaging Mrs Stewart's precious shawl in the process.

"You have come—oh, is not this too dandy?" she exclaimed, hands clasped rapturously. "When did you get here, Connie? How long do you stay? Which hotel do you stop at? But there—you must come to our place!"

Overwhelmed by this excited barrage of questioning, Connie was scarce able to supply a word in reply, but whilst Miss Drinker introduced her new set of acquaintances, and delved into plans for this and that excursion, she was miserably conscious of the countrified appearance which her own drab muslin must present.

The Drinkers' set, although not, Connie suspected, precisely the sort with which Mr Musgrave might be likely to associate, were none the less undeniably smart. She caught one young lady of the party studying her with an air of frank superiority, and her colour rose. She wished with all her heart that she had not come.

They were everyone without exception proof of a well-heeled background. Lizzie-May especially, was looking every inch the London belle, in a robe of spangled tulle over turquoise satin, and with a neckline cut so low that Connie could not help staring. Her blonde hair was dressed becomingly in a Grecian knot and caught about by a fillet of matching velvet ribbon.

Connie's spirits sank. Nothing in her own meagre wardrobe could begin to hold its own against such sophistication. What passed for high fashion in Winchester, or even Bath, must be laughably second-rate here. With forced spirits she told herself it was of no consequence, she would be in town only a few days, when she became aware of the one pair of eyes she had been dreading regarding her unwaveringly from the perimeter of the little group.

For an instant, their glances met, his searching, Connie's in a face first white then scarlet, hesitant for fear of what she might find there.

She was conscious of acknowledging his brief, respectful bow, then he was gone, melting into the thinning crowd as though he had never been, leaving her in a consternation, which she felt everyone around her must see.

In fact the Earl's momentary appearance had been apparent only to herself, and the awkwardness was alleviated by Mrs Drinker voicing a strong desire to be gone, the night air being treacherous to her chest.

"You know very well this dampness brings on my rheumatiz, Lizzie-May," she complained, wringing Connie's hand in a hearty gesture of farewell. "Our carriage is waiting, Miss Osborne. Be sure and drop by now. Our afternoons are Tuesdays and Fridays. Come along, Lizzie-May! Miss Osborne's party will doubtless come looking for her presently. Come along, I say!"

"Connie, honey, I shall send you a line by the Twopenny Post!"

Lizzie-May's farewell screech reached Connie

as Mrs Drinker bundled her daughter into their carriage. In the same instant as the vehicle rolled forwards, Mr Musgrave emerged from behind a pillar and with purposeful deliberation, tucked her arm through his before she had power to protest, shielding her from the press of humanity still surging about the carriage stances.

"And what brings you to London, Miss Osborne?" he enquired, drawing her into the shadow of the theatre. "Am I to assume that you have mellowed your prejudice—or is it merely that curiosity has got the better of you?"

His eyes held a glint of mockery or satisfaction, Connie was not certain which, but behind the lingering, caressing glance that she knew of old, she sensed the still raw vestige of his pride. Was it possible that she had hurt him more deeply than she knew?

For an instant, she hesitated, then the remembrance of what had gone before, the bitter intimacy of that glance between himself and the red-haired opera dancer—what name had the play-bill carried?—Désirée D'Erlon, that was it—the bitter recollection knifed uppermost in her mind. Proudly, her chin lifted.

"I would have you know, sir, that it is business of a private nature and—and that alone, which brings me here! I—I did not bargain on our meeting this way . . ."

Trembling, she extended her hand. "You need not put yourself about, Mr Musgrave. My friends should be—why, there they are!" she broke off, with a relieved smile, perceiving the Scottish couple in the glow of a linkboy's torch on the theatre steps. Turning to him, and struggling to keep her voice steady, she said, "G-Goodbye, Mr Musgrave. It is not likely we shall encounter each other again . . ."

"I should not count upon that, Miss Osborne," he returned softly, leading her up to a worried Mrs Stewart. "When it comes to obstinacy, I assure you I can prove as 'curst stubborn as yourself.'"

Before she could prevent him, he had taken her hand and kissed it lightly. "Remember that, my prickly burr!"

With a respectful bow to Mrs Stewart, he left her, striding back towards the lighted theatre. Off to meet his opera dancer, thought Connie, dully. Then Mr Stewart was helping her into their carriage, and they were jolting back to Brand's.

"Who was yon fine-looking gentleman?" demanded Mrs Stewart, in tones of appreciative admiration. "Did you see his ring, James? I'd no' be astonished if it was worth two hundred!" She regarded Connie with renewed curiosity.

"Is he maybe your intended?"

"My—No, of a certainty he is not!" declared Connie, hotly. "Mr Musgrave is merely an—an acquaintance."

She gazed out at the darkened streets, thankful that Mrs Stewart could not see the agitation in her face. She would not see him again! She would not! And yet, he had warned her to expect him, in that impudently careless manner of his . . .

Angrily, she wiped at her cheek with the back of her glove. On Friday, she would return to Rundell and Bridge, accept whatever sum they offered, pay back his five hundred pounds or as much as she could, and bespeak a seat on the first Mail coach to Salisbury.

Nine

DURING THE NEXT few days, Connie felt more lonely than she had ever been in her life. Mrs Drinker sent round a note, worded in a hysterical scrawl, with the intelligence that Lizzie-May had caught fever, and what was she to do? Connie immediately took a hackney coach to Manchester Street, where she found her friend in bed, red-nosed and feverish, and complaining of the headache.

Mrs Drinker was prostrated with visions of typhus but having examined Lizzie-May's pulse, Connie felt reasonably satisfied that her friend was suffering from nothing more alarming than a severe head-cold, induced, no doubt, by the scant garments she had worn to the Opera. As a precautionary measure, however, a doctor was summoned and Connie left Lizzie-May's bedside only when the girl had fallen into a fitful sleep.

Thankfully, Mrs Stewart saw to it that Connie was not left alone to brood. Their mornings were employed shopping in Mayfair. The good-hearted matron was swift to perceive that Connie's means did not extend to the extravagances of Bruton Street, however much she lingered over the fashionable delights in the bow-fronted windows, and with tactful understanding suggested an excursion to Grafton House, where prices were a good deal more reasonable.

Connie required no great persuasion to open her reticule there. Pretty, coloured muslins at only three and sixpence per yard, and silk stockings costing twelve shillings a pair were too fine an opportunity to miss, so she did not mind in the least having to wait at the crowded counter a full twenty minutes. Mrs Stewart drew her attention to a tray of finely worked Bugle trimming, and Connie bought two ells, feeling deliciously wicked over such unaccustomed extravagance.

Leaving Grafton House they set their steps to St James's Square, where Connie lost her heart to a charming Queensware dinner service in the window of Wedgwood's showrooms, but prudently cast temptation behind her. Although it was now almost noon, Mrs Stewart insisted upon 'a wee daunder doon to peek at Carlton House'.

Connie did not share her companion's gushing adulation of the Prince Regent but she was obliged to own a secret admiration of his tasteful residence, isolated behind a screen of Ionic columns, with two imposing gateways flanking Pall Mall, and guarded by scarlet-clad sentries sloping arms.

To Mrs Stewart's disappointment there was no sign of the Regent's yellow chariot, and it was agreed to return to Brand's. They were walking down Jermyn Street, when Mrs Stewart suddenly drew Connie's attention to an open curricle parked opposite, exclaiming, in excited undertones, "Well, I declare! If yon's no' your gentleman coming down those steps, dearie! I'd mind on they braw shoulders anywhere!"

Thankful for the concealing brim of her bonnet, Connie glanced warily across the street. It was him, looking dashing in a brown coat which fitted without a crease, his hair lightly ruffled by the soft March breeze. He swung himself on to the box, and she saw him glance up at the house from which he had just come.

A girl's face was framed momentarily at an upstairs window. Connie glimpsed the delicate grace of her, both hands raised to her lips, blowing a languid kiss. With a dull ache, she knew it to be his ballerina.

He lifted his tall crowned beaver hat to the window with exaggerated politeness as he took the ribbons, and almost before Connie realised, the curricle with its diminutive Tiger perched in the rear had rounded the corner, leaving her staring after it in wordless stupefaction.

"Bless me, child, you've gone pale as a half-baked scone!" clucked Mrs Stewart, in concern. "And sure as the Devil's in Ireland, I've left my smelling-salts behind."

"It is mere fatigue," stammered Connie, recovering swiftly. "We do seem to have walked unconscionably far this morning."

As Connie had predicted, Lizzie-May improved rapidly after a few days in bed, and by the end of the week she had regained her accustomed spirits. An excursion to Sadler's Wells Theatre, in Islington village, was immediately agreed upon, in order that Connie might enjoy the antics of the famous Grimaldi, whose

genius as an acrobat, juggler, swordsman, singer
and dancer was only surpassed by his clownish
artistry and the sheer magic of his humour.

Suspecting that the melodrama and farce of
Sadler's Wells appealed to Lizzie-May's palate
rather more than any opera staged at the King's
Theatre, Connie readily agreed to make up the
party.

"We shall call for you at seven, honey." Lizzie-May buttoned Connie's pelisse up to the
throat, and hugged her in high glee. "Oh, and
do bring a wrap. The breeze from the river can
be amazingly cool."

That same afternoon, Connie returned to
Rundell and Bridge and this time the head
salesman was all but grovelling at her feet. She
could barely suppress her amusement as he
rushed off to find Mr Rundell. He seemed to be
gone an interminable age, and she had begun
imagining all manner of horrors, that the diamonds had been mislaid, that they were
worthless even, when Mr Rundell appeared,
beaming. He seemed to sense her qualms, and
chuckled.

"There is no cause to look hobbled, dear
ma'am, I assure you."

He made her sit down. "These are fine
stones, remarkably fine. I have no hesitation in
offering you—" He named a figure, and Connie
gasped aloud, she could not stop herself.

"Well, Miss Osborne, what do you say?"

"Yes—oh yes, thank you!" she whispered, overcome. Never, in her wildest imaginings had she
counted on such a sum. Surely now, her be-
loved Monksford would be safe. She looked up,

quivering with emotion. "Oh, sir, you have no conception of what this means!"

"I may tell you that your stones did not even reach our window display!" he smiled, well pleased at her reaction. "They were snapped up almost immediately, and are in the most worthy hands. I shall write out a cheque this instant, dear ma'am, and Simms shall send out for a carriage to convey you to your hotel."

"You are exceedingly kind," whispered Connie. Her heart was singing. Lord Chievely, the odiousness of his wager, all were swept away, forgotten, in the exhilaration of the moment. Only one cloud marred her happiness. And that, no amount of money could alter.

Lord Chievely adjusted his cravat to a more pleasing angle and glanced beyond the looking-glass to the hunched figure of his cousin, who was grappling with a boot-hook, with an air of frenzied determination.

"For the Lord's sake, Sibbie, have Benson pull 'em off for you!" implored the Earl, unable to suffer his cousin's contortions any longer. "If you do not make haste, you'll be abominably late. Where did you say you are bound?"

"Sadler's Wells," ground Mr Sibbald, wrenching off his left boot with a force which all but laid him on his back. "This is the fourth time there in a sennight, Chievely! I wish that Drinker girl might develop a passion for something other than farce!" He glared accusingly at the Earl.

"Why is it *you* succeeded in sliding out of these fiendish invitations?"

"Firmness, Sibbie! One swiftly learns that an

excess of pleasure is ruinous to the life-span. I
caution you, old man, ere you sink into dissipa-
tion!" He accepted Mr Sibbald's indignant
snort with equanimity. "To be honest, I had
rather accompany you to the play. If, as I suspect, Miss Osborne is one of your party, be sure
to convey my deepest respects."

He swung an evening cloak over his shoulders and picked up his hat and cane. "I fear I
must leave now, Sibbie. The fleshpots of
Vauxhall are not to be denied."

"What pleasure is to be got in a rackety
hang-out like Vauxhall?" demanded Mr Sibbald, in aggrieved tones, struggling to brush his
hair into an imitation of his cousin's modish
locks.

Lord Chievely favoured him with a wicked
grin.

"That, Sibbie, rather depends upon where
one cares to look!"

Mrs Drinker's carriage called for Connie
punctually at eight. She had expected her
friends to stop by en route to the play, but to
her surprise, Connie found herself the sole occupant, the coachman intimating that his in-
structions were to bring her directly to Manchester Street.

She found Lizzie-May in a state of high vexation, her Mama at pains to countering it, and
Lord Chievely, writhing scarlet-faced before
them, in an opera hat and tails.

"Oh, Connie!" cried Lizzie-May, with the air
of a tragedy queen. "We cannot go!" She turned
an accusing eye upon the gentleman of the

party. "Lord Chievely has mislaid the theatre-tickets!"

"I had them with me when I left! I—I know I had!" stuttered Mr Sibbald, groping unsuccessfully in his pockets. "Must have pulled 'em out with my handkerchief. Oh, M-Moses!"

"Oh, Lord Chievely, how could you be so negligent?" declared Lizzie-May, in a rush of frustration. "I particularly desired Connie to see Joseph Grimaldi; it is altogether too bad!"

"Hold your tongue, Lizzie-May!" hissed Mrs Drinker, bundling her daughter to one side. "Do you wish to scare him off?"

"Oh, please!" pleaded Connie, feeling a pang of sympathy for his stricken lordship. "May we not propose another suggestion? You have given such glowing accounts of Vauxhall Gardens in your letters, Miss Drinker. May we not go there instead?"

"No-No!" stammered Mr Sibbald, in horror. "N-Not Vauxhall!"

"And whyever not?" demanded Lizzie-May, fixing him with an air of bristling authority. "I call it a splendid idea, Connie! I wish it were a masquerade night there, for it is the greatest sport then! But no matter!" She took Connie's arm, her spirits soaring anew, and pointedly handed Mr Sibbald his hat, saying, "We are quite ready, your Earlship."

Mr Sibbald gulped. He sensed impending doom, and did not in the least know what to do about it.

From the many differing accounts abounding with regard to the pleasure gardens, Connie was prepared to find Vauxhall gay, spectacular

and perhaps a trifle vulgar. She was totally
taken aback by the sheer size it encompassed—
almost twelve acres, laid out in spacious sun-
dappled walks, sheltered by high hedges and
trees, and opening at every turn on to rustic
bridges spanning miniature cascades, Greek
temples and grottos, and where, simply by
choosing a sequestered arbour or little-trodden
path, the shrieks of laughter, music and general
hum of gaiety mellowed to the tinkle and plash
of a fountain or the evening chirrup of a
thrush.

There was, it seemed, something to suit every taste in this wonderland of entertainment.
Class distinction did not exist; there were as
many shrill, Cockney voices in the pushing,
good-natured press around the Punch and Judy
booth as there were top hats and silks.

A burly fellow carrying a small boy astride
his shoulders made room for Connie and Lizzie-May to obtain a closer view of the antics of
Bruno bear, warning them, in a genial undertone, to keep a firm hold on their reticules.

"Crawling wiv cut-purses an' sharpers, missies.
Chouse you of your wery spit, they would!
Watch wot your about, I says."

Connie assured him they would vouchsafe his
advice. One must expect so popular a rendez-
vous as Vauxhall to pull as many rogues, but on
a balmy spring evening as this, such unsavoury
considerations seemed unforgivable.

She was thankful that only Lord Chievely
had come to make up their party. After wit-
nessing his undoubted liaison with that D'Erlon
girl, in Jermyn Street, Connie could not have
borne to face Noel Musgrave a second time. She

told herself that she was glad—glad to have her suspicions confirmed. He was in every way as great a fribble as his cousin. Her head insisted—but her heart refused to accept the obvious.

When Lizzie-May had satisfied herself that the principal delights were thoroughly impressed on her friend, when Connie had exclaimed over the myriad lamps strung overhead amidst the foliage, and Roubiliac's fine statue of Mr Handel had been suitably admired, Mrs Drinker sent his lordship in search of a supper-booth close to the Rotunda, where they might listen to the orchestra and partake of a light refreshment.

They had not long settled themselves when Lizzie-May declared her intention of stepping inside the pavilion to watch the country dancing, and without further ado hauled off Lord Chievely to do the honours.

Left with Mrs Drinker, Connie was endeavouring to assist that finicky matron in choosing between the custard and syllabub, when a dark-haired young gentleman, standing nearby with some friends, graciously deposited a dish of each on their table, remarking, with a confidential aside, "I recommend the syllabub, ma'am. It is laced with wine!"

Straightening, he smiled down at Connie.

"Forgive my impertinence in encroaching upon your privacy, but I have been lost in admiration of your charming companion these full twenty minutes." He inclined slightly towards Connie, saying, with an optimistic grin, "Will you not take pity, ma'am, on a gracious wretch who loves to dance?"

Connie hesitated, reluctant to acquiesce to such free manners, but Mrs Drinker, misinter-

True.
Unexpected
taste

© Lorillard, U.S.A., 1978

5 MG TAR

Newport

Newport

MENTHOL KINGS

Alive with pleasure!

preting this reticence, shooed her to her feet with a brusque nod. "You go way ahead, Miss Osborne! I like to see young folks enjoyin' themselves."

To refuse was impossible, without appearing rude or prudish. Connie had to own there was nothing in the gentleman's appearance to alarm. About her own age, or perhaps a little older, she surmised; well-spoken, with a faintly rakish air in his manner and dress which was by no means unattractive.

His name, he informed her, as he led her into a set, was Roger Thursby. Doubtless she had heard of his uncle, Sir Willoughby Thursby, the Member for Chelmsford? Connie confessed she had not, but he seemed not the least put out, and rattled away amiably as they went down the dance, extracting her life history, it seemed, in so many minutes. Hampshire—ah, yes, good hunting country, although he confessed to a preference for Melton.

Connie's initial shyness melted under his easy personality, and she found her mood responding to his, so that when the figure ended and the orchestra struck up the voluptuous strains of the waltz, she was so enjoying herself that it was with very real regret that she knew it behove her to refuse.

No unmarried young lady careful of her reputation must even consider so shocking a venture, yet her eyes were wistful as she begged off. Mr Thursby seemed to understand her reasons, and elected to remain by her side, apparently content to be an onlooker also. Yet, before the hesitant refusal had well left her tongue, Connie's heart missed a beat. Standing close by the orchestra, on the near side of the floor, in company with a coterie of gentlemen and their ladies, stood Noel Musgrave.

Upon his arm was a good-looking creature, raven-haired, with an excellent figure encompassed in floating white gauze. She was laughing up into his face with bold flirtatiousness, and he . . . Connie turned away, sick at heart.

It was then, for no explicable reason, other than pique, that she determined he should see how little she cared! Let him flirt outrageously with his—his harem of women, if he so chose!

Breathlessly, she touched Mr Thursby's arm.

"I—I have changed my mind, sir. Nothing would give me greater pleasure than to waltz."

"I am delighted to know it!" he smiled, regarding her with quizzical satisfaction. "Come, let us show everyone how a waltz ought to be performed!"

Masterfully, he swept her into the maze of swirling couples. Connie blushed as his arm tightened about her waist. Only one other man had held her so close, and he . . . Fiercely, she tried to push Noel Musgrave from her mind, an impossible undertaking when every beat of the dance brought her closer to where he stood.

She detected the look of startled recognition, the tightening at his mouth, and her chin lifted. Roger Thursby smiled down at her and she took infinite pleasure in his attention, knowing that a certain gentleman must be burning with curiosity.

With deliberate perversity, she widened her smile, throwing back her head and evincing every delight in her partner's society, whilst the compelling rhythm of the waltz swept her along in reckless disregard for convention.

Three times they circled the floor, thrice Connie caught Mr Musgrave's keen eye upon her as she passed, thrice she hid her aching heart in a display of flirtatious abandon, a circumstance which young Mr Thursby was not slow to appreciate.

As he led her from the floor at the music's end, Connie glimpsed the white anger on the face of her tormentor, and knew that she had succeeded. Mr Musgrave's mouth was compressed in a hard line, and his eyes sparkled dangerously. She saw him excuse himself from his partner with a whispered word, and watched him stride swiftly into the crowd without a backward glance.

"Connie! Mama begs that you will rejoin us for supper." It was Lizzie-May, and Connie could see that her friend was not a little taken aback by the uncharacteristic laxity she herself had displayed on the floor. The implication caused her to blush hotly. Was it, then, only the 'goers', the immodest jades who indulged in that exhilarating new dance? Panic seized her. What must the Drinkers think of her? What had she done?

Turning to Mr Thursby, she whispered, scarlet-cheeked, "You must excuse me . . . I—I would not have you believe me to be . . ."

His mouth curved in a grin. "I imagine only that you were enjoying our waltz, Miss Osborne. Surely nothing else signifies?"

Mrs Drinker was not to be found, and whilst Lizzie-May, with marked reluctance, departed in search of her parent, Connie sat down at the vacated supper-booth with Mr Thursby, thankful of an excuse to recover her composure.

Mr Sibbald was not enjoying his evening at Vauxhall. He had never successfully mastered the art of dancing, and in an evil moment had allowed Miss Drinker to lead him into the Boulanger. Before the dance was well over, Mr Sibbald had successfully decimated the steps of the couples on either side, trodden on eight pairs of toes and earned so many abusive protestations as to force Miss Drinker to trot him smartly from the reach of further destruction.

Now, just when he was retreated to a rout-bench to console his jangled nerves with a lemonade, a cousinly hand upon his shoulder signified worse to come.

"Sibbie," hissed the Earl, in a menacing undertone. "What in Hades is going on? You are meant to be in Islington!"

"L—Lost 'em!" moaned Mr Sibbald, edging defensively to the end of the rout-bench. "Lost the p-play tickets. Miss Drinker made us come here by way of compensation." He gulped nervously.

"Not my fault, Chievely. Wouldn't listen!"

His cousin's grim features darkened. "Where is Miss Osborne?" he interrupted, tersely. "And why is she not being chaperoned as she ought?"

Mr Sibbald blinked. "But she is—least, she was." He cast about him vaguely, peering at the sea of dancing couples.

"Bound to be here somewhere, old man."

The Earl seized him by the shoulder, urgently. "Find her, Sibbie!"

Mr Thursby's dark eyes watched lazily as Connie took a hesitant sip of the punch he had ordered. Vauxhall punch tasted strange, Connie decided, wryly, not at all like the fruit cup she was used to, but having a strong burning flavour which attacked her throat and made her head swim. She would have preferred not to finish it, but he pressed her, something about the fireworks being about to begin, and she must drink quickly, else they might not catch the Spectacular.

Connie's head felt muzzy as she stood up, but Mr Thursby took her hand, saying, urgently, "This way! It's a short cut."

He was drawing her down a side alley, so thickly grown with trees that hardly any light penetrated. Connie stopped, uncertainly.

"But . . . it appears so fearfully gloomy! The crowds—they are all taking the other avenues. Are you quite certain . . . ?"

Impatiently, he seized her arm. "I tell you, we avoid the crush by this route! Come on!"

Roughly, he propelled her into the funereal depths of the overhanging foliage. It was very still, and impossible to see one's footing. Connie clutched involuntarily at his hand, to steady herself. He laughed softly, and, without warning, she found herself pinned in an inflexible hold.

"That's more like it," he murmured, coaxingly. "I think we need not bother with the fireworks. You and I, my dear, are eminently capable of igniting a few sparks of our own."

Connie tried to scream but her throat was dry with fear. She strove to push him away, but he caught her fast, forcing his mouth down on hers, and though she struggled like a wild-cat, her efforts merely served to amuse him.

"So you wish to play hard to get?" he mocked, softly. "You surprise me. Provincial chits are normally hot for a little sport in the bushes!"

She felt his fingers rip at the thin muslin of her gown. With a frantic summoning of her strength, Connie kicked out, clawing her nails frenziedly down his cheek, her breath coming in hysterical sobs. A strangled oath broke from him, and his grip relaxed.

Seizing her chance, Connie twisted free and fled, stumbling over her skirts and clutching at the torn bodice, conscious that it was in shreds.

She could hear her molester's footsteps pounding behind her. Blindly, she reached the end of the dark avenue, half fainting with terror. The roar and brilliance of the fireworks beyond dazzled her momentarily, and in that same instant, a shadowy figure barred her path, causing her to scream, terror-stricken. He had headed her off, somehow . . . she was trapped . . .

And then she stumbled. She was aware of an indrawn exclamation, but her senses were reeling, and she realised that she was going to faint.

For several minutes the world went black. Presently, Connie became aware of strong arms supporting her. She opened her eyes, tears of relief flowing down her cheeks.

"Noel," she whispered, shakily. "Oh, thank God!"

Ten

～～～～～～～

"CONSTANCE! ... SWEET LUCIFER, what has happened here?" ejaculated the Earl, perceiving fully her distressed condition, and the rent in her gown. He swore softly, and leaped for the direction she had come, but the avenue appeared deserted.

Eyes ablaze, he returned to Connie, who was still shaking and hysterical from her ordeal. Sweeping off his silk evening-cloak, the Earl wrapped it about her shoulders, and drew her to him, saying, urgently, "Was it Thursby, Constance? By Heaven, I swear I'll kill him!"

She nodded dumbly, burying her face in both hands. "He ... Oh, Noel ..."

"I shall find him!" gritted the Earl, satisfied. Grimly, he took her face between his hands. "Connie ... if he touched you at all, you must tell me!"

Connie felt the blood leap to her cheeks. It was impossible not to understand his meaning. Trembling, she looked up.

"N-no ... I—I managed to—to ..."

"What the deuce possessed you to take up with that young rip?" he demanded, angrily. "Don't you know better than to go into the Dark Walk with any Tom, Dick or Harry?"

"The Dark Walk! . . ." Little wonder, after her uninhibited behaviour earlier, that Thursby should assume her willingness to philander. The shame of it, the burning degradation, engulfed her in its enormity. Through hot tears, she heard herself whisper, "I—I did not know . . ."

"Hush, my child," he soothed, drawing her firmly into his arms. "It's all over. I have you safe."

Gently he rubbed the wetness from her face with the back of his thumb, feeling her body shake convulsively against his. As though comforting a child, he murmured reassurances until the stark terror, which had made her grey eyes appear enormous, was banished in quiet.

"And now," he said, swinging her effortlessly into his arms, "I intend taking you away from this place."

Ignoring the stares directed from every side, he strode with her to his carriage, and after despatching his Tiger with a scribbled note of explanation to Mr Sibbald and the Drinkers, ordered him to drive at once to Berkeley Square.

"From tonight you are to reside with my Grandmama," he said, firmly, when they were comfortably on their way.

"But—but that is totally impossible! The Exeter Mail leaves from Lad Lane tomorrow evening at half past seven! . . . I—I must be on it."

He twisted round to face her, his body tensed. An uncomfortable silence followed, during which Connie's heart pounded fiercely against her ribs. She felt him lean back against the seat, and heard the quiet reproof in his voice as he said heavily, "So you intended to leave—just like that— with ne'er a word to anyone! Why, Constance?"

"My business is accomplished . . . there is no reason for me to remain," she heard herself reply, wearily. "And you are unjust. Miss Drinker was party to my intentions. You must know I would not be so uncivil as to do otherwise."

He digested her words in silence. "But *I* was not to be informed until after you were gone, is that it?" he remarked, at length. "Why are you so bent upon avoiding me, Constance? No—it is of no consequence," he added, quickly sensing the droop of her head, the stifled moan as the carriage lurched her against him. Gently but firmly, his arm secured her against his shoulder, and, as though of its own volition, Connie's head relaxed naturally against his breast.

Her ladyship had already retired, and her butler was about to bolt the outer doors, but Lady Fielding's grandson was used to being obeyed and in less time than Connie knew how the dying fire in the pleasant library had been rekindled, and she was ensconced before it, in a deep wing-chair, with Mr Musgrave's evening-cloak still about her shoulders.

Its owner, eyes dark with concern, measured a draught of golden liquid from a decanter and raised it to her lips, saying, firmly, "I wish you to drink this. As much as you can."

Not until Connie had swallowed down the contents did she realise that he had given her brandy. Fire seared her insides, taking her breath away, but almost in the same instant the nausea lessened, and she managed a tremulous smile.

"Good girl," he remarked approvingly, removing the glass. "Now, do you feel like telling me what happened?"

Haltingly, Connie related the evening's events. Mr Musgrave listened in grim silence, and his brows were snapped together so thunderously that she was almost afraid to look at him.

Involuntarily, her fingers went to the ripped vestiges of her gown. Another man might have taken advantage of her situation, but he was not like that. Her heart glowed.

He was regarding her soberly. "There is one part I do not fully understand. What in God's name prompted you to goad him on in such determined fashion? That was hardly in character, I should have thought."

His eyes were troubled, searching her face keenly so that she had to turn away, unable to return his glance.

"I . . ." She gestured helplessly. I wanted to make you jealous. The words were on the tip of her tongue, but she bit them back. She suspected he was blaming himself for the incident, as it was. That, and her pride, reduced her to silence.

He leaned against the book-lined shelves, regarding her thoughtfully. "Would you rather I concocted an explanation for your sad appearance, or do not you mind Grandmama learning the whole? I must give instruction to have her informed of your arrival, but should you rather I kept silent about—"

Connie could make no direct reply. There was a great lump in her throat. She gazed up at him, eyes big with gratitude.

"How may I ever express my gratitude?" she whispered, huskily. "I—I feel so bitterly ashamed. All those abominable things I said to you at Monksford . . . Had you not happened on the scene tonight I . . ." She regarded him in curiosity. "How did you know where I was gone?"

"I didn't," he admitted, ruefully. "But Thursby's reputation as a blackguard is common knowledge, and I feared to leave you any longer in his company, even," he added, with a smile, "at risk of a sharp set-down from yourself on the grounds of my being monstrously overbusy!"

He observed her colour heighten, and continued, gently, "Miss Drinker glimpsed you briefly just before the illuminations commenced. She had the foresight to apprise my cousin, and from his account of your direction, I guessed all too correctly what your friend Thursby had in mind."

He came nearer and stood, almost diffidently, by the side of the wing-chair. "If you insist upon laurels, you might assure me that we are friends again," he remarked, softly. "Are we, Constance?"

He had to strain to catch her whispered reply. Connie's heart was in a turmoil, but what else could she say but yes?

The Earl arrived early in Berkeley Square the next morning and sauntered into his grandmama's elegant boudoir, where he found the two ladies deep in conversation over a cosy breakfast. At his entrance, Connie half rose from a sofa, one hand flying self-consciously to the gauzy wrapper of lilac trimmed with swans-down, lent her by Mr Musgrave's sprightly relative.

"Be at ease, child," remonstrated the Dowager Lady Fielding, chuckling. "My grandson is used to seeing females with rather less wrapping on than *yours* this side of the day!"

She favoured his upshot eyebrows with an impudent wink, and proffered a thin cheek to be kissed. "Pray, what brings you here, young man, at such an ungodly hour? Do not you realise my hair is still in curl-papers?"

The Earl grinned at this scold, dropping an affectionate peck on the satin bow of his grandmama's amazing boudoir cap. Even now, when he was all of four and thirty, her ladyship continued to regard him with the same indulgent disapproval as when he had been five.

"I suspected Miss Osborne might be in need of her trunk," he smiled, looking across at Connie, who was in agonies over the toasted muffins. Her long, dark hair hung loose about her shoulders, giving her, she knew, an absurdly little-girl appearance, but worse, much, much worse, was the recollection of how she had so wantonly cast herself into his keeping during the carriage ride to Lady Fielding's.

Even as her guilt at such abandoned behaviour diffused under a surging and even more shocking tide of joy, he sat himself next her, so that her disconcertment was complete, and she dropped her spoon.

The Earl stooped swiftly to retrieve it. Connie did the same, and their foreheads bumped smartly, causing them both to laugh.

"You have regained the roses in your cheeks,

I see," he observed, helping himself to coffee. "Firstly, however, I must confess to having cancelled your seat on the Mail."

"It would appear, sir, you have been inordinately active on my behalf," returned Connie, favouring him with a rueful smile.

His mouth quirked. "Your friend Thursby will testify to that."

Connie's eyes flew to his. "You—you have seen him?"

The Earl's jaw tightened. "Assuredly, my dear. He will not trouble you again."

Seeing the swift alarm in her face, he added, gently, "No, Constance, I've not killed him."

"I warrant you gave him more kicks than half-pence!" declared the Dowager, with relish. For all her five and seventy years she was alert as a gazelle; a small, bird-like creature, whose mischievous eyes missed nothing, and who, despite stiffening joints, insisted upon being driven round the Ring, in Hyde Park, every evening at five, so as to keep abreast of the on-dits of the carriage set.

"I can deliver a facer when needs must," murmured the Earl, resting his gaze on Connie's bent head. "After leaving here, I returned to Vauxhall. The young fool was still in the Rotunda, cool as you please. Naturally, he denied all knowledge of the affair. Once outside, however, I persuaded his memory to recover wondrously! And I did allow him first move, Bright-Eyes."

The Earl spoke lightly, but nothing could disguise the burning passion in his glance. "I fear he will survive. That sort always do."

"Wh-What did you do to him?" whispered Connie.

"Flung him in a bush. I ought to have chosen the river—but I feared to pollute the water supply. By the by," he added, turning the subject adroitly, "that Mrs Stewart has been amazingly helpful over your trunk. If any item has been overlooked, only tell me so, and I shall fetch it in a wink."

Connie thanked him, brought alive to the deficiencies of her appearance, and begged leave to be excused. The Earl watched her go, a thoughtful expression on his face.

"A pretty mannered child, that," observed Lady Fielding, the minute Connie was out of earshot. "But, merciful Heaven, Chievely, do you realise she has brought her parlour-maid to wait upon her? I have never heard the like!"

"The wench is now upstairs, unpacking the trunk," returned his lordship, smiling to himself at the outraged expression on his relative's face. "You will find Miss Osborne an exceptional young lady, Grandmama." He looked sharply at her. "I trust you have kept good guard of your tongue, my love. She must not suspect my real identity."

"Not a syllable have I breathed!" declared his grandmama, snatching off her pince-nez. "But I tell you, young man, I consider it quite monstrous to deceive the girl as you are doing!"

"Do you imagine I do not realise it?" Despairingly, the Earl pushed a hand through his fair locks. "Oh, Grandmama, it seemed so harmless, at first." He stared fixedly at the floor. "Monksford is in appalling shape—but you already knew that from my letters. It's not Miss

Osborne's fault. She has done everything possible, short of selling up. And that, she refuses to do . . . least of all to me!"

"Is Monksford the reason behind this all-absorbing interest in her?" demanded Lady Fielding, sharply. His lordship lifted an eyebrow.

"You are well enough acquainted with my views, Grandmama. Wedlock is a padlock. And when the time comes, I elect to choose my own gaoler, so I shall thank you not to match-make, my love!"

"Pshaw!" snorted his relative, impatiently. "As though I should presume! But this Miss Osborne is a cut above your usual try-ons, Chievely, and I shall not countenance your making sheep's eyes at her, unless you mean well by it! What about this degrading wager? Does it still go on?"

"It does," he replied, bluntly. "I desired to drop out, for Miss Osborne's sake, but Frome would hear none of it. It is the devil of a situation."

"Whatever made you consent to such a distasteful arrangement?"

"I wanted Monksford," explained the Earl patiently.

"And what if the girl had been ugly as Aesop?" rasped the Dowager, grimly. "Or an adventuress, like your shameless French piece? And, if one may enquire, where does she stand, in all this? Kept in the wings, I daresay, on the boil!"

"You know better than to probe after such affairs," reproached her grandson, gently. "If only Constance were that sort—it would be no end simple. But she's . . . different. She don't give a button for my title." A queer little smile pulled at his mouth.

"Ironic, don't you agree? When we first met, I considered it famous not to reveal myself to her. And now—now that I want to, I—dare not . . ."

"How long do you suppose you are capable of enacting this absurd double-life? Why, everyone who is anyone knows you for Chievely!"

The Earl crossed to the long, leaded windows and stood looking out at the green Square below. "It is become a mare's nest," he admitted, quietly. "Oh, not on account of Mrs Drinker and her daughter. They do not mix quite in our set, although dodging encounters at the play and such are become something of a sport, I grant you. It's Sibbie—he's being deucedly decent, but the strain is turning him green at the gills. I have him lodging with me, did I mention?"

"Your cousin Sibbald," commented her ladyship, "requires prudent handling. That boy never did possess a strong head, Chievely."

She polished her glass carefully with a handkerchief as she spoke. "What is more, I consider it gross sacrilege for any gentleman of the cloth to be so making a cake of himself! Get him back to Weevelthorpe or—or Wyvencoop, or wherever his parish is, before the Church authorities hear of this escapade! Pray, what bounce has he slipped the Bishop of Upton for this extended leave of absence?"

"Oh, the usual—sick relative."

His grandmama gave an indignant snort. "It

is beyond my comprehension why the Fates have not struck you both down. I quite tremble to think of it!"

"If it affords you any satisfaction, my love, Sibbie has sermonised me stiff on the fires awaiting below," grimaced the Earl, kissing her brow penitently. "Au revoir. I am taking myself off to Jackson's, for an hour at the muffles. I shall return promptly at two o'clock, for Miss Osborne. We are bound for the Tower."

"Indeed! And is she aware of this?"

"Not yet," responded his lordship, cheerfully. "I rely upon you, my love, to convince her of its merits."

The Tower of London is a melancholy haunt, and Connie confessed to shivers as Mr Musgrave and she explored its ancient battlements. He proved an excellent guide, relating all manner of scraps which he knew would interest her, and revealing a keen knowledge of history which he confessed to having nurtured since childhood; but the chill dungeons and turreted staircases were all too reminiscent of the bloody deeds done in their shadows and Connie was relieved when they emerged into the sunlight of Tower Green.

The ravens amused her, and they spent some time feeding them with crusts brought for the purpose. Mr Musgrave proposed viewing the Crown jewels, and they duly repaired to one of the vaults, where, to Connie's amazement, the priceless gems were housed in nothing more grand than a smoky cupboard, dimly lit by two tallow candles, and grudgingly unlocked to them by an ancient harridan of the most un-gainly appearance.

"May the powers of Darkness rot her gar-ters!" whispered Mr Musgrave, winking at Con-nie, after this creature had shuffled back to her knitting with a disparaging spit in their direc-tion. Connie stifled a giggle, but she was never-theless thankful for the reassuring warmth of his hand under her arm.

They could not leave the Tower without in-specting the Royal Menagerie. Connie was im-mensely saddened to see how wretched the animals looked. The lions, especially, appeared cruelly restricted in their narrow cages and it seemed to her unnatural that such noble beasts should be thus incarcerated.

"Tell me, how does my little sweetheart in Bath progress?" enquired the Earl, as they walked towards his curricle. "She has neglected our correspondence monstrously of late."

"I received a letter only the day before I left Monksford," replied Connie. "And I may tell you Fanny is diseasedly anxious to learn which of your colts has the most go for the Derby— Azor or Prince Oriol."

"She don't intend to stack a bundle on 'em, I trust?" he laughed, thinking to himself how lovely she looked, with the blue ribbons of her bonnet-strings nestling against her glossy dark side-curls.

"I am not perfectly certain, but Fanny writes that the girls are to organise a school sweep-stake, and will I please forward some money! I dislike of all things putting her in the sullens, but . . ." Her eyes darkened with trouble.

"Oh, Mr Musgrave, what if gaming should be in her blood? You know how it is with Uncle Maurie."

"It will not come to such a pass with your sister," he reassured. "The blame must lie to my account, for having filled her head with racing flummery."

"She has persuaded her friends to back your Azor," smiled Connie, greatly relieved. "But they particularly request reassurance that he will not plunge."

"My stars!" The Earl burst out laughing. "I had better pen a letter to her myself. She'd do better to have 'em put their shirts on Oriol."

They stopped at St Paul's, on the return journey. It was years since the Earl had voluntarily elected to enter this bastion to Wren's genius but to his immense surprise, he found himself taking a genuine interest in the imposing beauty of the interior, although it must be said that his gaze more often than not followed Connie, who, oblivious to his surveillance, was drinking in every facet of the cathedral, with shining eyes.

"One obtains a cracking panorama from up there," he remarked, indicating the corkscrew flight to the Whispering Gallery. He grinned at her wickedly. "Are you game to attempt it?"

Never for a second imagining that she would accept the challenge, his lordship received the rudest shock of his life when Miss Osborne declared she would like it of all things.

"So long as your leg does not mind," she added, anxiously.

The Earl assured her that his leg would not

in the least object, and ruefully led the way to
the seemingly never-ending flight of steps.

"Great Heaven, are you saying my grandson
actually climbed to the top of St Paul's?" Lady
Fielding put up her glass in horrified fascination. "My dear child, have you any notion how
honoured you are? Wild horses would not drag
him to such exertion!"

"But it was Mr Musgrave's idea!" protested
Connie, anxious to give credit where it was
due. "And would you believe, your ladyship,
the whispers really do echo amazingly! Mr
Musgrave tried several times, though I allow his
words did not always come across distinctly."

"I fancy it is just as well," murmured Lady
Fielding, turning a caustic eye on her grandson,
who had flopped into a chair and was studying
the carved gilt looking-glass over the chimneypiece with an intent desperation.

"And—er—how many steps did you say there
were, my dear?"

"One hundred and sixteen," faltered Connie,
looking apologetically towards Mr Musgrave.

"Dear me!" The Dowager's mouth quivered.
"One might almost consider it a Judgment."
Her bright eyes regarded Connie with new re-
spect. A girl who could coax her grandson up St
Paul's might achieve anything.

Before the Earl took his leave, Connie drew
him aside. All afternoon she had wished to
broach the subject of his loan, but something
held her back. She anticipated his annoyance
and desired nothing to spoil their golden afternoon together. But it must be done.

He followed her upstairs to her bed-chamber

but when she handed him the document, his mouth hardened and he shook his head firmly.

"Wait," she whispered, removing her bonnet. "There is something else."

With a pair of nail scissors, she unpicked the blue silk lining from the bonnet's crown, and drew out two slips of paper. One, she held out to him, saying, with quiet pride, "It was for this I came to town. Will—will you be so obliging as to keep it safe for me, Mr Musgrave?"

The Earl took the slip of paper, then his eyebrows shot up alarmingly. "God's Teeth! Do you mean to tell me you have been going about town with a cheque for this figure sewn inside your bonnet? In Heaven's name, girl, are you moon-calfed?"

"Of a certainty I am not!" retorted Connie, hotly. Her indignation gave place to a reluctant smile. "Will you have the charge of it?"

"It shall be deposited in the bank this very hour!" He looked deeply at her. "Was it the veriest wrench to part with them, Bright-Eyes?"

Her eyes flew open in amazement. "You know! . . . I—I presume Miss Drinker informed you . . . Yes, it entailed an excessive heart-searching," she continued, in a quiet voice. "But—oh, do not you see? Monksford is safe! Now Lord Chievely shall never have it!"

Instantly, a deep colour surmounted her cheeks. "Oh—how grossly uncivil of me! . . . He is your cousin, after all."

Biting her lip, she pushed the other cheque into his hands. "This is to revoke your loan, Mr Musgrave. I truly never conceived of my being in a position to repay you so promptly."

Her eyes brightened. "Tomorrow, I shall call on Granby and Fairbrother. They will put me in the way of a dependable building contractor."

"Allow me to handle this for you," he suggested. "They may attempt to chouse you, being a woman, and inexperienced in such matters—but I'll be damned if they swindle me!"

"I suspect no one would dare!" laughed Connie, dimpling at him. "You look so forbidding when you cut up stiff."

"I? Cut up stiff?" he echoed, stung. "And what may I have to be vexed about, pray?"

"I am persuaded you were only funning when you suggested we climb those abominable steps," she answered, candidly.

The Earl's brows snapped together, then a slight quivering about his mouth betrayed appreciation of this confidence.

"You minx! I do not recall when I enjoyed an afternoon more!" He smiled at her, boyishly. "Will you allow me to show you another side of London? A side most people never give themselves the opportunity to see?"

"Oh, I will!" she breathed, intrigued.

"You must be up betimes to view London in this guise," he warned, enjoying her eagerness. "Not later than six of the clock." He fingered the brim of his high-crowned beaver hat. "Not this week, my girl, for I wish you may recover fully from your ordeal of last night, but soon . . . I promise it. But this will not serve!" he exclaimed, glancing round the neat bed-chamber. "Your reputation must not be exposed a second longer."

He patted his breast pocket. "I shall attend to

the cheque and your other business at once. You shall hear from me soon."

He proved as good as his word. Within the week, plans for the restoration of Monksford had been drawn up by his own hand for her consideration, and they were so exactly what was required that Connie marvelled, not merely at the obvious thought and detail exercised over their construction, but at how meticulously his memory served him.

His lordship could scarcely reveal that those same plans had been worked on and completed months before. But if Connie's unquestioning nature reassured him to the continuing duplicity, the staff of Lady Fielding's household were understandably nonplussed as to why her ladyship's grandson must now at all times be addressed as plain Mr Musgrave.

"Damn their gossiping tongues!" expostulated the Earl fiercely, when his grandmama broached the problem. "If any one of the them so much as breathes my rank to Constance, I shall have him horse-whipped!"

"Really, Chievely, you put me quite out of patience! You will break the girl's heart in any event—would it not be a kindness to do it at once?"

The Earl rested one arm along the white marble mantelshelf. "I dare not tell her," he said, quietly. "Not yet."

"No? Then remember this! A woman will forgive a man almost anything—but never for having deceived her!"

Lady Fielding contemplated the brooding hunch of the lithe shoulders, with a wisdom born of long years. "Especially when she happens to be in love with him."

Up shot the Earl's head. He stared.

"She would not confide that!"

"What need? It is plain as pie! And I shall tell you another thing, young man. You are not half good enough for her!"

Eleven

THIS EXCHANGE WAS to remain with Lord Chievely, pricking him into a dilemma of conscience. Constance was not a child, but he knew her to be almost totally inexperienced with men. Their relationship was a fragile thing, to be nurtured like a tender shoot. She had trusted him once, and he had fouled matters abominably. He could not bear to see that expression in her eyes a second time—that deep, destroying anguish, as a puppy might look who has received a sudden kick from a loved master . . . No, Chievely, he told himself, this time there must be no mistake.

For Mr Sibbald, however, the realisation had long since dawned that his mistake, as well intentioned as ever paved the road to Hades, was to be penanced by a visitation, in the mettlesome form of Miss Lizzie-May Drinker. The Almighty, in his wisdom, had decreed her to be his pestilence but Mr Sibbald nurtured a resentful suspicion that the divine Hand was being fiendishly over-vengeful.

Even Pharaoh had been punished with nothing more dire than a rash of boils and frogs. Had Lizzie-May been visited on Egypt, it was odds on

149

that Moses would have found himself grievously underemployed.

So pondered Mr Sibbald one blustery April afternoon as, with Miss Drinker on his arm, he flicked a half-hearted paw in acknowledgement of her Mama's vociferous wave, and braced himself to embark with his companion on a saunter to Kensington Gardens.

The instant they were out of Manchester Street, however, Lizzie-May grabbed his coat-sleeve vehemently.

"Signal that hackney carriage yonder!" she insisted, yanking his arm upwards and shaking it about, as though manipulating a marionette. As the hack drew alongside, she hailed the whip with her parasol, and commanded him to set them down in St Martin's Street.

"S-St Martin's Street?" stuttered Mr Sibbald, gaping. "But we're bound for Kensington village! The Round Pond, you said!"

"Aw, that was merely to placate Mama!" giggled Lizzie-May, pushing him firmly into the hack, with a conspiratorial wink.

"This girl's from Red River country, Mister, and I aim to see some fun! I've had a snoutful of them hick monuments and greenery! We are going to see a mill!"

Mr Sibbald gulped. "A m-mill? You mean, a—a prize-fight? But—but I've never . . . mean to say, they don't allow females to that sort of affair!"

"They will this one!" Miss Drinker's eyes sparked with excitement as the hack pulled away. "It's been my ambition to attend a milling since I was knee-high to a cotton seed! My cousin Bertram now—he boxes for Harvard, see,

and I'll bet a hundred grand of anyone's shin-
plaster that he could make a blancmanger out
of this Tom Crib of yours!"

Whilst the hack rattled towards St Martin's
Street and the unspeakable Fives Court, Mr
Sibbald learned that Cousin Bertram could tool
Four-in-Hand like a Jehu, was a regular out-and-
outer sportsman, having twice been champion
of the State horse trials, swam like a duck with
two tails, handled a fancy oar, fenced with the
best, and was an excellent shot, or, as Lizzie-
May put it, 'a beaut with the hardware!'

"Bertram don't suffer no truck with horn-
swogglers!" she declared, in a carrying voice, for
the especial benefit of the hack-driver, who had
the cut of face which positively invited suspicions of over-charging.

"I sure do miss him," she added wistfully, to
herself.

"That's a relief," muttered Mr Sibbald, betrayed into thinking aloud. Miss Drinker fixed
him with a narrowed eye.

"Might I hear that again, Lord Chievely?"

"B-B-Bad for the teeth!" stammered her companion, casting wildly around for escape. "M-
Molasses, that is."

Miss Drinker threw him a peculiar glance,
but wisely declined to comment, having been
forewarned by Mama of his lordship's eccentric-
ities.

"It surely is grievin' that Cousin Bertram has
sights on turning a black-coat," she sighed,
scraping despondently with her toe at the
straw-lined floor of the hack. "I don't rightly
consider it decent of him."

"B-Black-coat?" blinked Mr Sibbald, at a loss to understand her drift.

"A preacher! All buttoned gaiters and no reading two-bit fiction on Sundays!" Her eyes rolled upwards expressively.

"You know . . ."

Mr Sibbald knew only too well. The hairs on his neck stood out and he could feel himself perspiring. Retribution—it was nothing less! The Sword of Damocles hung in the air, and Mr Sibbald felt his knees turn to jelly.

In strictly measured doses, Miss Drinker was bearable. Angling for a coronet at her parent's behest, she was lethal as Epsom Salts. He had hitherto sustained himself with the comforting knowledge that sooner or later truth must prevail. But a Miss Drinker partial to preachers! A defeated groan escaped him. Had there been a pistol to hand, he would in all probability have shot himself.

"Don't allow no petticoats!" snapped the ticket clerk imperiously, upon their arrival. "Fives Court h'is a gen'l'men's preserve!"

He slammed down the wooden shutter, all but guillotining Mr Sibbald's fingers in so doing. This treatment produced an unaccountable effect. Mr Sibbald promptly determined to gain access for Miss Drinker at any price, and seizing her parasol, he rapped resoundingly on the wooden partition, trembling the while at his temerity.

Up flew the shutter, down came the parasol— and the clerk staggered backwards, emitting a strangled howl of pain.

"Oh, M-Moses!" ejaculated the hero, turning pale at sight of the rising lump on his victim's brow. "I do beg your pardon! I—oh m-my lungs and l-liver—"

"Don't back down!" hissed Lizzie-May, giving him an encouraging prod. "I got to see this mill!"

Mr Sibbald nodded weakly and requested her to be so obliging as to wait for him by the outer door, fearing that language such as the clerk might choose to employ would be totally unsuitable for a lady's ear.

His companion shrugged. "S'pose. I'll just mosey over to them prints on the wall."

She strolled off, confident in his powers to smooth matters. Mr Sibbald gulped, feeling his heart performing a fandango and his neck-cloth intent upon strangling him. The clerk wore an ugly scowl, and the lump had progressed to the size of an egg. Casting heroism to the winds, Mr Sibbald extracted a half-crown from his pocket and laid it quakingly on the counter.

"T-Two tickets, if you please," he croaked, in a small voice.

The clerk's eyes bulged. "You konked me skull!" he accused, an unpleasant curve twisting his thick lips.

Another half-crown piece. The clerk's nose twitched. But no tickets.

"N-Now see here, my man!" stuttered Mr Sibbald, hackles rising. "You have no authority to refuse me admission! It may interest you to learn that—"

Glorious inspiration. If he were to be damned for his transgressions, better to be hung for a sheep than a goat.

"That I am the Earl of Chievely!"

A burst of intemperate laughter greeted this disclosure.

" 'Ere! Ned!" cackled the clerk, bellowing to an unseen companion in the inner office. "This 'ere joker finks 'e's Lord Chievely!"

The other fellow stuck a grinning countenance round the window.

"An' I'm King George!" he scoffed, good-naturedly.

"Sorry, mate, but we 'appens to know wot 'is Nibs looks like, 'im bein' a reg'lar at Fives, like."

"M-Mean to say, I'm his *c-cousin*!" gurgled Mr Sibbald, hurriedly, praying that Miss Drinker might not overhear. "W-Will you accept half a guinea?"

"Your honour's over-generous, ain't he, Charlie?" grinned the man, nudging the clerk. "Two it is! An' straight through for the ring—Your lordship!"

With dignity, Mr Sibbald collected Miss Drinker, who expressed herself mighty impressed by his firmness of manner, and together they entered the brick-walled arena. The mill was already in progress, and the air thick with yells of encouragement and expletive-peppered advice, as the excited spectators pressed forwards, those at the front crushed against the raised platform, those behind drumming clenched fists on the near-most pair of shoulders.

Miss Drinker elbowed herself a stance near the ringside with remarkable ease, to the astonishment of Mr Sibbald, who tottered in her wake, subjected to the most unparliamentary abuse from the press of bodies.

The bout in progress proved to be a charity affair, held in aid of the widow and children of

'Bouncing' Bob Rafferty, the Irish pugilist, who had met an untimely end under the wheels of a runaway chaise. The Elite of the Fancy were participating, and the ring was meantime occupied by Tom Spring, that giant of the sport, and the Champion himself, Tom Cribb, supremely fit, and, at six and thirty, living proof of the skill which had successfully wrested the title from the legendary Jem Belcher back in 1809.

After making play a short time, Spring planted a smashing right hook on the Champion's jaw. Cribb retreated, counter-punching, to the accompaniment of a deafening roar from the spectators, then deftly caught Spring a tremendous blow to the face, lacerating the upper lip and causing his opponent to reel backwards against the ropes.

In his excitement, Mr Sibbald found his beaver hat pushed firmly over his eyes, and his chin pinned against an uncompromising chest. Upon regaining his vision, he discovered the chest belonged to a purple-faced giant, whose wrathful glare and bulging eye intimated distaste of the Sibbald presence upon his left toecap.

"How dare you, sir?" growled the giant, grabbing Mr Sibbald by the lapels so that he was lifted off the ground. "What do you intend by winding me in the gizzard?"

Mr Sibbald was by no standards accounted bright, but from the manner in which the gentleman was shaking him about, he knew better than to argue.

"F-Frightfully clumsy of me, old b-bean!" he spluttered, feeling his teeth chatter uncomfortably. "I s-say, d'you mind awfully putting me down? N-Never could stand heights."

The words had scarcely left his mouth, when, from the lofty eminence above the giant's shoulders, his gaze froze into stupefied horror.

Standing directly behind Lizzie-May, in a snappy frock-coat of Dandy blue, Mr Sibbald perceived the chilly eye and bare upper lip of an all-too familiar figure. Far from being buried deep in rural Somerset, but alive and well and rooting for Tom Cribb with the righteous fury of a Juvenal, was The Right Reverend, the Lord Bishop of Upton.

"Do you mean to tell me that you simply abandoned Miss Drinker and ran?" demanded the Earl, fastening an astonished eye upon the quivering figure stretched limply on the chaise-longue.

"Like H-Hades!" admitted his cousin, clutching at a brandy. He cast a despairing glance round the Earl's tastefully furnished morning-room. A racing calendar was tucked behind a corner of the Canaletto over the chimneypiece and a stack of invitations and calling cards littered a salver upon the mahogany sideboard.

Two long windows slanted late afternoon sunshine on to a sabre-foot sofa table, upon which reposed an open copy of Weatherby's *General Stud Book*, a decanter of Cognac, and serving as book-mark, the questionable statuette of a multi-bosomed Indian goddess of Fertility, carved in jade.

Mr Sibbald, however, noticed nothing of these touches. His eyes were on stalks, and his lower lip trembled convulsively.

"Old Rumble-Belly! Here . . . in town!" he moaned, brokenly. "Nemesis . . . that's what it is! Oh, Chievely, what's to be done?"

"Did he recognise you?" interrupted the Earl.

"How the b-blazes do I know?" babbled Mr Sibbald, mopping at his brow. "That Philistine was shaking my insides to pulp! But it was Bishop R-Rumbelow, I tell you—there's not a phiz to touch his—not anywhere! That cold, m-malevolent stare . . ."

He shuddered, and applied himself to the brandy.

The Earl pursed thoughtful lips, and took a turn about the room.

"Now why should your bishop be in town, dressed like a Turk, and selling his soul to the Devil at the Fives Court? I understood he was vastly down upon such plebian amusements?"

"He is! Pagan, he calls it!" Mr Sibbald licked a dry lip. "And as for gaming! . . . Threatened to dish the Dean for catching him at backgammon! Why, the poor old horse was merely playing for comfit stakes."

He fixed his cousin with an arctic glare. "There is nothing in the situation to warrant your amusement, coz!"

"You are dashed right—there's not!" returned Lord Chievely, frowning. "I strongly suspect you mean to ditch me, and leg it for Wivelsham." Perceiving the guilt-ridden countenance before him, he broke into a sympathetic smile. "Lord, I don't reproach you, Sibbie." He fingered the gold signet ring which he habitually wore with a contemplative detachment. "Do you feel able to withstand the siege another six weeks? You have my solemn oath that come

Derby day, my troth will have been plighted,
and this tomfoolery at an end!"

Mr Sibbald uttered a hollow groan. "Could
not you offer for Miss Drinker instead?"

"Miss Drinker," declared the Earl, pleasantly,
"is an invigorating companion, but she is unable to offer Monksford as a dowry."

For the first time, Mr Sibbald stirred from
his recumbent laying-out on the chaise-longue.
He sat up abruptly, staring hard at his cousin.

"You do not seriously intend to—" Then, observing the set line of the Earl's jaw, "Jove, but
you are a mercenary wretch, Chievely! I would
not have believed it of you."

"You are at liberty to conclude what you will,
Sibbie," remarked his lordship, evenly. Picking
up an amethyst-handled paper knife, he broke
the seal on a stack of unopened correspondence.
"Might I count upon your keeping out of trouble during the next sennight or so? My racing
calendar will necessitate a spell at Cambridge,
in preparation for race week."

He glanced up, smiling faintly. "I trust you
mean to back my colt, old man. Oriol will be
the strongest Bit of Blood in the field, mark my
words."

"I am backing nothing!" gritted Mr Sibbald,
falling back against the cushions, with a Sid-
dons-like gesture of ill-usage. "I'm in trouble
enough!"

Twelve

MRS DRINKER REMAINED ill satisfied at the progress of her daughter's matrimonial aspirations. Her wrath on discovering Lizzie-May's illicit exploration to the Fives Court had been terrible, and its brunt naturally fell upon the hapless Mr Sibbald, as the evil genius instigating her daughter's steps to ruin.

The result was a growing impatience at Lizzie-May's avowed preference for her Cousin Bertram, and when, one morning, a letter arrived bearing that young gentleman's unmistakable hand, Mrs Drinker's spleen ignited.

"You dare to correspond with that good-for-nothin' jackanapes behind your Momma's back, Miss?" she snapped, snatching the letter from her daughter's protesting hand.

"You are a wicked, ungrateful girl, that's what!"

Trembling with rage, she broke open the seal. "Well, let us see what your fine cousin has to say for himself!"

"Momma . . . Do not! I—I implore you!" whispered Lizzie-May, colouring. "You—you must not read my mail! It—it is despicable—wicked . . ." Bright tears welled in her eyes. "I—I love Bertram, if you must know. Sure, he don't match your requirements of what's fittin'—Bertram ain't grand enough spoke or—or Midas enough to be acceptable! But he pleases me, Momma—don't that count?"

"Any more of such sentimental hooey, Miss, an' you'll go straight home to Louisiana!" rasped Mrs Drinker. She ran a bulging eye over the closely worded script. Utter silence of what, to her quaking daughter, appeared interminable minutes, followed, then in a strangled sort of gasp Mrs Drinker demanded, "Lizzie-May, have you—any inkling of what this—this improper communication contains?" Her bosom heaved with wrath. "Answer me, child, or I'll slipper your hide! Has that boy been makin' up to you?"

"Momma . . . I—I demand that you hand over what is mine!" flashed Lizzie-May, white-faced, confronting her rabid parent with an air of authority which surprised even herself.

"Bertram and I have nothing to hide. We—we're promised, so there! And you'll never make me accept Lord Chievely—not in a thousand years!"

"Go to your room, child!" thundered her Mama, barely able to speak for rage. "As for this shameless garbage!"

Advancing to the chimneypiece, she tore the letter firmly in two.

"There's but one fittin' repository for such impertinence!"

"No!" screamed Lizzie-May, struggling to get at the letter. "You must not . . . Ooooh!" A broken sob escaped her, as the greedy flames devoured her cousin's epistle. Choked with grief, she rushed from the room and locked herself in her bed-chamber, deaf to all threats and entreaties.

Connie did not see Mr Musgrave for almost three weeks. He was gone out of town, and although he called before departing she was not at home, having arranged to accompany the Drinkers to the Royal Academy exhibition of paintings at Somerset House.

She was greatly dismayed at having missed him, a circumstance which Lady Fielding was not slow to notice.

"You care excessively for that grandson of mine, do you not?" she commented, glancing up shrewdly from her game of Patience. "I do not mean to put you to the blush, child, but some matters are self-evident."

Connie, in the act of parcelling a pair of kid slippers to send to Fanny, almost dropped the sealing wax in disconcertment.

Lady Fielding never minced words.

"How can one fail to like Mr Musgrave?" she stammered, fencing for words. "I am immensely in his debt. It is but natural that I—"

"Do not allow yourself to become over-partial, my dear," ventured her ladyship, gently. "Come—sit by me. I wish to talk plainly."

She waited until Connie had taken a chair opposite, before continuing, with a careful choosing of her words. "My grandson is possessed of considerable charm, Miss Osborne. He is moreover, by no means a poor man. Such was not always the case. He inherited almost nothing from his father. Only by dint of his years in India with my late brother, and a sound business sense, is his fortune what it is."

She leaned forwards purposefully, bright eyes taking in the girl's bent head, the manner in which the slim fingers were twined nervously about her knees. "Constance—my grandson has known many women. I—I should not wish you to mistake his attentiveness for any deeper significance."

Connie glanced up swiftly. "I assure you, ma'am—"

"Now, do not fly at me, pray! I am grown inordinately fond of you, child, so hear me out." Turning over a playing-card, she said, "I am persuaded Noel does care for you, in his fashion, but . . . to be plain, there is a matter which he has deliberately kept from you."

"I expect you mean Mademoiselle D'Erlon," said Connie, quietly. "I—I realised some time ago that she was your grandson's mistress."

"Did you, indeed!" murmured the old lady, taken aback by this admission. "Young gels have no business to know of such affairs!"

"I am five and twenty, ma'am," returned Connie, dispiritedly, unclasping her hands. "Have they been—I mean, have they known each other for long?"

"Been hanging after her these six months past," sniffed Lady Fielding, slapping down a Four of Clubs with a ferocity which spoke volumes. "The brazen creature don't have to dance—he squanders enough upon her to square the National Debt! Sheer vanity on her part, nothing less! And constantly unfaithful! It is beyond my understanding why Noel puts up with her."

Connie stared down at her hands, only half-listening. Six months! Désirée was as much part of his life, then, as any woman might be. Dimly, she heard Lady Fielding say,

". . . presumably she means to be at Epsom with him. For my part, I have no intention of attending. So many obnoxious persons are permitted there nowadays!"

She patted Connie's hand warmly, having resolved, by the wobble in the girl's voice, to abandon any introduction of her grandson's true identity.

"No, child, you and I shall remain in town. You would not care for Epsom, my dear. Nothing but four-flushers, gypsies and bad language."

Connie's spirits sank. Lady Fielding was a dear, but time lagged heavily in Berkeley Square without Mr Musgrave. From the first, the appeal of the races had fired her with delight. She wanted so much to see his colts in action, had taken it for certain that Lady Fielding would be there. It was a bitter blow.

"I do not visualise being able to remain in town so long, your ladyship," replied Connie, determined those amiable but all-seeing eyes should not detect her heaviness of heart. "I must return to Monksford before the contractor's men arrive. There will be a great deal to do, and—and Uncle Maurie writes that my housekeeper has begun the spring wash, and—"

"And I suppose you will be informing me next that it is your intention to plunge up to your elbows in soap suds!" declared Lady Fielding in amusement, not the least fooled by this spate of excuses. "Noel is determined upon your remaining in town until you are properly rested. He tells me you have been wearing yourself to a wraith with worry over that great barracks of a house, so you may as well prepare to be my guest for some weeks yet, my dear."

Her eyes twinkled with satisfaction over the pince-nez.

"I must own my pleasure in your society, child. Now, why do not we call upon my mantua-maker this afternoon? Her spring collection must be ready for inspection, I feel sure. Something in saffron crape, perhaps—or—*yes,* rose pink! We must make the most of your pretty dark hair, child."

. . . . .

After the frosty reception meted out by Mrs Drinker, it would have been no surprise had Mr Sibbald lain low for a period, but his was a nature which attracted disaster unaided, and with his cousin gone out of town, he became sole recipient of Lizzie-May's attentions. He found a change had been wrought in her spirits, however, to no small degree, for her accustomed ebullience was gone, and in its place a detached reticence which unnerved him.

She made little effort to converse, leaving the onus upon himself, but after having exhausted the state of the weather, the state of the country, the habits of the lesser spotted woodpecker and everything else he could think of, Mr Sibbald despairingly wondered why he had ever found her former prattle so wearisome.

Thinking himself on safe ground, he ventured one afternoon to embark on the prowess of her athletically minded cousin. Miss Drinker's countenance altered alarmingly. For one ghastly moment, he thought her about to cry.

"Steady on, old horse!" muttered Mr Sibbald,

fishing for a handkerchief to assist matters. "Mustn't uncork the waterspouts here!"

They were standing in Pall Mall, having paused to watch the sentries change at St James's Palace opposite. He produced a crumpled offering of cambric. "Here—use this."

"You're real sweet." Lizzie-May wiped her eyes, and looked a shade embarrasseed. "I'm a little down, I guess."

She walked on in silence, then, as though having made up her mind, said quickly, "My lord, I got to ask you a question. It may sound mighty presumptious but . . ." She took a deep breath. "Do you aim to offer for me?"

A constricted choking emanated from her companion, causing several passersby to regard him in alarm. "I . . . I . . . No!" he croaked.

"Hallelujah for that!" declared Miss Drinker, in feeling tones. "Oh! . . . Do not misunderstand!" she added, hastily, seeing him redden. "It's been just dandy having you take me about, sir! But," she bit her lower lip, "it's Momma, see. She's sore as a bear over Bertram's letter. I—I guess you ought to learn the whole story."

It had started to mizzle, and the pavements were pushing with damp broadcloth and bonnets, as people hurried to find shelter. Mr Sibbald listened in awe as his companion unburdened herself. He could not help but feel their surroundings grossly inappropriate, pressed as they were into an apothecary's doorway in company with at least three other persons, each of whom was displaying a surreptitious interest in the unfolding saga.

"And now Bertram is forbidden to mail me

any correspondence!" finished Lizzie-May, staring gloomily at the wet cobbles.

"All the same, he might send 'em to a different address," mused Mr Sibbald, scenting personal salvation and determined to pursue it. "Sort of private receiving-office, where one might collect his letters unbeknown to the old tig-m-mean to say, without your Mama turning shirty."

"Now you're talkin'! That's a real ripsnorter! I shall have Bertram mail all letters to you!" Her round face lit up with renewed hope. "I just know you will oblige us, your Earlship! Oh! I could hug you, sure as die!"

"H-Hold on!" spluttered Mr Sibbald, in alarm, not altogether certain that he ought to sanction this arrangement, and even less happy at what the Earl would have to say on the subject.

"Aw, there's no call for sportin' your tragedy mask!" soothed Miss Drinker, confidently. "Let's see now."

She rooted deep within her reticule and produced a shopping list. "I have placed our order for tea with Berry's, and collected Momma's copy of *Christabel* from the circulating library. She's plum stuck on your poet Coleridge at the moment. Say . . . you gone sick or somethin'?" she demanded, struck by his glassy stare which appeared fixed on the approach of a pair of elegant gentlemen, walking arm in arm.

One, with an air of ludicrous affectation, led a small poodle dog. His companion, a bored-looking dandy, having enormously padded shoulders to his morning-coat, carried a jewel-top cane and minced along with a comical, exaggerated gait. Miss Drinker would have liked to study this absurd creature further, but Lord Chievely was propelling her into a shop with indecent haste, muttering something about their sheltering from the rain.

"But the shower is over!" objected Lizzie-May, trying to look over his shoulder at the objects of his alarm.

"Ah . . . yes. But the sun—heatstroke, you know. M-Much safer in the shade!" babbled her companion, coaxingly.

Miss Drinker privately conjectured that it was he who appeared to be suffering the effects of the sun, although she considered his odd behaviour more probably due to the gentlemen being gaming acquaintances from the Tulip set, whose notes-of-hand his lordship had not got around to settling.

She was not far wrong. Mr Sibbald was mentally congratulating himself in having recognised his cousin's fellow gamester Mr Lucian Frome, to whom he had been introduced some weeks before at a convivial evening in the Earl's rooms, and in whose sharp mind the association must immediately register. The other gentleman was Mr Frome's boon companion, the celebrated Mr 'Poodle' Byng, whose French dog was as much part of his ensemble as his gloves or quizzing-glass.

A deprecating cough recalled Mr Sibbald to the fact that he had sought refuge in some sort of gentlemen's outfitters. An elderly relic, wearing half-spectacles, was peering expectantly at him from behind the counter. The Sibbald brain groped for a suitable purchase. The stock on display appeared as fossilised as the counterhand, and the shop itself smelled pungently of camphor.

Patently aware of Miss Drinker's dare-if-you-will gaze upon him, Mr Sibbald screwed up an air of seeming nonchalance, and defiantly asked to be shown the range of flannel drawers.

"Has sir a preference for the short leg or the long?" enquired the aged counter-hand, solicitously, opening a wooden drawer. Sir choked down an ill-chosen retort, and hastily turned his back on the open shop-door, where Mr Frome and his fellow dandy might be observed in leisurely discourse outside.

"Do I want the short leg?" hissed Mr Sibbald, willing the smirking Lizzie-May to come to his aid. Miss Drinker elevated twin eyebrows in affronted mirth.

"Lordy, I'm a carefully-nurtured girl, sir!" she giggled, enjoying the situation hugely. "I guess you had best bespeak three sets of the other. Your English winters are mighty cold!"

Endeavouring to sound as if ordering three pairs of loathsome flannel drawers was an everyday occurrence with him, Mr Sibbald did as she suggested, colouring furiously at her frank reminder that he would likely be plagued grievously with the itch, and that nothing served so well as a liberal shaking of Fullers Earth.

"Connie's Uncle Pinchbeck don't use nothin' else," she confided, in a wicked undertone, as they quit the shop (with Mr Sibbald's shrinking profile slunk into his coat-collar, and his hat brim well over his eyes). "Say! . . . He might give you the reckoning of 'em, I guess! Don't wear no other type. Momma asked him," she added, by way of explanation.

"Sir Maurice may have 'em—with my compliments," muttered Mr Sibbald, distinctly ruffled. He was not in the habit of discussing such personal preferences with anyone but his laundrywoman. He wondered if all American maidens were reared to be so free-spoken. Moreover—and this rankled above everything—he was a cambric man when it came to underlinen!

Thirteen

CONNIE WAS ENGROSSED in writing to Sir Maurice late one Sunday evening when a light tap at the door of her bed-chamber roused her. Lady Fielding had already bidden her good-night, and she could not imagine who else it might be.

"Mr Musgrave! Oh, whenever did you return?"

Her eyes could not conceal the pleasure she felt. He took her hand and pressed it gently, laying a warning finger to his lips.

"I called to persuade you to come riding tomorrow." His expression held a suppressed devilment, which even the dim flutter of the candle could not hide.

"Can you be ready by half after six?"

"Half after—Oh! Do you mean? . . ." Her eyes shone. "I—I assumed you had forgotten—"

"How could I?" he said, softly. He came farther into the room, and Connie saw that his top-boots were travel-stained. It struck her that he must have come directly to Berkeley Square. Perceiving her glance of enquiry, he smiled. "I wished to catch you before you retired."

He hesitated, self-consciously it seemed. "Everything will be perfectly proper, Constance. I have arranged for a groom to accompany us."

"Oh . . . I was not thinking of any such foolishness!" whispered Connie, turning hot with embarrassment.

"I know," he replied, softly, "but others might."

. . . . .

Early next morning, Connie dressed with care in the new riding habit which Lady Fielding had persuaded her to have made. It was practical yet eye-catching, in rich indigo superfine, and its short jacket was becomingly figure hugging, with a capuchin collar cut low in front to reveal the ruffle of white lace at her throat. To go with it there was an impudent black silk top-hat with a high crown and veil, and Connie knew, with secret satisfaction, that she would not disgrace her escort.

Taking up her gloves she hastened downstairs, past the sleepy-eyed housemaids already going about their duties, and made her way to the mews, where Mr Musgrave had promised to meet her.

He was already there, standing beside his beautiful black stallion, Satan, and impeccable as always in a dark riding coat and corded breeches. At her approach he looked up eagerly, only to pause, an expression hard to define stealing over his countenance.

"How lovely you are . . ." he said, softly. "Like Diana herself." Then the boyish anticipation returned to his eyes as a groom rounded the stable yard, leading her mount.

"Well, Bright-Eyes, and what do you say to my surprise?"

"It—it's *Firebrand!*" Connie stood stock still,

unable to speak for emotion. "I—I can scarce believe it! However did you manage—"

Blinking back tears, she darted forwards, laying her cheek close to the chestnut's silky neck. Firebrand whickered his delight, and nuzzled gently at her face.

"I judged he might relieve your homesickness a little," explained the Earl, enjoying her pleasure. He viewed the chestnut with an expert eye. "He's a knowing looker, this one. Pure thoroughbred. I'd give my eyes to own him. Let me hand you up."

Connie threaded the reins and watched him swing himself into Satan's saddle, then, with the groom riding a respectful distance behind, they trotted out of the mews, and into the murky light of early morning London.

It was still mid-May, with a faint mist rising from the river as they rode across Westminster Bridge towards the Surrey shore. Through the light swirl, it was just possible to discern the grey, Parliament buildings of St Stephen's Hall, flanked by the low, willowed banks. Downstream, Somerset House rose from the water like a Venetian palace. And linking both banks, the Thames, greenish-grey, with barges and wherries stirring to face a new day, and brown and white sails fluttering in the light breeze.

As they rode Mr Musgrave told Connie how, after having completed his affairs, he had taken chaise for Monksford, to apprise Sir Maurice in detail of the contractor's plans and of the proposed starting date.

"I hesitated to inform you of my intention," he explained with an apologetic smile, "because I knew that you would certainly wish to accompany me, and—to be frank, I feared I should return to town alone."

They had reined in at Southwark, to view the river. Connie fondled Firebrand's ear absently, absorbed in his words. The mist had cleared, and the watery sunshine was breaking through, transforming the fluffy white clouds to a glowing pinkish-gold, and as he spoke it seemed as if the morning were in tune with the happiness in her heart, as the rays gilded the tumbledown rooftops and mastheads behind them, painting the drab surroundings with a mystic splendour.

Lady Fielding's words rang in her ears, but his eyes were regarding her with such unmistakable tenderness that her body thrilled, and the wild, sweet knowledge of it compelled her to look quickly away, for fear he might consider her immodest.

"Would you have returned with me, Constance?" he asked, very softly, stretching out a hand to touch hers.

"If—if you had wished it," she stammered, suddenly shy.

He appeared satisfied, for he touched Satan's bridle-rein, and they continued on their way, a tacit understanding forged between them.

Recrossing the river they entered the City which, unlike the fashionable West End, was bustling with activity. Letter-carriers in scarlet coats bearing hand-bells and leather postbags, were going from door to door. Fresh-faced milkmaids, grimy chimney-sweep urchins and bakers in white aprons bearing trays of hot loaves shouted themselves hoarse above the city's wakening din.

An apprentice, taking down the shutters of a bow-fronted, dimple-paned gunsmith's window, paused to whistle after Connie's trim figure. Connie smiled back, thrilling to the bustle of this other, exciting London, which lived and worked alongside the square of Quality May-fair, and which she was seeing with new eyes.

They met draught-horses lumbering into brewers' yards, hackney coachmen waiting at their stances, even a little crossing-sweeper child shouldering his brooms with stoical deter-mination outside the Mansion House. Newsven-dors shouted each other down at street corners, and pretty, mob-capped housemaids gawped from upstairs' windows at the sight of gentle-folks so early risen from bed.

It was fascinating, thought Connie in delight, as if, by some sorcery, she was eavesdropping upon another world, peopled with cheerful faces and energetic hands, who emerged, gnome-like, at dawn, and disappeared when the fashion-able world came awake.

By nine o'clock they were skirting the northern boundary of the capital, along the macadamised New Road, which linked the vil-lages of Paddington and Islington. The pleasing scents of meadow-sweet and freshly mown hay caused Connie to breathe the air appreciatively, for they were the fragrances of spring, and re-minded her of Monksford.

The violets would be peeping shyly in the mossy copse, she supposed, and the hawthorn buds, delicately fringed with green, opening to the sun, beneath the rambling stone balustrade in the rose garden . . . This was the first year she had not been there to see them unfold.

I ought to feel guilty, she thought, chastened. But with Noel Musgrave riding not a bridle-length away, it was inexplicably hard to focus one's mind on duty.

The quiet stretches of the New Road enabled them to gallop flat out along the final length, bringing them to the Tyburn turnpike and into Hyde Park. As they trotted beneath a canopy of bursting horse-chestnut trees, the Earl turned to Connie, noting with satisfaction the keen bloom in her cheeks, and more particularly, the becoming tendrils of soft brown hair escaping from her riding hat. Not for the first time did his lordship wonder what had possessed him to take the groom along.

Wheeling his stallion in the direction of the Row, he shouted, "Let us see what that horse of yours is capable of, Bright-Eyes! I'll race you the length of the Serpentine!"

With a flick of the bridle, he was away, with Connie hard behind, urging Firebrand to exert his all. Down the sandy avenue of Rotten Row they thundered abreast, leaving the bemused groom far behind, and dispersing a family of unsuspecting ducks who had strayed on to the track.

The Earl reached the finishing point first and dismounted, watching Connie rein to a triumphant halt only seconds behind. Her eyes were aglow with the zest of their gallop, and as he held out his arms to help her dismount, she uttered a sigh of pure satisfaction.

"Oh, how I have been aching to do that for ever so long! If only there had been fences to jump I should be blissfully content!"

"I have never encountered a girl with such

command of a horse," he said, smiling in genuine admiration. "Nor an animal with such go!"

Firebrand licked at his hand as if in total concurrence.

"If you are agreeable, I should like to have him stud with my brood-mare Nimbus after the racing season. We should produce a first-rater, Constance—I am confident of it. What do you say?"

"Why . . . to be sure!" she agreed, after initial surprise. "Firebrand is pure bred, you know, and not the least temperamental, despite his name." She patted the stallion's neck lovingly.

"He is the finest mount in the whole world."

The Earl looked down at her animated face, his expression sober. Taking both her hands in his he held them lightly, then, with a despairing gesture, released her, saying in an unsteady whisper, "Oh, Bright-Eyes . . . there is so much I want to say to you."

Connie glanced hesitantly into his eyes, longing to abandon herself to the wave of emotion which surged through her at the anguished pleading in his tone. She felt him draw her to a nearby bench overlooking the lake. She was immensely conscious of him as he sat, shoulders hunched slightly forwards, absorbed in the pattern of sunlight dappling the expanse of the Serpentine to a silver hue.

Unexpectedly he scooped up a handful of pebbles and flung them, causing ever-widening ripples to break the smooth surface as they fell.

"Do not you sometimes feel that life is akin to this water, Connie?" he mused, breaking their silence for the first time. "A vast, mirrored

surface, over which we chart our course . . .
until we encounter something—or someone
. . . who disturbs our well-ordered pattern—
sending ripples to question our cherished be-
liefs."

His voice had dropped to a low-pitched mon-
osyllable. Connie sensed that it was important
he continue. She had never found him in this
mood before, and it troubled her, but she remained quietly by his side, willing her presence
to transmit the comfort he needed.

"I often was used to come here, as a young-
ster of five or so," he remarked, staring at the
lake. "Always with my nurse. Do you realise,
Constance, that I was fully three years old before I understood that the beautiful lady in
silks and furs who occasionally looked in at me
in the nursery was actually my Mama?"

His voice was bitter, the jaw-line hard.

"Not every woman is born to motherhood, I
imagine. She was like . . . like an exotic but-
terfly, flitting from one lover to the next. My father tolerated her indiscretions, because he
loved her . . ."

He snapped off a frond of fern growing at his
feet, and rubbed it thoughtfully between his
fingers. "Strange, how such memories remain
with one. I fashioned a little horse for her once,
from a piece of wood. I worked on it for
weeks." He forced a wry smile. "Mama gave it
to her spaniel to worry. Not that she intended
to be uncaring or hurtful—I believe she was
simply incapable of considering anyone's
feelings but her own."

Instinctively, Connie's hand crept into his.
Their fingers entwined naturally, and she felt

him relax. She wanted to lay his head against her breast, to stroke his hair, convince him that she understood, that she loved him, had always loved him. But she did not dare.

"Is that why you have never married, Noel?" she asked, softly.

He glanced up then, and she saw that a momentary gleam of amusement had crept into his eyes at her question.

"If you mean, is that why I grew up such an abominable flirt, then I expect it is." The light vanished as swiftly as it had come.

"I vowed no woman should have the opportunity to make me suffer as my father suffered! I convinced myself that wedlock had no advantage to offer which might not be had elsewhere. So—I love and leave 'em broken-hearted, as they say."

He stood up unexpectedly, pulling her with him, and said, almost angrily, "Shall I break yours also, Connie? Grandmama says I shall, and she is not generally mistaken."

"Noel . . . Don't! Don't punish yourself—I do understand! Oh, how I wish I might make up to you for every hateful moment of hurt! I—I cannot bear to see you look so—so . . ."

The sentence was never finished, for his arms tightened about her, and he was deliberately tipping back her head against his shoulder. Very gently, he kissed her. Connie gasped with surprise, causing her mouth to open under his. His lips sought hers, not gently this time, but with a burning insistence which deprived her of all feeling. She could not have resisted had she desired.

"Connie, oh, Connie, my little love!" he whispered, hoarsely. "I did not intend this should happen—I swear!"

Tenderly, he removed her riding hat, and gazed deeply into her eyes for a long moment. Then, with a little groan, he cradled her face against his cheek, fingers winding gently through the dark tendrils at the nape of her neck.

"It's no good, little one," he murmured, softly. "I love you. I think I've done so from that first day at Monksford, when you walked into my life. I mistook you for a 'curst governess. Did I ever tell you?"

His arms slipped about her waist, and he held her from him, a new, graver expression on his face. "There is so much about me of which you know nothing, Bright-Eyes. You have given me your trust . . . and God knows I do not deserve it."

At the agonised remorse in his voice, Connie looked up wonderingly and her hand stole up to touch his cheek. A strangled groan escaped the Earl, and he crushed her to him with a desperation born of fear, whispering, urgently, "Oh, my heart's dearest, I cannot bear the thought of losing you! Say you will love me, Bright-Eyes, come what may!"

"There never can be anyone else, Noel," choked Connie, into his lapel. Her body ached to respond to him, to release the multitude of emotions which had for so long been suppressed within her. But she had already been hurt once, and whilst she had given her lips to the wine-sweet urgency of his kiss, her heart cried out a warning.

She leaned against him, hating herself for

doubting. She nerved herself to speak—but the words refused to come. Désirée D'Erlon and what she stood for remained, an unbridgeable gulf, between pain and perfect happiness.

He was regarding her with uncertainty. "Connie?" Then his expression darkened. Sternly, almost fiercely, he pulled her close, and asked, simply, "Constance, will you marry me?"

It was nearing eleven when they rode back to Berkeley Square. Neither spoke much. Connie's face, however, held a quiet radiance. Noel loved her, as deeply and intensely as she needed him. It was enough; more than any dowd of five and twenty had a right to expect, she reminded herself. Surely, please God, if she might only satisfy him, as he deserved, surely then Noel would no longer have need of Désirée.

She glanced shyly at him, as he trotted Satan a head's-length in front, loving his every characteristic, the long, masculine fingers handling the ribbons, the set of the finely chiselled mouth, the way his light hair grew softly into the nape of his neck. She wondered what his thoughts were.

Connie smiled to herself, recalling with what mortification she had stirred from his arms, to discover their groom desperately attempting to render himself inconspicuous behind a tree. Her abandoned lover, apparently immune to the embarrassment of their discovery, had merely raised one wicked eyebrow and grinned, relishing her scarlet-cheeked confusion with infuriating calm.

The unfortunate groom, whose embarrassment was almost equal to her own, was speedily compromised with a substantial bribe, and Connie had the comparative solace of knowing that his word might be relied upon.

What worried her most, however, was how Lady Fielding would accept their news. Connie was under no illusion that whilst the old lady genuinely liked her, she must doubtless expect her personable grandson to secure a brilliant match. This sobering reminder occupied her thoughts as they re-entered the mews. She wondered if perhaps the same doubt had occurred to Noel also, for there was a troubled look in his eyes as he helped her from the saddle.

"Connie," he began, hesitantly, catching her to him fractionally, "should you mind awfully, my darling, if—if we were to keep our betrothal secret for the present?"

She stared wide-eyed, trying to understand.

"You mean—not tell anyone . . . not even your grandmama?"

"Believe me, I'd not ask such a thing unless there was sound cause." There was a deep-seated wretchedness in his voice.

"Trust me, Connie. If only—" He stopped, and again she glimpsed the haunted expression in his face. Then, in a rush, he burst out, "No, by God! I'll have no pretence between us! Connie . . . I have a confession to make, only I fear that when I tell you, I—I may forfeit your love for ever."

"Never!" whispered Connie, vehemently, catching at his hand. "Whatever the reason, Noel, I—I shall listen . . . it cannot be so dire, after all."

He means to broach the subject of Désirée

D'Erlon, she realised, with a flutter of panic.
How typical of him to wish her to know the
worst, before committing herself to a public announcement of their betrothal. His honesty
would countenance nothing less.

"We shall talk of it—later," she said softly,
forcing a smile. "Besides, I shall like of all
things to savour the knowledge of our happiness, before informing the *Gazette*."

His eyes thanked her, then he was unbuck-
ling the girth straps on Firebrand's saddle and
turning to exchange a word with the stable lad
who had come forward to lead the animals
away.

Lady Fielding was awaiting them in the
morning-room, considerably irate. She had
spent a harassing hour with Mr Sibbald, who
had arrived hoping to find his cousin, and who
had departed sooner than he intended, in her
ladyship's carriage, sporting a large rent on the
seat of his Unmentionables.

The jaws which had accomplished this dis-
tressing feat were presently engaged in demol-
ishing a steak. St George, having spent a
considerable part of the previous day being
transported from rural Berkshire in a carter's
dray, was understandably crabbed, and merely
yawned at Connie's delighted exclamation.

"Gormless animal!" snorted her ladyship,
balefully. "What sin I have committed to
deserve the housing of him is beyond my comprehension!"

"I do not choose to have you ladies un-
guarded at night, after the attempted burglary
at Lord Granville's," declared her grandson in

firm tones, keeping a careful eye on his maligned pet as Connie knelt to fondle the shaggy fur.

"Humbug! Every door and window in this house is—Lud! What in the world have you been at, child?" she demanded, staring incredulously at Connie's hair, which, for several reasons, was less than neat.

"Such a breeze as there is by the river, Grandmama," put in the Earl promptly, winking at Connie with the eye farthest from his relative. She responded with a deep blush, and hastened upstairs, fearful that Lady Fielding's shrewd mind would analyse the situation.

Her ladyship glanced out of the window, where the planetrees in the Square barely ruffled so much as a leaf.

"Your cousin called, in a monstrous fangle," she remarked, favouring the Earl with penetrating interest. "It seems he encountered your friend Mr Frome this morning, and is bidden remind you that there is but eighteen days left in which to stitch yourself up or forfeit the wager."

"Confound Frome! And why did not Sibbie wait here for our return?"

"He intended to," retorted Lady Fielding, in grim amusement. "He had the misfortune, however, to trip over that animal yonder, and was unable to sit. It bit him," she explained, as an afterthought. "And another thing! Benson had just taken receipt of this letter for you. Sibbald brought it along."

She indicated a communication propped against the Ormolu clock on the mantelshelf. "It don't bear a frank, and the spelling is formidable. That must only indicate bad news!"

"Oh, the devil!" A groan escaped Lord Chievely, as he frowned over the contents. "It's from O'Malley. Oriol has contracted navicular disease! Fears the nerve may have to be severed! I must return there at once!"

His face looked all at once tired. "Oh, Grandmama, after the hopes I entertained . . . He would have pulled it off! But now . . ."

The bitter disappointment showed bleak in his eyes. "And now Frome. I foresee that business recoiling upon me also." He laughed mirthlessly. "I begin to believe I was destined to lose out on happiness, Grandmama."

Late that night, Connie stood by the window in her bed-chamber, gazing out at the darkened Square below. The gas lamps, a recent innovation and to her eyes quite wonderful, cast sweeping pools of light so bright that they completely transcended the old oil burners still in use in lesser parts of town. Somewhere, beyond Lansdowne House opposite, a night-watchman's cry broke the stillness, and an owl answered mournfully from a gently swaying branch over the way.

Downstairs, a clock chimed three. Connie redrew the window-curtain and stood for some minutes before the guttering candle flame on her dressing-table, absorbed in the pattern of light playing on the gold signet ring on her finger.

Noel's own ring, which he had taken from his finger and slipped on hers, only a few hours earlier, before going North. Gently she traced the entwined initials, surmounted by a crest, both so minute that it was impossible to distinguish them.

"I want you to have this, Connie," he had said softly. "It is too large for your hand, I know, but I would have you accept it, dearest, as a token of our understanding."

Then, tenderly, he had turned her face up, and she was conscious of the dark hunger in his eyes, the trembling of his fingers as he parted her lips to meet his.

"Oh, my darling—my dearest love!"

The words were spoken beneath his breath, and Connie, lashes wet with tears at the imminence of their parting, clung to him dumbly, with her face buried in his driving coat, and the beat of his heart against her cheek.

"Think of me, little one."

Then he was gone, striding purposefully to the stairs, his jaw firmly set. A few minutes later she heard the carriage draw away, leaving her alone, with the feel of his caped coat still rough against her skin.

Fourteen

∽◯∽◯∽◯∽

THE NEWS THAT the Chievely colt was out of
the running circulated like wildfire. Around
the select green baize gaming-tables of Brooks's
Club and White's, and in the lesser taverns and
areas of entertainment where the fraternity of
the curry-comb waxed strong, punters were generally agreed that Chievely's second colt, Azor,
was too inexperienced to present much of a
show.

As might be expected, Miss Drinker devoured
every detail of the impending event with mounting excitement. Ruff's *Guide to the Turf* became her Testament, and Mr Sibbald found
himself plied with such penetrating questions
on form that he was obliged to scurry after every available scrap of racing literature, but with
the Earl not there to instruct him thoroughly,
he found himself becoming disastrously unstuck.

Miss Drinker, who had long since compared
his lordship's reputation with personal acquaintance, and found him wanting, declared
herself unable to comprehend why a peer so
closely bound to the Turf should be unable to
name the grey which had secured him the St
Leger, and disbelief sharpened to suspicion.

"Your mount was Filho da Puta!" she accused, flourishing a racing manual under his nose. "Jumpin' Jehosaphat! One don't forget a name like that!"

"'Course! A regular goer of a filly," mumbled Mr Sibbald, pretending what he hoped was intelligent interest.

"It states here that Filho da Puta was a colt!"

Lizzie-May regarded him with a narrowed eye. "If your stables were not so celebrated, I'd wager you know as little of flat-racing as my Great-Aunt Jemimy! If you are holding out on me, I'd as soon know!" Her good-natured face scanned his in frank appraisal. "Fact is, somethin' tells me that I've been gammoned!"

Mr Sibbald squirmed with unease. "Wh-What causes you to think so?" he gulped.

Miss Drinker sprawled comfortably over a sofa and considered. "You act mighty jumpy for a lord—and your reputation of Lothario simply don't figure." She hugged one knee with an air of contemplation. "What's more, if you expressed any genuine interest in securing this wager I hear talk of, you'd be down wind like a shot, 'stead of leaving the field to your cousin! So—when you don't display a shine for Connie, with so much at stake, I figure there must be a darned good reason."

She favoured him with a candid eye. "Ain't that so?"

Mr Sibbald felt his heart lurch unpleasantly. Miss Drinker was too sharp by half but he knew her to be a sensible, warm-hearted girl. Most importantly, she was Miss Osborne's particular friend. Offering up a silent prayer in respect of the consequences, he croaked, "M-Miss Drinker . . . can you keep a secret?"

St George's entry into the correct life of Berkeley Square swiftly aroused anxieties. His pedigree may have been native-bred but his code was pure Jacobin. It was Liberty, Equality and Fraternity to the end and he upheld it unswervingly.

Equality in that he deemed it his right to appropriate her ladyship's most comfortable chairs; Fraternity in that he treated all men as brothers—and all women, too, for more than one elderly spinster was reported as having been treated for the vapours after encountering St George in the Square; and Liberty because the instant the front door should be opened he was gone, streaking for the trees to the imminent danger of any human unwise enough to impede his progress.

Sympathising with this mania for fresh air, Connie willingly undertook the task of exercising him. St James's Park was their usual venue, as it was relatively near and possessed a gloriously long canal of water in which St George delighted to chase sticks and ducks and other low life.

Cats were his especial forte, and Connie was thankful they were a scarce commodity in the Square, for St George had the constitution of a boa constrictor and was known to have devoured a silk stocking and a copy of the *Morning Post*, besides having regurgitated a Methodist pamphlet (which, Lady Fielding dryly remarked, said much for his spiritual good sense) .

Connie's affection for the sheepdog was very

real, not only because she loved animals but because he belonged to Noel. Cambridge did not seem so far away, with St George's head upon her lap.

There were Noel's letters also, filled with tender endearments, which she had re-read so often that she knew each page by heart. This frequent delivery of mail occasioned glances of apprehension from Lady Fielding, although tact forbade any enquiry after their source. And there was Noel's ring, which Connie pressed every night to her lips before going to sleep, and which was dearer to her than any other thing she possessed.

Two days, she thought, exultantly. Two more days, and he will be back! She could scarce wait for Mrs Drinker's rout on Thursday. To be reunited with him once again, to be swept close in the waltz, to re-affirm their love, oh so tenderly, under the stars . . .

She would wear the round gown which he liked best, although it was neither her newest nor most fashionable.

'White becomes you above everything,' he had written. And she knew he was right. No other colour lent such a bloom, such softness. Or was it another reason, an altogether special chemistry which caused her to be in such looks? Smiling, Connie touched the folds of shimmering spider gauze, and gave herself up to daydreams.

The rooms in Manchester Street were well filled by the hour of Mr Sibbald's arrival on the Thursday evening. Banks of flowers exuded fragrance from staircase and alcoves. A trio had

been engaged, and a buxom soprano, whose
voice was reported to be inordinately fine (and
for whose exorbitant fee Mrs Drinker intended
to exact every last half-penny worth of performance).

The doors connecting the back and front
salons had been fastened back for dancing, and
candelabra and an elaborate epergne overflow-
ing with fruit and trailing vine leaves graced
the long polished table in the dining-room.

In hopes of avoiding his hostess, in whose
memory the incident of the Fives Court lingered unquenched, Mr Sibbald judged the
deserted dining-room a sensible refuge. An ap-
petising aroma drifted from the kitchens adjoining, and he was peering through the half-open
doors, in hopes of ascertaining the menu, when
a booming voice from the far end of the room
caused him to spin round, as if stung.

In the doorway, conversing animatedly with
Lizzie-May, stood none other than the Bishop of
Upton.

Whimpering with terror, Mr Sibbald shot
through the double doors and collapsed against
a wall in a nerveless heap. Every second he
expected to hear his name being barked in that
blood-chilling rasp which never failed to reduce
him to quivering idiocy.

Nothing of the sort followed. Hardly able to
believe his escape, Mr Sibbald inched open one
eye, and discovered his hiding place to be a
darkish entry, with a further set of doors leading from it to the kitchens proper. A linen
closet covered one wall, on the outside of which
was hung a neatly laundered table-maid's uni-
form, complete with starched laced cap.

When his courage felt equal to plucking itself from the soles of his black evening pumps, Mr Sibbald stuck a bulging eye to the crack of light showing through from the dining-room. Miss Drinker was just out of vision, but he could hear her well enough, and from the conversation, it emerged that the Bishop had taken it upon himself to escort the young lady homewards from St Martin's Street, of bitter memory.

"I can't rightly express our pleasure that you have come tonight, sir!" declared Lizzie-May, cheerfully. "We simply had to despatch an invitation, after your exceeding kindness to me. 'Course, Momma was high as ripe cheese when she found where I'd been, but I reckon she was sore at findin' a flea on her bonnet, after we'd been to Astley's Amphitheatre. You ought to go see the cute dancing horses there, Bishop! There just ain't nothin' in all Brighton to beat 'em! You been back there at all since we met last Fall?"

"I am happy to report my gout has improved sufficiently to enable me to contemplate taking the air on the Steyne again this year. The ozone . . . the cry of the gulls, the bathing-machines . . ."

"The big spy-glass on the Marine Parade to ogle the bathers!" giggled Lizzie-May, wickedly. "And the Old Ship Hotel, where you partnered Momma at whist! I guess you have been practising no end of card tricks over the winter months, Bishop."

"I flatter myself that my expertise is improved, certainly. Indeed, only yesterday I indulged—would you believe—in a most entertaining game of rouge-et-noir!"

Stunned by these treacherous revelations, Mr Sibbald could merely gape from his retreat behind the double doors, vainly trying to equate this smirking, worldly card-sharp with the Bishop Rumblelow of his nightmares. He could discern the weasel-like, self-important figure, done up in dark evening coat and silk breeches, with a flash of white stocking below the knee, reminiscent of a diminutive magpie.

The Bishop, moreover, had discarded his sober clerical neckwear in favour of a crisp starcher, and although this in itself was reason for incredulity, what sagged the Sibbald jaw-line still further was the new wig adorning his vinegary senior's balding dome.

Of lustrous chestnut, it was crimped to a degree worthy of the Regent himself, and upon any aging roué would have aroused no undue comment; but coupled with the Bishop's foxy countenance, it looked diabolically flash.

Mr Sibbald was not permitted to dwell upon its merits or otherwise. The parade-ground tones of Mrs Drinker bellowed from the hall, ordering her guests into dinner. Next moment, the room was filling up alarmingly. Mr. Sibbald glimpsed Miss Osborne's troubled countenance, as she looked vainly about her before taking her allotted place at table. It was some minutes before he realised she had almost certainly come alone. The empty place at her side must be set for his cousin, but of the Earl there was no sign.

It took Mr Sibbald only a couple of seconds to realise that under no circumstances could he

hope to slip unnoticed through the crowded
dining-room to freedom. The guests had already taken their seats. His appearance must
inevitably be apparent to all, whereupon the
Bishop would expose him unhesitatingly as his
curate, with every attending horror. Worse,
Miss Osborne must suffer publicly the shock of
the Earl's deceit.

There was but one hope left. Mr Sibbald
stripped off his evening coat and cravat, and
struggled heroically into the blue-striped servant frock and white apron. This . . . *this*
was the depths of degradation now, but what
choice had he? With a dry mouth he pulled on
the lace cap, arranging it well over his ears, and
frantically hauling forward a curl or two to
create the effect of femininity.

Just as he was nerving himself to nip smartly
through the roomful of guests, the double doors
from the kitchens swung open, and a very stout,
harassed-looking female servant emerged, bearing a large soup tureen.

On espying the cowering Mr Sibbald, she
pulled up in surprise, then a black scowl descended on her features, and she snapped
crossly, "I expec's you be the hired help what's
takin' Moll's place! By the holy Mother, 'tis a
warm backside you warrant for neglectin' to be
punctual! Take this!"

Without ceremony, she dumped the tureen
of soup into Mr Sibbald's keeping. "Now get
in there sharpish! An' mind—not more'n three
ladlefuls apiece!"

Connie gazed down at her empty plate, un-
mindful of the buzz of voices about her. He had

not come! The choking hurt of it blotted every other thought from her mind. Mistily, she glanced at the empty place by her side. What could possibly have kept him?

Only that morning they had been reunited. He had sent round flowers for her to wear, and the tender note which had accompanied them had indicated no change of plan.

But she had waited in vain for his carriage. Finally Lady Fielding had ordered her own horses to be put to, and Connie, with no heart for the evening's entertainment, had arrived alone, hopeful of discovering Noel already there.

It was so utterly unlike him. Some grave mischance must have prevented his coming—yet he would surely realise her anxiety and send some message.

She had taken such pains over her toilet that evening. The looking-glass had told her she had never looked more lovely, with her gleaming hair caught up into a coil of soft ringlets, and his corsage of rosebuds and ferns nestling against her creamy bosom.

Connie's melancholy was banished momentarily by a talkative Mrs Bunbury, whose spouse sat on Connie's left, and who insisted upon his relaying the exciting rumour concerning the Princess Charlotte, daughter of the Regent, whose marriage to Prince Leopold of Saxe-Coburg had taken place last May.

"Bunbury! Inform Miss Osborne that the Princess is three months gone."

"Three months," muttered the crimson-faced Mr Bunbury.

"And not before time!" sniffed his lady, in a carrying voice. "Mind you, the Princess is such a boisterous, inelegant creature, I should not be at all surprised to find her produce an heir to the Throne with four legs and fetlocks."

Connie wished more ardently than ever that Noel might be present to give this tiresome matron one of his masterly set-downs, but her reply faltered in mid-sentence as a bevy of servants approached to serve the soup course, under the watchful eye of the butler, who stood at the sideboard.

The wench who had so arrested Connie's attention was a raw-boned, angular creature, whose unusually masculine hands were wielding a soup ladle with a nervous, twitching action, and whose face seemed set to bury itself in her distinctly flat bosom.

A startled gasp of recognition broke from Connie, stifled as swiftly by the unlovely creature's terror-stricken glance as their eyes met. As the soup ladle drew near, Connie pressed both lips fiercely together for fear of disgracing herself.

"Ssssh!" hissed Mr Sibbald, before Connie had power to utter a word. "D-Don't give me away, Miss Osborne!"

He leaned over to dole out a splash of soup, continuing, in an urgent whisper, "Where's my cousin?"

Utterly bemused at this latest folly, Connie shook her head.

"I—I was about to ask the self-same question of you!" she answered, faintly. "My lord . . . What is this . . ."

"Chicken broth!" muttered the maiden, sti-

fling a curse as a drop of hot soup scalded his
fingers. With a hitch of his skirts, he melted
along the line of guests before Miss Osborne
might question him further.

Quite unable to tear her eyes away, Connie
followed his progress, nonplussed as to the reason behind this eccentric pantomime.

"I declare, Miss Osborne! You are quite in
the clouds! One would think you had never encountered a serving wench before!"

Not one of such a singular description, was
Connie's private conjecture, forcing her attention back to Mrs Bunbury. She could only marvel at his lordship's brazen self-possession.

It was then a delighted smile lit up her face
as she observed him in the throes of a new pre-
dicament. Seated close by Mrs Drinker at the
end of the long table was an elderly gentleman,
wonderfully got up in a chestnut wig, and it
was evident that Lord Chievely had aroused
within him feelings of the most amorous
nature.

Mr Sibbald could have confirmed her suspicions. Vanity had prompted the short-sighted
cleric to discard his accustomed spectacles, a
fact which had nerved Mr Sibbald to approach
and attend to his wants (miraculously without
mishap).

He had thought to slink off, unnoticed, when
a light caress on the thigh nearmost to the
Bishop almost caused him to drop the tureen.

"Whass your name, pretty chil?" hiccuped the
Bishop, emboldened to un-Christian intentions
by the effects of claret.

"S'funny," he muttered, peering into Mr Sib-

bald's aghast countenance. "R'mind me—
hic!—of a curate of mine. Come now, you
mus'—mus' not be shy," he chided, grabbing at
Mr Sibbald's straining hand. "Not—*hic*—not al-
waysh modes'—what?"

A playful tweak to his rear sent Mr Sibbald
charging for the safety of the kitchens. That a
highly respected Divine should so forget himself as to frolic with a serving-wench! Heaven
help me, moaned Mr Sibbald, to himself, if ever old Rumble-belly learns the truth.

After soup, the main courses were brought
around, the servants offering the various dishes
so that everyone could help themselves. This
was a new and more convenient method of serving, introduced from Germany, but it only had
the effect of prolonging Mr Sibbald's agony.

By the time the cloth was removed, and the
port and stomachic ginger placed before the
gentlemen, my lord Bishop had fallen into a
light stupor, with his head sunk forwards on to
his chest, and his new wig askew. The ladies
withdrew to the salon and Mr Sibbald made an
unsuccessful attempt to slip from the kitchens.

"Oh, no, you don't, miss!" declared the stout
virago. "There be a stack of dirty crockery to
scour 'fore you gets out of 'ere! An' I wants 'em
so's I can see me face lookin' back at me!"

Lord Chievely had an excellent reason for
failing to attend the rout at Manchester Street.
Earlier that evening he had dined at White's,
and was not long engaged in studying the bill
of fare, when he was joined by a fellow-mem-
ber, Mr Fitzroy Montague.

"I should not choose the boiled fowl, old fellow," advised Mr Montague, conversationally. "Raggett had been laundering his stockings in the water again."

The Earl smiled at this standing joke told against the club's owner, whose menus were celebrated for their sheer unwholesomeness.

"A luncheon of cold beef will serve. I am going on to a rout, where I trust the victuals may prove rather more edifying."

Mr Montague helped himself to a measure of claret from the bottle which the Earl had ordered. "Yes, I know—the Drinker girl's crush. Heard you had got acquainted in that line. Friend of a friend of my sister Emily, don't you know," he added, by way of explanation.

"Strictly between you and I, old fellow, do not you judge the girl something of a Cit to be—"

"You know Miss Drinker!" It was more an affirmation than a question. The Earl set down his wine-glass, his expression guarded.

"Oh, not socially!" declared Mr Montague, hastily. "Rather too hearty for my taste, Chievely. But Miss Hope says—oh, you must know whom I mean—fizzy little honey with flirty eyes—Miss Hope met your Southern belle last week, apparently, and is thinking of taking her up."

"Arabella never was one to restrict her circle of acquaintance," observed his lordship, dryly.

"Nor you, old fellow—by accounts," grinned his companion. "The Drinker girl means to set you up as the prize exhibit tonight. According to Miss Hope, the girl's mother is confident of reeling you in—deuced fanatical about it, in fact. By the by, ensure to honour the Hope with a brace of country dances—she is to be at this crush tonight."

"Is she, by Jove!" muttered the Earl, privately scouring his brain for a way out of this disastrous situation. God in Heaven, he conjectured, grimly, it is madness to go through with this thing! If Bella Hope was to be at the Drinkers' rout, he had as well prepare to lose Constance there and then.

And Sibbie! His cousin would already be at Albany preparing to leave for the confounded affair. Unless I am able to prevent him, thought the Earl, he will walk in unsuspecting and the instant Bella Hope sets eyes on him there will be the Devil to pay!

" 'Course, don't believe it for a second, myself," declared Mr Montague, preparing to attack a beefsteak with relish. "Mean to say, never seen you hanging about this Drinker girl." He favoured the Earl with a knowing wink. "No—since your old Derby screw has come unstuck, Chievely, I mean to put my blunt on your Hampshire filly instead!"

"Goodbye, Monty." With a hurried excuse, his lordship collected his hat and left the club. But when he reached his rooms, it was to find Mr Sibbald already departed.

Having had his escape so vilely thwarted, it was well after ten before Mr Sibbald was empowered to snatch up his evening coat and cravat from the gloomy entry, and steal across the now deserted dining-room, with some idea of securing a quiet corner in which to rid himself of his striped frock. The sound of music and laughter from above assured him that the rout was well advanced, and upon gaining the hall, he sat himself on the bottommost tread of the staircase to wrestle with his apron-strings, which had knotted disastrously behind his back.

Engrossed in this operation, he failed to hear a soft footfall approaching, until a hiccup startled him into awareness. Bishop Rumbelow swayed unsteadily before him, brandishing an empty wine-glass, and wearing a glint in his bloodshot eye that caused Mr Sibbald to leap smartly to his feet.

"I's my li'l shwee'heart!" declared the Bishop, in tones of round satisfaction, stumbling forwards with arms out-stretched.

"One kiss—jus' one!"

Mr Sibbald uttered a shriek, and galloped upstairs at the double, hitching his long skirts frantically up to his knees. The amorous cleric, mistaking this glimpse of shapely underpinnings for encouragement, clambered enthusiastically after him with an agility incredible in one so overcome.

Gasping for breath, Mr Sibbald clung to the stair-rail, wildly debating the wisdom of gate-crashing the rout in the salon nearby. His pursuer's grunts, however, decided him that the safest course must be to gain the upper floor where, with luck, he might conceal himself in one of the bed-chambers.

At the head of the next staircase stood a Grecian pedestal, on which had been arranged a display of lilacs. Mr Sibbald tossed aside the basket of flowers, and heaved the ornate pedestal across the stair-head, where he hoped it might temporarily halt his unwanted suitor.

My Lord Bishop, however, merely paused

long enough to select a bouquet for his love, stepped delicately over the obstruction, and trotted after his perspiring quarry, whom he espied disappearing through a doorway at the end of the passage.

Too late, Mr Sibbald realised his folly. He was trapped in a chamber, three storeys from ground level, and with exposure but a minute or so away. Stumbling to the window, he flung up the sash and peered down. This side of the house skirted a small yard, with what appeared to be a mews adjoining. And—unbelievably—a strong growth of ivy clung to the wall!

Without further ado, Mr. Sibbald threw a leg over the sill, hitched his skirts over, and grasped feverishly at the sinewy tendrils of greenery.

Seeing his prize set to flee, the Bishop of Upton burst into the room and locked himself around the Sibbald ankle. Mr Sibbald gave vent to a terrified yell, being half in and half out the window, with the ground sickeningly far off. Gritting his teeth, he mouthed a silent prayer, and kicked out, sending his senior flying backside foremost on to the bed and freeing himself to clamber tortuously downwards.

As luck would have it a sharp-eyed stable lad espied his perilous descent, and being under the impression that a burglary had been committed, immediately set up a hue and cry. By now on the point of collapse, Mr Sibbald tottered along the low roof of the stables, closed his eyes tightly, and launched himself into the gloom.

He landed softly in a mound of straw, but even as he dazedly groped about to regain his

balance, the cries of his pursuers grew more
clamorous. The only available means of escape
was a saddled bay mare, tethered outside its
stall, and regarding him with what seemed to
Mr Sibbald the most unsavoury stare.

A rush of footsteps clattering over the
cobbles decided the issue. Mr Sibbald clambered feverishly astride the horse, which reared
up, neighing loudly, and took off at an almighty
gallop, with Mr Sibbald clinging to its mane,
and the shouts of "Stop thief!" reverberating in
his ears. Out of the mews they shot, and into
the darkened streets.

After the discovery of his cousin's departure
for Manchester Street, Lord Chievely sought
the counsel of Lady Fielding, whose denuncia-
tions he was obliged to receive before apprising
her of the reason behind his absence that evening.

"What reason am I to give Miss Osborne for
you?" demanded his grandmama, scathingly.
"You had best present an excellent case, young
man, for that child was positively crushed! I
have never been more annoyed with you!" She
glared at him. "Well?"

"You will tell no bounces on my behalf,
Grandmama," replied the Earl, firmly. "Tomorrow, I mean to confess the whole to Constance." His mouth tightened. "She must
decide then what our relationship is to be."

"And where are you bound meantime?"
asked Lady Fielding quickly, alarmed at the
grim resolution in his manner.

"To get drunk!" declared the Earl, forcefully.

In actual fact, he passed the remainder of

that evening in the billiard-room of White's. It was shortly after three in the morning when he returned to Albany, to be met by Benson with the intelligence that his cousin had been arrested for horse-stealing, and was presently in the custody of Spanish Place police office, where he was to appear next morning before the magistrate.

"Horse-stealing?" echoed the Earl. "What the blazes has he got himself into now?" He sank into a wing-chair. "Tell me the whole."

Benson coughed discreetly and gazed at the ceiling.

"Mr Sibbald is reported as being in possession of—ahem—items of female attire, my lord. The constable who called with the disturbing intelligence bade me inform your lordship that these circumstances are to be brought before the Court, together with the other charges."

"Other charges?" repeated his lordship, faintly.

Benson cleared his throat. "Mr Sibbald is further accused of having assaulted a night-watchman, causing irreparable damage to the said night-watchman's wooden shelter, employing abusive language towards the arresting officer, and of being in unlawful possession of certain garments as worn by female persons in domestic employment."

"Oh, my sweet heaven!" muttered the Earl, covering his eyes. "He's done it this time! Fetch me a pot of strong coffee, Benson. I shall require a clear head to disentangle this mess!"

Mr Sibbald had spent an uncomfortable night in the cells, where he had deliberated long upon his horrific chain of misfortune. What weighed most heavily on his mind was the fact of his having inadvertently allowed the arresting constable to extract his true identity, even though he had rallied sufficiently to maintain silence on the nature of his gainful employment.

It was visibly heartening, therefore, to espy his cousin's tall figure in the public benches. Mr Sibbald managed a wan smile as an officer led him into the dock. But the worst was yet to come.

The presiding magistrate took his seat, the clerk called the first case, and Mr Sibbald was prodded to his feet, only to discover himself gazing into the bewigged and stony face of the giant from the Fives Court.

With such a Justice in command of his fate, Mr Sibbald was as good as finished. Vaguely, he recalled hearing the black list of his crimes being read out, baulked as the prime witness, an aged Charley sporting a fine black eye, recounted in an aggrieved whine how the accused had allowed his old screw to plough recklessly through Government property (which only the Almighty knew as how he weren't occupying at the time) .

"Into mid-air, straight, I wur, yer Honour, wive me stave knocked Gawd knows where, till the bleedin' article twangs back on me from the cobbles. Damn near close me daylights proper!"

Further evidence was submitted, in the shape of two scraps of blue-striped cotton which corresponded exactly to the torn garment as worn by the accused, at the time of his arrest, and the case was complete.

"Lord, I fully expected the horse to be brought in, any second!" expostulated the Earl, wrathfully, as he drove his shattered cousin back to Albany, having parted with the sum of fifty pounds bail in order to effect his release. "I daresay you realise this farce will have the town by the ears! That 'curst reporter from *The Times* was gone like a bullet the minute your case was over!"

Mr Sibbald moaned softly. His cousin's anger came hard, after the anguish of the past twelve hours. Stealing a glance at the grim mouth, he said, in a flat voice, "Seems I've confounded everything, coz."

Lord Chievely stared ahead to the space between his pair's twitching ears. In a tone of heavy finality, he said, "Yes, old man. I greatly fear you have."

Mrs Drinker stared incredulously at the uniformed constable facing her across the octagon table in her front drawing-room.

"Do I wish to press charges against *whom*?" she queried, hoping that the maid had gotten the fellow to wipe his boots first.

"Against Mr Augustus Sibbald, ma'am, the gentleman what was apprehended in possession of certain effects, as before stated."

"But, I tell you, officer, we know nothing of this—this Sibbald! I never heard tell of him before! Why, this is the first we know of our being burgled!"

The constable looked embarrassed. "It's delicate like, ma'am. Turns out he's kinsman to

Lord Chievely, who, we understand, attended
your little gathering last night. Under the circumstances—"

"You quite mistake the matter, my good fellow! Lord Chievely did not set foot here, nor
did he have the grace to send his refusal! Why,
I had most fifty folks itchin' to be introduced,
and he darned well don't show up!" Her bosom
heaved with vexation.

"And when next I encounter that gangling,
chinless popinjay I'll—say, what's gotten you,
mister?"

The constable was frowning. "Can you
describe his lordship, ma'am?"

"Can I?" declared Mrs Drinker, wrathfully.
"How's this!"

The constable listened, with a narrowed eye.
When she had done, he remained silent for a
minute or so, then, with a deprecating cough,
declared, slowly, "Seems you've been took for a
juggins, ma'am. You've given a crack picture of
this 'ere cove Sibbald. Why, ma'am! . . ."

But Mrs Drinker, with a moan, lay prostrated
at his feet.

Fifteen

AT THAT SAME moment Connie was setting off
with St George and a dutiful footman, to take
the air and allow her shaggy friend his accustomed freedom in St James's Park.

She promised herself to be returned within
the hour, for Mr Musgrave had left word with
his grandmama that he would be calling at
three, especially to see Constance. There was a
particular matter he must settle, and Connie
knew without enquiring that it must concern
his non-appearance at the rout. If Lady Fielding knew the cause, she steadfastly refused to
be drawn, and Connie suspected, with some
trepidation, that his absence must needs have
been prompted by some issue of particular
gravity.

It was a close, humid afternoon, with a
promise of thunder in the air. Their destination, when they reached it, proved lushly green,
with buttercups and tiny dog-violets thrusting
their heads above the grass. Thankfully there
were few persons about with whom St George
might fraternise, and Connie decided it would
be safe to unhook his leash.

Unfortunately, St George had detected some
three hundred yards away a coquettish white

tail, which instinct told him belonged to the female of the species, and immediately he
streaked off, crashing through the undergrowth,
alarming the grazing cows, in and out of the
canal, with bedraggled tail flying, and barking
enthusiastically.

The footman was hampered in his efforts at
pursuit on account of his narrow livery but
Connie, heart in mouth for fear of what St
George might accomplish, picked up her skirts
and ran despairingly after the sheepdog.

When flushed and out of breath she finally
tracked him down, St George was circling
round a dainty French poodle, whose owner,
considerably harassed, was making ineffectual
attempts to shoo him off with the point of his
white-thorn cane.

Whoever the gentleman might be, concluded
Connie, with distaste, he favoured inordinate
stylishness of dress. His coat was worn wide
open to display to advantage a rose-coloured
waistcoat lavishly embellished with fobs and
chains. His skin-tight pantaloons were gathered
up into a wasp's waist, and his head, poking stiffly from a high and crispy starched cravat, was
crowned by a shiny silk hat, under which
sprang a crop of lavishly pomaded red-gold
curls.

At her approach the gentleman looked up
stiffly, and she perceived the nosegay in his but-
tonhole to be fairly quivering.

"Madam!" he protested, in a peevish voice.
"Have the goodness to restrain this—this mon-
grel! I have my pedigree to consider." A dawn-
ing horror suffused his haughty countenance.

" 'Gad! . . . I declare it's Chievely's ani-mal!"

With trembling fingers, he tore off one ele-gant pea-green glove and stuck a quizzing-glass to his nose.

"The devil—it is!"

"No, no!" cried Connie, stooping to secure the leash to St George's collar. "You mistake the matter, sir. This is St George, who belongs to Lord Chievely's cousin, Mr Musgrave."

Mr Byng stared from Connie to the goggle-eyed footman, who had sidled up, and was hovering a discreet couple of yards off.

"My good girl," he drawled, inspecting her as though she were an insect. "Whom you may be I have no desire to discover, but this—this bag-ful of fleas is the property of Noel Chievely, as I live!"

"You—you are wrong . . . you must be! Thomas—"

She turned pleading eyes to the silent foot-man, whose face was a study. "Have the good-ness to explain . . ." In desperation, Connie forced her eyes back to the dandified creature, although an icy coldness was gripping at her heart.

"You must have heard of Mr Musgrave, sir, indeed you must!" she whispered, tearfully. "He is the finest gentleman in all the world, and—and his grandmama is Lady Fielding, and—and his colt was to win at Epsom next week, only it is gone lame, you know, and . . . and . . ." Bright tears rolled down her cheeks, and her voice was a high, hysterical sob. "And if he is not my Mr Musgrave, sir, then who . . ."

Connie knew the answer even before it was asked. He had deceived her—more surely, more cunningly, than ever she could have deemed possible! Noel—her own, darling Noel—who had held her against his heart, and silenced her mouth with his kisses; Noel, who had made life an enchantment; Noel who could coax her into laughter with his teasing nonsense; Noel, who had pledged their love with the ring from his own finger . . . Noel was the despised Earl of Chievely.

All these months, all these glorious, bitter-sweet months, he had used her, seduced her feelings with single-minded determination. She ought to have guessed he would not quit the fight so lightly. Monksford was his obsession, and she, like a fool, had given it him on a platter.

Everything fell into place now. Bitterly, Connie recalled the peculiar glances and whispered asides of the housemaids in Berkeley Square. They had known, they all knew, what a dupe she was! Lady Fielding's reticence, the apologetic, half-begun revelations . . . Noel's cousin, who had been coerced into aiding in this diabolical outrage . . .

She felt a sudden, contemptuous anger towards that gangling, incompetent figure—an anger which cooled as swiftly as it had come. He was not a bad sort, the victim of a will stronger than his own, and he could not, after all, help looking like a fish.

She became aware that the disdainful features of the manmilliner were quivering in a spasm of mirth. In a strangled voice Connie heard herself say, "Thomas . . . I beg you

will attend to St George. I—must return immediately. I . . . I cannot . . ."

"But Miss . . ."

"Oh, please, please let me be!" With a sob,
she turned on her heel, summoning as much
dignity as she could muster, leaving Mr Byng
and the footman staring after her wordlessly.

But she could not face returning—not yet.
How long she remained by the canal with her
thoughts, Connie had no notion, but long
shadows were lengthening the Square when she
entered it from Hill Street. She went quietly
upstairs to her room, and set about bathing her
reddened eyes and brushing her hair with
mechanical precision, unable even to suffer the
agitated concern of her maid. Her brain felt
numb—incapable of clear thinking, and her
heart felt as though it had been torn out.

"Constance—my dear child!" Noel's grandmama, white-faced and clutching at her stick,
stood in the doorway. "Thomas has told me . . ."

She extended a hand, but Connie did not
move—indeed, she was afraid to. More than
anything, she desired to fling herself into those
outstretched arms, to sob out her heartache and
bewilderment against Lady Fielding's understanding breast, but pride froze her limbs.

For what seemed an age, Connie remained,
with head held high, her throat working pain-
fully. Then, replacing the hairbrush on the
dressing-table, she said, dully, "I—I shall be excessively grateful, your ladyship, if Thomas
may be permitted to summon a hackney coach.
My abigail is already seeing to my trunk . . .
Rose!" She motioned the girl to leave them.

"Constance—you must not go—you shall not,

without first talking out this—this sorry affair
with Chievely! He is wretchedly upset . . . a
full hour he waited here, hoping for your return. Oh, my child, you must not walk out on
him in this manner . . . You—you do not understand what it would mean!"

Despite her own crushing agony, Connie perceived that the old lady was deeply affected.
Drawing forward a chair, she pressed Lady
Fielding into it, saying, in a faltering voice,
"I—I shall see Noel . . . if—if it truly means
so much to you, ma'am. But I cannot remain
. . . it is quite finished."

She tugged at the bell-pull, sudden decision
overtaking her.

"Matthews will care for you, whilst I am gone
out. If I am to go through with this, it must be
accomplished instantly, else I . . . I n-never
shall."

"You will not find my grandson at his
rooms," warned her ladyship, quietly. "He is—
he is gone to call upon Mademoiselle D'Erlon."

Connie hesitated. "In that case, I shall of a
certainty find him there, if I make haste," she
declared, stoutly.

Large drops of rain were falling fast, but
Connie was too agitated to mind. As she
reached the end of Berkeley Street, the heavens
opened. Lightning danced off the pavements
and the street swiftly became a running, muddy
stream. Connie had always been apprehensive
of thunderstorms, yet she knew that to take
shelter would break her iron control—compel
her to turn back.

Blindly, hardly able to see for the downpour,

she ran across the cobbled thoroughfare, narrowly escaping the wheels of a whiskey and pair, and gained the Burlington House corner.

In answer to Connie's imperative rap on the knocker, the front door of Mademoiselle D'Erlon's apartment in Jermyn Street was opened by a sulky maidservant who resolutely began closing it again at sight of the dirty, dripping figure on the doorstep. Connie's sprig muslin was saturated and splashed with mud, and her dark hair clung wetly to her forehead. She realised what a fright she must look, but she did not care—nothing mattered, except she see Noel.

"I dunno as 'ow I ought to admit the likes of you!" declared the maid, rudely, in answer to Connie's urgent request.

"You best step into the hall—no farther, mind!—I don't want no puddles to clean up."

She flounced off, leaving Connie to glance about her. Désirée was kept in evident style, she surmised, wryly. A white-painted spiral staircase adjoined the hall and even as she stood, striving to regain her breath and her courage, she heard Noel's deep, familiar voice coming from an open doorway in the gallery above.

Without pausing to consider, Connie flew up the stairs, conscious of the maid's indignant cries behind her. At the commotion his head came round the door, and she saw the incredulous disbelief in his eyes.

"Constance! . . . However do you come to be here?" Swiftly, he came towards her, observing her sodden gown and the white tiredness in her face. A sharp alarm darkened his eyes. "Connie, my dearest, whatever is amiss?"

He made as if to take her into his arms, but Connie twisted free, her fingers fumbling at the clasp of the fine gold chain around her neck, from which she had hung his ring for safe-keeping. With a sob she wrenched it free, saying, chokily, "You must find another hand to wear this, Lord Chievely! I—I pray you may not find it necessary to deceive its owner, as . . . as you have me."

"Noel? *Qu'est ce que brouhaha? . . . Ma foi!* Mais 'oo is zis so wet lady?"

Mademoiselle D'Erlon appeared from the bed-chamber wearing a diaphanous wrapper of white lace, with her vivid auburn curls spilling over one creamy shoulder, and dainty feet thrust into white fur slippers. She stared from the Earl to Connie in questioning curiosity. The Earl's face was grey, and his eyes never left Connie's tear-wet countenance.

In a voice heavy with defeat, he said quietly, "This is Miss Osborne, Désirée, the lady of whom I was telling you." To Connie, he said, in a near whisper, "So you know . . . Oh, Connie . . ."

"You lied to me." Connie spoke flatly, without expression. "Everything you professed—all your f-fine words . . . all lies."

"No, by God!" His eyes blazed with an anguished desperation. "I love you more than anything on earth, Connie!"

Urgently, he pulled her against him, forcing her to look into his face. "There was simply no other way, my darling! Do you imagine I have enjoyed deceiving you?"

His arms tightened about her, and the naked hurt in his eyes twisted her insides so agonisingly that she wanted to cry out.

"All my life, I have been searching for someone who might love me for myself. All the success and wealth in the world counts for nothing unless one has someone to share it with."

His voice broke on the words, but he recovered, after a pause, saying, unsteadily, "Those three months with you at Monksford were the happiest I had ever known. Do you imagine you are so easy to forget, Constance?"

Connie gave a little moan, as though he had struck her a blow. "Do not! . . . You have no right to pretend." A brittle laugh escaped her, that more resembled a sob. "I thought you so honourable, so—so fine . . . Oh, why did you let me fall in love with you, Noel?"

Connie had determined not to break down, but the tears were fairly slipping down her cheeks now, so that his face was a blur. She was aware that his mistress had shooed the inquisitive maid-servant downstairs, and that she herself had tactfully withdrawn to the bed-chamber, closing the door softly behind her.

Through the haze of grief and tears, Connie heard Noel say, firmly, "This is no place to be discussing our affairs. You are wet through, besides. Let me take you home, else you will contract pneumonia."

"I—I wish nothing further from you!" whispered Connie, shrinking from him. "I came only because your grandmama desired it . . . Oh God! Such fools we women are!"

"Nevertheless, there is a cheque for a considerable sum deposited in Child's bank, which you shall certainly have from me!" he stated, quietly. "And another item which must not be forgot."

A bitter-sad smile relieved his countenance. "Do not you guess to what I am referring, Connie?"

She shook her head wordlessly, fighting to staunch her tears.

"Oh, Bright-Eyes . . . Did you never once suspect that I was the purchaser of your diamonds?"

"You? . . ." Connie swayed, so numbing was this fresh blow. "Oh, do not say it!" Fiercely, she bit into her clenched fist to blot out the irony of it. "Are you not content with breaking my heart?" she whispered. "Need you dance upon the fragments as well?"

Feverishly, she sought in her reticule for a handkerchief. "What have I to do with those diamonds now?"

"I meant them to be your wedding gift," he answered, very quietly, passing her his own neatly folded handkerchief. "None other shall wear them."

With superhuman effort, Connie held back the lump of tears in her throat. "So that is what you had in mind as exchange! Monksford—with myself as part of the fittings! Do you fancy me such a dullard, my lord? You know very well I should feel morally obliged to—to . . ." Proudly, her chin lifted.

"Keep your stones, Lord Chievely. I am not obliged to wed anyone—least of all you!"

At the scorn in her words, the Earl's face contorted, as if a whip-lash had been laid across it.

"God!" he muttered. "That it should come to this between us!"

Casting off his coat, he set it about her resisting shoulders, remarking, grimly, "Let me not have your death to my account, at the least. Come."

The short carriage drive to Berkeley Square was accomplished in silence. Connie would not suffer him to see her indoors, but he stubbornly refused to drive off until the butler had ushered her inside.

"*Connie!*"

A small figure, ringlets flying, streaked downstairs and threw herself into Connie's astonished arms. "Is not this the most famous surprise? Uncle Maurie promised I might come—he wrote to St Ursula's for especial leave—truly he did! So now we are to go! Oh, do say you are not in a miff, Connie!"

Wordlessly, Connie hugged her young sister. "Oh, how perfectly delightful . . . And Uncle Maurie, too!"

She smiled mistily above Fanny's dark curls to the beaming figure in the ancient cutaway peering over the baluster-rail.

"I have missed you both so!"

Sir Maurice heaved a relieved sigh, having harboured doubts as to how his elder niece might view young Fanny's absence from school.

"Come for the Derby, Conn," he boomed. "Me and the young 'un—bespoke rooms at the Spread Eagle, in Epsom. Pays to gauge the Blood early—catch 'em at their exercise on the Downs, what?"

He tapped his nose confidently, and descended a farther step or two, demanding, in querulous tones, "What's griping that Yankee woman, Conn? Flounced in, with her nostrils smoking, not ten minutes since—bellowing for Musgrave's insides like a Philistine! Somethin's up, Conn."

Shortly after nine next day, Lord Chievely stood in his book-lined morning-room, tersely facing a triumphant Mrs Drinker. Lizzie-May fidgeted uneasily on the chaise-longue, her cheeks perfectly white under the brim of her chipstraw bonnet, and her hands clasping and unclasping in a frenzy of agitation.

Ignoring the fast-cooling breakfast which his lordship had abandoned at their unexpected entrance, Mrs Drinker snatched up the Earl's unopened copy of *The Morning Post* and flourished it under his nose.

"Judge for yourself!" she shrilled. "Now, sir, back out if you dare!"

The Earl stared at the *Gazette* column. His face drained of colour, and he remained like stone, a hard, white line about his mouth and in his eyes an expression of stunned horror.

'A marriage has been arranged,' the announcement ran, 'between Adrian Noel, Eleventh Earl of Chievely, and Elizabeth Mary, only daughter of Mrs Dorothea Drinker and the late Mr Hubert Drinker, of Belmont, Baton Rouge, Louisiana.'

Sixteen

~~~~~~~~~~~~~~~~~~~~~~~~~~~~~~~

ABSOLUTE SILENCE FOLLOWED. Lizzie-May pulled
nervously at her glove, not daring to glance up.
After what seemed an age, the Earl deposited
the newspaper by the side of his breakfast cup,
and quietly enquired, "What means this?"

Miss Drinker immediately sprang to her feet,
breaking into an incoherent explanation, which
her Mama speedily silenced.

"It means, Lord Chievely, that your betrothal
to my little girl is at this moment bein' picked
over in every breakfast parlour in Mayfair!"
Mrs Drinker's triumphant screech rose to a cre-
scendo. "Well, sir?"

The Earl's mouth compressed dangerously.
"As the fortunate recipient of your daughter's
hand, is one permitted to ask why?"

Mrs Drinker seated herself complacently on
the gondola-style chaise-longue and regarded
him with caustic deliberation.

"Now see here, your Earlship! I ain't a vin-
dictive woman, but when my flesh and blood
gets took for a loopy, it's scalp-huntin' time, yes
sir! The way I figures it is this! No further
charges against your nincompoop kinsman Sibbald, on my part, and a helluva practical appreciation upon yours!"

"You tie a pretty parcel, ma'am." The remark was made with icy civility. "Upon my honour, I congratulate you!" Turning to Lizzie-May, who stood pale and embarrassed before the window, he said, "Your personable nature alone might have secured the objective, Miss Drinker, without having recourse to—ensnarement."

"You do not understand—I—I knew nothing of this! I swear . . ." Lizzie-May was close to tears. "This is entirely Momma's doing!" An anguished moan escaped her, and she sank into a chair, her plump shoulders heaving piteously. "Do you imagine I wish to marry you? It—it's B-Bertram I love, and . . ." Her face crumpled suddenly, and she burst into loud sobs, burying her cheeks amongst the cushions.

"I had forgotten Bertram." The Earl looked thoughtful.

"What do you know of my nephew, pray?" demanded Mrs Drinker, in sudden suspicion.

The Earl intercepted Lizzie-May's momentary stiffening, the unspoken pleading in the swift turn of her head. Shrugging, he replied, dryly, "Of your nephew, ma'am? Absolutely nothing, above that he is a veritable Corinthian, with a mania for religion."

Mrs Drinker snorted derisively. "Got no option! He ain't fitted for no decent occupation, and too poor to be a gentleman!"

"That is unfair, Momma! Bertram knows heaps about animals, and how to treat 'em when they get sick! Why, he's broke in more horses than I've had hot dinners!"

"Any hick hayseed can do as much!" Mrs Drinker's eyes, swivelling round, stopped further protestation with the effectiveness of a bullet. "I don't aim to acknowledge no two dollar horse-doctor as my kin! Nor no preacher! We Drinkers come of superior stock, child! And you had best remember it!"

"I cannot allow you to harangue my betrothed, ma'am," demurred his lordship, with the beginnings of a smile. "Neither must you raise your voice at so early an hour. My neighbours, you understand, are nocturnal creatures, who habitually carouse till five of the morning, and will damn my eyes for allowing any threat to their repose."

Ignoring Mrs Drinker's stupefied gaze, he crossed quickly to Lizzie-May's disconsolate figure, and raised her, saying gently, "After the initial surprise, I confess myself favourably attracted to our union. It is my hope that you may speedily be of like mind."

Lizzie-May gaped at him, aghast. "N-No! . . . You are not serious? I—I understood Connie and you . . . I shan't marry you! No one shall make me!"

Wildly, she whirled away from him. "I—I shall place an intimation of my own in the *Gazette*—"

"Belt your lip, Lizzie-May!" hissed Mrs Drinker. She fixed the Earl with an incredulous stare. "You mean—you'll take her? No spoofin'?"

"Nothing shall alter my enthusiasm," declared the Earl, firmly. "But come! This calls for celebration! Champagne—or shall you first partake of coffee?"

"Lizzie-May will take a cup—I got to get home!" Mrs Drinker settled her bonnet, and enveloped her daughter in a constricting embrace.

"You leave all arrangements to your Momma, honey! I mean to contact Gunther's this instant—they did us such a fine Escalope de Veau Milanaise for our little get-together the other evening! And you must be wed by special licence! Dear Lord Chievely will know how to set about that. Oh, and your bride-gown, honey! We shall stop by Madame D'Arbignon's of Bruton Street after luncheon—worked silver tissue, with a cap of blossoms, just such as your cousin Maud wore, 'cept yours must cost more! If this ain't the grandest day of my life! How dear Hubert would be proud."

She wiped affectedly at her eyes, and in the same breath dug her daughter in the ribs, adding, in a hissed undertone, "Don't forget, Lizzie-May, Maud only managed a trumpery, four-stone ruby!"

"Momma—how can you?" whispered Lizzie-May, crimson-faced, but her parent was already sweeping to the door, which Benson was holding dutifully ajar, leaving her alone with the Earl.

Lord Chievely fetched a cup and saucer from the sideboard, and lifted the lid of the coffee-pot with a dubious frown. Miss Drinker put forth a restraining hand.

"I—I don't wish no coffee, truly." She bit her lip, at a loss for words. "Lord Chievely . . . sir, I—I guess it's a real honour for a girl to be sought in marriage by a genuine English Earl, but—"

"I was used to believing so," mused his lordship, smiling faintly. "But if I am to be jilted for the second time within four-and-twenty hours, I begin to question the truth of it."

The smile died on his lips, and he turned swiftly away, so that only his profile was visible. Miss Drinker regarded him in awed silence, too much astonished to reply. At length, she stammered, disbelieving, "Not—not Connie? Gee, no—why, she was so . . ."

The Earl's jaw tightened, but he did not answer. When he finally spoke, it was to observe, in casual vein, "You have had no letter from your cousin for some time."

She glanced up, on the defensive. "Since you have delivered me none, sir, I—I guess Momma must have written to warn him off."

Resolutely, she extracted a handkerchief from her reticule, and blew her nose. "He vowed nothin' would stop our runnin' in double harness, but—" She favoured him with a wan smile. "I guess he's found someone else."

"In which event, you may view with less repugnance the prospect of becoming my wife?" The Earl spoke lightly, but the question brought a surge of colour to her cheeks.

"Sir, I . . . I did not intend my refusal as a slight. There never can be anybody I'd plump for half so readily as Bertram, but—" Her lips trembled. "Seems he don't want me, so . . . so I guess I might learn to do my duty by you, Lord Chievely, even if I d-don't love you . . ."

The words ended in a stifled sob. His lordship regarded her keenly for some minutes, then, as though satisfied, he took an envelope from the inner pockets of his waistcoat.

"In that case, my dear, I may deliver this letter to you without qualm," he remarked, handing it to her. "It arrived only this morning, and in my preoccupation I regrettably mistook it for my own. The seal is broken, as you observe," he added, apologetically, "and I must caution you that the contents ensure an end of any future correspondence with your cousin."

He directed her blanched countenance to the letter.

"But read it for yourself."

The intelligence of Noel's betrothal to Lizzie-May shattered Connie more surely than anything which had gone before. Any flicker of conciliation must be extinguished by that wounding announcement in the *Gazette*. The chasm was final, irrevocable—the shock as numbing as a physical blow.

Equally astounded, Lady Fielding had been so incensed as to summon her barouche immediately, only to find her grandson departed with Miss Drinker to transact business with Messrs Rundell and Bridge.

She returned visibly upset, and Connie, who had been unable to bespeak a seat on the Mail before Monday evening, spent an anxious two days, trusting fervently that the grief of this new worry might not affect the old lady's recurring heart condition.

Herself exhausted from weeping and lack of sleep, Connie strove to banish all thought of the crushing news from her mind. She had seen off young Fanny that morning with a brave face, resolved that nothing must cloud the child's excitement at the impending treat.

With a heavy heart, Connie surveyed the neat bed-chamber which had been her retreat these last hours from the curious and pitying faces of the servants. Nothing was out of place.

Her bonnet and pelisse lay over a chair in readiness for departure, the trunk was fastened down.

"Constance." Lady Fielding had entered, so softly that Connie looked up, startled. "Will not you reconsider? I implore you!"

She drew Connie to a chair and sat opposite, taking the slim hands in her own. "Oh, Constance—you are so—so right for Chievely! He loves you—surely you must realise that?"

The thin fingers tightened involuntarily. "He has been hurt enough in his life . . . You must not desert him now!"

"And what of my hurt?" Connie retrieved her hand, as if stung. "Do not my feelings count? He has humiliated me—nothing can alter the fact!"

Pierced to the heart she turned ravaged eyes to Noel's grandmother, her voice threatening to drown in the flood of tears pressing upwards in her throat. "He has taken the life from me! I—I ought to hate him for what he has done, but I . . . can feel nothing . . . nothing."

"Allow me to send for him," urged Lady Fielding. "This preposterous betrothal must be ended at once! Chievely and you were intended for each other, child."

"It was with Noel Musgrave that I fell in love, ma'am." Connie's voice was low, unmoved. "I knew only that he was good and honourable. It was for these qualities that I loved him . . . and for himself. But Noel Chievely can have no claim on my regard. I—I have my pride."

Lady Fielding regarded her soberly for some

minutes. There was an ominous silence in the room, broken only by the relentless tick of the clock. Connie fidgeted uneasily, steadfastly lowering her eyes. Finally the old lady broke the silence.

"My daughter—Noel's mother—had little time for infants. Ever more at ease with horses and dogs. And yet Noel was passionately attached to her. It broke him completely when she ran off with Egrinton." She stopped, perceiving Connie's altered expression.

"Has not Noel told you?"

Connie shook her head, dumb with conflicting emotions.

"My dear, such a scandal as there was! The Duke was a married man, notorious for his profligacy, to be sure, but to desert a young wife, with five little ones and another on the way! . . . I loved my daughter, but her irresponsibility in the matter was indefensible."

She sighed softly. "I hoped she might regain her senses, but it was not to be. the divorce came as a crippling shock to Chievely. An eight year old is incapable of understanding such things. From that day, it was as if he had built an inner wall to insulate himself from further hurt."

She glanced keenly at Connie, but Connie's dark head remained lowered. "I was in Stockholm at the time—my husband, Sir Edward, was Ambassador—else we should have taken him at once! Consequently, Noel was reared by a succession of nurses and governesses. Is it any wonder that he should view the world, and women in particular, with cynicism?"

Connie closed her eyes, unable to trust herself to reply.

"That wall has persisted," continued Lady Fielding, softly. "I suspect you and I are the only two women who have ever been suffered to break it down. In you, Constance, my grandson found what he has sought all these years and never known—a deep, unselfish attachment, untainted by greed, and unprejudiced by knowledge of his worldly indiscretions." She paused. "Did Chievely impart to you his reason for calling upon that Frenchwoman the other day?"

Connie stiffened. "His intentions, ma'am, can be of no interest—"

"He went there," interposed Lady Fielding, quietly, "to pay her off."

The sound of wheels stopping outside reached their ears. Connie rose, her face strained and bleak. A glance confirmed that the carriage was waiting to convey her to the departure terminal of the Western Mail. Calling upon Rose to make haste, she slipped on her pelisse, fumbling at the fastening with shaking fingers.

"You truly mean to go?" Lady Fielding halfrose, agitation flooding her countenance. Hating herself, but resolved, Connie kissed the thin cheek fervently, saying, in an unsteady whisper, "It is best. I—I never shall forget your kindness—"

"I will not hear of the Mail! You—you must wait! . . . contrive to engage a post-chaise—"

The sentence was never completed. With a low moan, Lady Fielding slumped forwards in the chair, one frail hand clawing at the armrest, the other clutched to her heart, as if in the throes of a seizure.

Shouting to the maid to have Thomas send out for a doctor immediately, Connie loosened the old lady's clothing and made her comfortable as possible, although a leaden presentiment gnawed within her.

Matthews, her ladyship's personal abigail, hastened in, and with the butler's assistance Lady Fielding was helped to her own room and put to bed. Connie hovered at the window, sick with fear, willing the doctor to make haste. Noel's grandmama was still conscious, though clearly in pain, and as Matthews bent over her she made a feeble attempt to mouth a word of instruction.

"What—what does she say?" whispered Connie.

Matthews drew on the bed-curtain with a swish. "She don't wish for nobody but Mr Lawrence. He's the old physician—no new-fangled notions with him!" She regarded Connie sceptically. "I can manage her ladyship, ma'am. I knows just how to handle her."

She spoke not unkindly but Connie felt herself dismissed. There existed an obvious bond between mistress and maid, and Connie did not doubt that Matthews could cope admirably.

The sense of rejection must have evidenced itself, however, for the maid was swift to add, in a gentler tone, "I should be happy to have you sit with m'lady, ma'am, once Mr Lawrence has gone."

Connie nodded, and returned to her own bed-chamber to have Rose unpack. There could be no question of their leaving now.

It was after eight when the doctor left, giving instruction that Lord Chievely be summoned without delay. Connie thanked him dumbly and hastened to the sick-room. The interior had been darkened, its only source of light the uncertain flicker from a pair of wax candles above the chimneypiece.

Trembling with apprehension, Connie approached the bed. To her relief the Dowager's respiration seemed less laboured, but she was under heavy sedation, and the doctor had looked grave. Wordless, Connie drew a chair close to the bedside, and settled to her vigil.

Would Noel never come? As the clock struck nine, then ten, she was seized with fear. Her mind sped to all manner of disaster. When, finally, Thomas returned, to report the caretaker at Albany giving it as how Lord Chievely was departed some three hours ago bound for Epsom, she was undecided whether to feel relief or dismay.

Throughout that night, as the frail figure on the pillows waxed restless, Connie never left her side, fighting sleep so as to be alert should the least change manifest itself. Matthews urged her to go to bed, but Connie refused. An inner voice told her that she herself was responsible in no small measure for the old lady's condition. If Lady Fielding had not fretted over my going, she decided miserably, this might never have occurred.

Compulsively, her gaze was drawn to the framed likeness on the bed-table. Noel's eyes laughed back at her, cramping her heart-strings . . .

Was it truly a mere four days since their bit-

ter parting? It seemed a lifetime. In the dark of
her despair, Connie's burdened feelings were
undergoing hard appraisal. Had Noel's deception been so very heinous? Had not her own anger and slighted pride distorted the issue to
unjustifiable magnitude? And was not her prejudice, fanned by the irresponsible gossip in the
newspapers, wholly to blame for the situation?

In her heart Connie knew that it was. God
alone understood how wretched was her need
of him. But Noel's pride was as great as her
own. Never again the comforting strength of his
arms about her, the sense of absurd joy that was
hers when their eyes met across a roomful of
people, the glow of happiness at simply being
near to him. Life without Noel was a mean-
ingless existence . . . But she had sent him
away, and that was that.

She must have slept without realising, for the
next thing Connie knew was Matthews shaking
her gently, sunlight shafting through the window-curtains, and the first drays and carriages
rumbling from the Square below.

"How is she?" whispered Connie, as the
abigail bent over to examine the patient, who
had stirred, and was looking about her in confused fashion.

"She'll do." Matthews smoothed back her
mistress's snowy hair with a satisfied nod. "Now
get you to bed, Miss Osborne. I shall see to it
that you are not woke unnecessary."

Connie slept for most of that day. About four
in the afternoon, she dressed and returned to the
sick-room, with St George at her heels, to find
the doctor packing his instrument case.

He nodded a greeting, pronouncing himself
well satisfied with his patient, now fallen into a
light doze, but who earlier had downed two
bowlfuls of broth with amazing despatch.

"Is not Lord Chievely arrived yet?" demanded the doctor, whipping his hat from the
reach of St George's inquisitive jaws. "She has
been asking for him continually!"

Connie bit her lower lip. "She must not!
. . . I—I know he will come soon!" She explained about the race, and its importance to
the Earl. "But such an engagement would
never prevent his return!" she insisted warmly.
"I—I am too sensible of his character to think
otherwise."

"Then why is not he here, in God's name?"
returned the doctor, irritably, closing the case
with a snap. "Epsom is but a ride of two hours
from town. Might there be any other reason for
his lordship's absence?"

The question was put in all innocence, yet
nevertheless, Connie's colour rose dramatically.
She could form only one explanation. He refuses to return whilst I remain here, she told
herself, and the realisation brought her close to
tears.

Mechanically, she busied herself in smoothing the over-sheet.

"I—I suspect Lord Chievely has excellent reasons for delaying his return, sir," she stammered, chokily. "But you need be no longer
concerned. I have the means to remedy the situation."

He looked relieved. "Splendid! My patient
must not suffer anxiety." He lowered his voice
confidentially. "Strictly between ourselves, Lady

Fielding goes on wondrously for her years. The constitution of a veritable horse!"

A muffled sound from the bed-curtains caused his head to jerk round smartly, but Lady Fielding had merely stirred in sleep. Settling his hat, Dr Lawrence inclined briefly to Connie, adding, "I shall wait upon my patient tomorrow. Until then, Miss Osborne, I bid you good-day."

"I shall not be here," replied Connie, quietly.

Seventeen

To be at Epsom for the Derby Stakes was the goal of every right-minded Englishman, and from dawn onwards the entire length of the turnpike road through Clapham and Mitcham witnessed a slow-moving cavalcade of transport, enveloped in choking dust clouds.

All along the course, drawn up three or four deep, were carriages of every description standing without their horses, and crowded outside and in with spectators. Forming their ring on a neighbouring crest were the bookmakers, yelling the odds as the hour of the race drew near, against a cacophany of din. The weathered gibbet stump which was the Betting Post was all but obliterated to view by the chaotic press of mounted punters cursing as they fought to get near.

Peers rubbed shoulders with pie-men, pickpockets, bank clerks and ballad hawkers upon this extraordinary day which might witness fortunes being lost and won, orange peel and lobster claws flung into the crowd, and a generating of excitement unparalleled in any other event of the calendar.

Beyond stretched the Downs, green on rolling green, creating a verdant backdrop to the lively pageant being enacted on their doorstep. Atop the central rise, known to decades of race-goers as The Hill, a sea of gypsy caravans proclaimed the Fair to be in full swing, with the ensuing noise unbelievable.

Below, catching the sunlight, the colourful silks of the jockeys were a dazzling display as they walked their mounts to the saddling enclosure. On the far side, the track itself, wide and inviting ran slightly uphill for the first half mile, lined so far along by wooden rails behind which the mass of pushing humanity permeated a steady hum of anticipation into the hot June air.

Young Fanny was having the time of her life. Since arriving she had gorged herself upon marchpane and gingerbread, coaxed Uncle Maurie into watching the spangled acrobats and the Fire Eater, and seen fit to steer him firmly from the tent of a skimpily clad female in Persian pantaloons, who promised, in strong Cockney tones, to reveal to him the wonders of the Orient for twopence.

They had left the Fair and were retracing their steps when an enormous telescope attracted Fanny's eye. It was carried by a gentleman whose overgrown stylishness struck a familiar chord.

"It's Lord Chievely!" Fanny dashed forwards, uttering a shriek of delight. "And Mr Musgrave is here also!"

The Earl, approaching in company with Lord Jersey and the Duke of Grafton, excused himself and swung the child high upon his shoulder with a total disregard for dignity.

"Burn me, sir, wherever did you secure

this—this object?" hollered his Grace, staring in undisguised fascination at Mr Sibbald's spyglass.

"I pray you do not refer to my cousin's starcher, Grafton," murmured the Earl, shaking a sorrowful head at the alarming cravat of scarlet and gold. "I know, Sibbie—they are my racing colours and I am in no position to object. Ah!" he broke off, smiling.

"Here is my betrothed come to root me out, gentlemen."

He extended a hand to Miss Drinker, who had breezed up in company with her Mama, saying, "My dear, allow me to present two veritable Lions of the Turf, whose stables eclipse mine prodigiously."

Deciding not to speculate on the chances of Mrs Drinker's amiability, Mr Sibbald muttered an excuse and sought out the roan, which his cousin had furbished for his use, at Tattersall's, with the resolve to place a modest bet on the Earl's Azor.

The Betting Post was still seething with riders, but he succeeded in nosing his mount into the queue, to the accompaniment of black looks from those gentlemen unfortunate enough to be clubbed and poked from behind by the monster spy-glass.

Mr Sibbald had not the faintest understanding of Turf jargon, but he approached a knowing-looking tipster, explaining with polite caution his desire to place a small wager, and how much did the gentleman advise?

"You 'aving me on, guv?" growled the bookmaker sourly, sticking a thumb behind the belt of silver coins at his waist.

"This 'ere ain't a bleedin' stock market! Whose next?"

A howl of hisses and earthy advice persuaded Mr Sibbald that his popularity with those queuing behind had sunk dangerously low. Greatly flustered, he strove to extricate his roan from the mêlée of horseflesh pressing in on all sides.

"Great Caesar's ghost!"

The startled ejaculation broke from the rider of a long-tailed grey. Mr. Sibbald glanced round —and his spy-glass clattered to the ground. In the saddle, with a jaw hanging somewhere in the region of his middle, sat Bishop Rumbelow.

The spy-glass lay in the dust, unretrieved. But the Bishop's reaction was totally unpredicted. In a flash he had whipped his grey to a smart turnabout, and was frenziedly clearing a path through the tight crowd as though his life depended on it.

In that split second, Mr Sibbald understood with blinding clarity how his entire future hung in the balance. Upon his immediate actions rested the basis of all further relationship between himself and his dreaded senior.

Taking a deep breath, he urged his animal in pursuit, clinging on grimly as the protesting roan shied at this unexpected exercise, resolved, above all, not to lose track of the squat figure astride the grey.

A bell rang loudly, followed by thunderous cheering from the massed crowds lining the course, but Mr Sibbald was closing the gap and had eyes for nothing else. They were now well clear of the Betting Post, with the Bishop of

Upton galloping hell for leather towards the stand opposite the starting flag.

Mr Sibbald's temperamental roan, however, saw no logic in the chase, and would have slowed down but for the timely aid of a faceless urchin in the crowd. With stinging accuracy, a catapult galvanized the unwilling brute to renewed vigour. As the searing pebble connected with its rump, the roan shot forwards, emitting an enraged whicker, and baring an ugly set of teeth in a manner boding ill for the luckless grey in front.

Past the stand they flashed, nose to tail, with the Bishop lashing desperately at his animal, and Mr Sibbald feeling his insides lurch unpleasantly, when an unexpected thinning amongst the spectators offered Bishop Rumbelow a means of escape.

Over the astonished crowds he sailed, clearing the barrier-rail and on to the track, followed doggedly by Mr Sibbald, with eyes tightly shut, and a stomach which had long since deserted him.

From his position in the stand, the Earl watched Azor go strongly with the leaders. Through field glasses, he could discern the little colt manoeuvre skilfully towards the inside lane, and his interest quickened. If Brady held that position, there was a chance of pulling it off. Azor and the young Irishman worked well together; the jockey knew how to coax the best from him. Lord Chievely's spirits lifted.

Now Azor had worked to third place, behind the Duke of Richmond's bay filly, the favourite. It was as if he were bent on dispelling the lack of confidence invested in him. The Earl watched, quietly confident, when suddenly Miss Drinker uttered a gasp, and grabbed at his arm.

"Snap my garters!" she yelped. "It's . . . it's your cousin! There . . . On the track!"

With appalled horror the Earl perceived the bizarre two-horse struggle being contested farther up the field. It was undeniably Sibbald, hanging grimly to the bridle-rein of another animal, whose rider bore a more than passing resemblance to the Bishop of Upton.

"God's Teeth! They'll be mown down any second!" The Earl paled. "In the name of reason, Sibbie, get out of the way!"

Whether or not Mr Sibbald heard his cousin's hoarse shout is unrecorded. Doubtless the thundering hooves bearing down on him had greater effect, for in that instant the danger of their situation apprehended itself simultaneously to the Bishop and himself.

As one, they bolted for the safety of the barrier-rail, not drawing rein until the field, grouped tightly together, had swung round Tattenham Corner on the final lap.

"S-S-Sibbald?" Bishop Rumbelow tottered from the saddle, grappling with the painful shock of nearly swallowing his teeth. A greenish tinge enhanced his weasel face, and he had lost his wig.

They appraised each other silently, the vinegary cleric and his curate. Mr Sibbald marvelled at the incongruity, caught out, as they were, like schoolboys found pilfering apples, and each attired in a blaze of worldly decadence as must damn them irretrievably should ever their sins leak back to Lambeth Palace.

"S-Sibbald? Is it really Sibbald?"

Bishop Rumbelow was babbling, helpless to assert himself. And in that instant, Mr Sibbald struck. The Bishop listened, dazed, as his curate, displaying alarming strength of purpose, calmly uncovered those dark exploits which he had believed safe for ever.

Brighton, the gaming tables, the oglings on the Marine Parade, even that regrettable incident with the serving-wench at the American woman's—Sibbald knew it all. Bishop Rumbelow ground his teeth and forced a waxy smile.

"Ahem—let us not judge over-hastily, my boy. I have always considered you a coming man, Sibbald." He cleared his throat with difficulty. "Perhaps an increase in stipend? . . . Arrumph! In other words, I shan't nark, if you don't!"

Mr Sibbald chewed a blade of grass with leisurely deliberation. How he wished the Earl might be there to witness this triumph. Never again would this rabbity, twitching creature strike terror to his soul. Bartering for survival before him, the Bishop looked almost pathetic. But now that the worm had turned, no sympathy must be spared. From now on, decided Mr Sibbald, marvelling at his own temerity, old Rumble-belly shall dance to a very different tune!

"An excellent compromise, Bishop," he agreed, pleasantly. "As I recall, the living of Haythorpe is presently vacant. Now, if you were to speak favourably on my behalf . . ."

"By Lucifer, Chievely, you are a sly one!" commented Lord Jersey, as surrounded by jubilant well-wishers the Earl was carried in a rush to lead in his victorious colt. "You keep us in the dark till the last possible moment, then your confounded screw leaves 'em standing! One in the eye for Richmond, what?"

The Earl hardly heard. He was frowning over a message just handed to him by a steward. After the presentation he excused himself and sought out Miss Drinker, explaining that he must return immediately to town.

"My grandmother is ill. Word was sent yesterday, it seems, but by some evil chance I failed to receive it." His face was grim. "Convey my apologies to your Mama, my dear, and to Sir Maurice and the little one, should you encounter them."

So saying, he strode to the exit gate where his carriage stood waiting.

"A moment, Chievely."

Mr Frome's world-weary voice emanated from a high-flyer phaeton drawn up nearby. "My heartiest, old stick. Pity the Hampshire rose declined to make it a double for you. I discount your American acquisition—must abide strictly by the rule-book, what?"

Tilting his hat brim over his nose, Mr Frome settled back in the carriage, remarking blandly, "Eight hundred of the best, Chievely, soon as you please. Bank-bills or cheque—I have no preference."

Normally, the Earl would have countered this sneer, but he paused only to acknowledge settlement of his dues, before nosing the curricle out from the press of vehicles and driving at a furious crack towards the London road.

. . . . .

Arrived at Berkeley Square, he took the stairs three at a time to his grandmother's bedchamber. Lady Fielding lay against the pillows, eyes closed. Tiptoeing to the drapery-hung bed, Lord Chievely bent and kissed her tenderly. A hand instantly fastened on his wrist, causing him to recoil, thunderstruck.

"Grandmama! I thought you asleep!"

"Asleep—dead, what difference!" was the scathing retort. "Heavens, boy, what has delayed you? Do you suppose I am able to feign sickness indefinitely?"

Her grandson's eyebrows shot upwards. "Are you saying this seizure of yours is . . . nothing but a pretence?" he queried, faintly.

"How else would Constance have consented to remain?" snapped Lady Fielding, defiantly. "To be sure, I suffered a slight turn—nothing to signify, and that old fool Lawrence has not the wit to see how I was spinning it out." Her eyes kindled. "Constitution of a horse, indeed! How dare he?"

The Earl was staring at her intently. "Constance is—here?"

His relative glared. "I do not profess to work miracles, young man! Of a certainty she is not! Did you expect her to be?"

She put on her spectacles and surveyed him with a scrutiny bordering on hope. "I am wholly ignorant of the contents of her letter, but it has brought you back with devastating alacrity!"

The Earl took Connie's letter from his pocket, and passed it to her, saying in muffled tones, "Where may I find her, Grandmama?"

"At this precise hour?" Lady Fielding glanced

up from her perusal of the crossed and closely worded script. "I should judge Constance to be anywhere between Hounslow and Staines."

She returned the letter, saying, firmly, "And if you are possessed of a measure of intellect, Chievely, you may read into these lines essentially more than meets the eye!"

Connie recalled her gaze from the last straggling cottages of Hartley Row flashing past the carriage window. They had been on the road just over four hours. Four hours in which despair and self-recrimination had chased turbulently through her mind, leaving her sorrowing.

She longed to stretch her cramped limbs, having had no opportunity to do so since stopping for dinner at Bagshot. A disapproving sniff from the travelling companion at her elbow, however, caused her to abandon the attempt. Miss Digweed was an uncommunicative maiden lady, journeying in company with her brother, a bragging half-pay major of Dragoons, whom Connie suspected to be rather less asleep than he pretended.

She blushed guiltily at these uncharitable reflections. It was, after all, generous that they should allow her to share their chaise as far as Basingstoke.

How she and Rose were to accomplish the distance beyond Basingstoke, Connie had not yet determined. She had jumped at the offer of sharing, for to await the availability of a private chaise would have entailed a delay of some hours. Such, she learned ruefully, was the penalty for desiring to travel on Derby day.

Leaning forward to exchange a word with her maid, Connie found her words drowned in the sudden thunder of hooves. A private chariot, drawn by four sweating post-horses, was momentarily framed in the carriage window. She glimpsed the blur of a crest on its door-panel, the peaked cap of a post-boy astride the leader, then the vehicle was swallowed into the dusk.

Twenty minutes later, the chaise carrying Connie and her travelling companions swept into the yard of the White Hart, at Hook, in or-der to change horses. In the one minute al-lowed for this lightning operation, a tall figure wrested open the carriage door and sprang lithely inside, depositing the astonished Rose into the lap of a gratified Major Digweed, and taking her place opposite Connie.

"Noel!" Connie's bemused exclamation be-came submerged in a blood-curdling shriek from Miss Digweed, as the chaise rocked for-wards once more, under the impetus of a fresh team.

"Murder!" screamed the spinster, convinced of being at the mercy of a blackguard highway-man. Her brother, for whom the journey had brightened considerably, rudely ordered her to be silent, which had the effect of prompting Miss Digweed to further octaves of hysteria.

Totally ignoring this scenario, Lord Chievely leaned forward urgently and shouted something unintelligible to Connie's ear.

"I said—'*Will you marry me?*'" roared his lordship, so violently that Miss Digweed shot al-most a foot in the air, in mid cry, and her brother abruptly left off pawing the struggling Rose.

Uncaring as to who might see, the Earl sought and found Connie's unresisting hand, tucking it firmly in his own, his eyes burning into hers with an intensity that caused her to tremble, even as her heart surged upwards in an ecstasy of happiness.

"But—but what of Lizzie-May?" she stammered, hardly trusting herself to reply. Two bright spots of colour burned her cheeks, and she sensed rather than saw the enraged scandalisation of the major's sister, who was making choking sounds in the corner.

"My adorable goose, Miss Drinker is hoping like Hades you will take me off her hands, so that she may honorably leg it for the altar with her Bertram, before Mama has power to stop 'em! The gallant hero dropped anchor at Cork last week, and by now I daresay, has already posted from Falmouth with the fixed intention of blowing my brains out!"

He favoured her with his familiar, impudent smile. "I intend to abduct you, Bright-Eyes, whether or not you choose, so—Confound this infernal noise!" he expostulated, as the spinster's howl of execration effectively obliterated any hopes of further exchange.

Sticking his head out the carriage window, the Earl ordered the post-boy to pull up, in terms which brooked no argument.

"Now, my girl," he declared, when they were descended, and his own chariot, which had been following closely behind, was come up, and Rose bundled briskly inside along with her mistress's trunk. "We have but one matter to settle."

Drawing Connie firmly towards him, he gazed deeply into her hesitant face. "Please, Constance . . . Grant me a second chance. I love you to distraction, dearest, and if you will not have me, I—I simply do not know how the devil I shall bear it."

"Noel . . ."

At that crack in the voice of the man she loved, Connie's uncertainty fled. In full view of her maid, the Digweeds, post-boys and anyone else who cared to observe, she turned up her mouth to receive his kiss.

Some fifteen minutes later, with the post-chaise bearing Miss Digweed and her attack of the vapours long lost to view, and Rose departed in the Earl's chariot to await their return at the White Hart half a mile back, Connie sat by the grassy verge, with Noel's arm securely about her, and her head resting blissfully under his chin.

"And tomorrow Monksford shall welcome the restoration of its rightful master," she murmured softly, as together they watched the last fiery blush of sunset dip behind the distant trees. "It seems incredible that I should ever have wished—"

She turned in his arms, adding hesitantly, "Noel—I did truly mean every word of my letter."

He cupped her face close. "About selling to me? And did you honestly imagine that I could be happy living at Monksford without you?"

Sternly, he looked into her upturned countenance. "Well?"

"It was my one hope," confessed Miss Osborne, disarmingly frank. "But, oh Noel . . . I have been so miserable."

"I have grieved you abominably," he said, soberly. "And for that, I can never forgive myself. But, Connie, you must not—you cannot believe that my farcical betrothal to your friend was anything other than a ruse to placate Mrs Drinker? Do you seriously imagine I would deliberately hurt you so?"

"I . . . I knew not what to conclude." Connie pondered his words, her brow wrinkling slightly. "But, Noel—how is Lizzie-May to manage? She inherits nothing until she comes of age. Surely her cousin is in no position to support a wife?"

"A little privation will test the strength of their feelings for each other. But do not be over-concerned, Bright-Eyes. I intend offering Bertram the management of the new stud farm I have long been planning. It just happens to be in Virginia," he added, smiling.

"Noel!" Connie flung her arms about his neck. "You are arranging this purposely for them—I know it! Why . . . what have you there?"

He had withdrawn from his packet a long, folded paper. Together they examined it. Connie had never before seen a special licence, but she was well aware of its significance.

"As I was obtaining a licence for Miss Drinker I noticed there might be no harm in securing another—just in case. You do realise this entitles us to be wed whenever and wherever we choose?" Tenderly, he kissed her on the nose.

"I'd marry you this very night if it were practical—but I know you will wish to have Grandmama and your uncle present, and the little one as bride-maid. We shall send word from the White Hart—lord, yes, and Sibbie must be told, and Miss Drinker, too!"

"And there is the fatted calf to kill, and the whole estate turned en fête to celebrate our nuptials!" laughed Connie.

He grinned boyishly. "Would next week be too soon for you, little love? I do have your ring—Miss Drinker helped me choose it and this time, I think, it will fit properly."

Connie's delighted gasp was all the assent required. Naturally, so felicitous an undertaking required suitable demonstrations of approval, and they were accomplishing this to their mutual satisfaction, when flying hooves and a blaring horn heralded the approach of a stage, painted chocolate, bedaubed all over in gilt letters, a Saracen's head on the hind boot, and packed outside and in with passengers, every one of which hooted enthusiastically in passing at seeing rustic pleasures being so ardently enjoyed.

"Deuce take 'em!" declared his lordship, releasing Connie with a stricken expression. "Am I never to be permitted to make love to you without grooms, post-boys, hysterical spinsters and Lord knows what else staring us out of countenance? I hope you realise, my girl, that every passenger aboard the Regulator will have the White Hart by the ears with accounts of how I have tumbled you in the hedgerows!"

"Do not dare to disillusion them, pray!" dimpled Connie, shaking a wisp of grass from her hair. "I feel so shockingly abandoned, my dearest lord, that it is as well you intend making an honest woman of me."

"I like the sound of that admission!" murmured Lord Chievely, with his most roguish twinkle, drawing her to her feet. "Excessively!"

About the Author

Roseleen Milne is a young writer from Aberdeen. Though BORROWED PLUMES is her first novel, in 1974 she was honored with an award by the Scottish Association of Writers. She has long been fascinated by the Georgian era, and is now at work on a second Regency novel.

More Big Bestsellers from SIGNET

☐ **THE RULING PASSION** by Shaun Herron.
(#E8042—$2.25)

☐ **CONSTANTINE CAY** by Catherine Dillon.
(#J8307—$1.95)

☐ **WHITE FIRES BURNING** by Catherine Dillon.
(#J8281—$1.95)

☐ **THE WHITE KHAN** by Catherine Dillon.
(#J8043—$1.95)*

☐ **KID ANDREW CODY AND JULIE SPARROW** by Tony Curtis.
(#E8010—$2.25)*

☐ **WINTER FIRE** by Susannah Leigh. (#E8011—$2.25)*

☐ **THE MESSENGER** by Mona Williams. (#J8012—$1.95)

☐ **LOVING SOMEONE GAY** by Don Clark.
(#J8013—$1.95)

☐ **FEAR OF FLYING** by Erica Jong. (#E7970—$2.25)

☐ **HOW TO SAVE YOUR OWN LIFE** by Erica Jong.
(#E7959—$2.50)*

☐ **HARVEST OF DESIRE** by Rochelle Larkin.
(#E8183—$2.25)

☐ **MISTRESS OF DESIRE** by Rochelle Larkin.
(#E7964—$2.25)*

☐ **THE FIRES OF GLENLOCHY** by Constance Heaven.
(#E7452—$1.75)

☐ **A PLACE OF STONES** by Constance Heaven.
(#W7046—$1.50)

☐ **THE QUEEN AND THE GYPSY** by Constance Heaven.
(#J7965—$1.95)

☐ **THE CHILDREN ARE DYING** by Ned O'Gorman.
(#E7960—$1.75)

☐ **DR. ATKINS' SUPER ENERGY COOKBOOK** by Fran Gare and Helen Monica, Introduction by Dr. Robert C. Atkins,
(#E7942—$2.25)*

☐ **TORCH SONG** by Anne Roiphe. (#J7901—$1.95)

☐ **OPERATION URANIUM SHIP** by Dennis Eisenberg, Eli Landau, and Menahem Portugali. (#E8001—$1.75)

*Price slightly higher in Canada

Have You Read These Bestsellers from SIGNET?

☐ **NIXON VS. NIXON** by Dr. David Abrahamsen.
(#E7902—$2.25)

☐ **ISLAND OF THE WINDS** by Athena Dallas-Damis.
(#J7905—$1.95)

☐ **CARRIE** by Stephen King. (#J7280—$1.95)

☐ **'SALEM'S LOT** by Stephen King. (#E8000—$2.25)

☐ **THE SHINING** by Stephen King. (#E7872—$2.50)

☐ **SLEEP POSITIONS: The Night Language of the Body** by
Dr. Samuel Dunkell. (#E7875—$2.25)

☐ **OAKHURST** by Walter Reed Johnson. (#J7874—$1.95)

☐ **FRENCH KISS** by Mark Logan. (#J7876—$1.95)

☐ **COMA** by Robin Cook. (#E8202—$2.50)

☐ **THE YEAR OF THE INTERN** by Robin Cook.
(#E7674—$1.75)

☐ **CALDO LARGO** by Earl Thompson. (#E7737—$2.25)

☐ **A GARDEN OF SAND** by Earl Thompson.
(#E8039—$2.50)

☐ **TATTOO** by Earl Thompson. (#E8038—$2.50)

☐ **MISTRESS OF DARKNESS** by Christopher Nicole.
(#J7782—$1.95)

☐ **DESIRES OF THY HEART** by Joan Carroll Cruz.
(#J7738—$1.95)

☐ **THE ACCURSED** by Paul Boorstin. (#E7745—$1.75)

☐ **THE RICH ARE WITH YOU ALWAYS** by Malcolm Mac-
donald. (#E7682—$2.25)

☐ **THE WORLD FROM ROUGH STONES** by Malcolm Mac-
donald. (#J6891—$1.95)

☐ **THE FRENCH BRIDE** by Evelyn Anthony.
(#J7683—$1.95)

☐ **TELL ME EVERYTHING** by Marie Brenner.
(#J7685—$1.95)

NAL/ABRAMS' BOOKS
ON ART, CRAFT AND SPORTS
in beautiful, large format, special concise editions—lavishly illustrated with many full-color plates.

☐ **THE ART OF WALT DISNEY: From Mickey Mouse to the Magic Kingdoms** by Christopher Finch. (#G9982—$7.95)

☐ **DISNEY'S AMERICA ON PARADE: A History of the U.S.A. in a Dazzling, Fun-Filled Pageant,** text by David Jacobs. (#G9974—$7.95)

☐ **FREDERIC REMINGTON** by Peter Hassrick. (#G9980—$6.95)

☐ **GRANDMA MOSES** by Otto Kallir. (#G9981—$6.95)

☐ **THE POSTER IN HISTORY** by Max Gallo. (#G9976—$7.95)

☐ **THE SCIENCE FICTION BOOK: An Illustrated History** by Franz Rottensteiner. (#G9978—$6.95)

☐ **NORMAN ROCKWELL: A Sixty Year Retrospective** by Thomas S. Buechner. (#G9969—$7.95)

☐ **THE PRO FOOTBALL EXPERIENCE** edited by David Boss, with an Introduction by Roger Kahn. (#G9984—$6.95)

☐ **THE DOLL** text by Carl Fox, photographs by H. Landshoff. (#G9987—$5.95)

☐ **DALI . . . DALI . . . DALI . . .** edited and arranged by Max Gérard. (#G9983—$6.95)

☐ **THOMAS HART BENTON** by Matthew Baigell. (#G9979—$6.95)

☐ **THE WORLD OF M. C. ESCHER** by M. C. Escher and J. L. Locher. (#G9970—$7.95)

THE NEW AMERICAN LIBRARY, INC.,
P.O. Box 999, Bergenfield, New Jersey 07621

Please send me the books I have checked above. I am enclosing $_____ (check or money order—no currency or C.O.D.'s). Please include the list price plus the following amounts per copy for postage and handling: 35¢ for SIGNETS; 50¢ for ABRAMS. Prices and numbers are subject to change without notice.

Name_____

Address_____

City_____State_____Zip Code_____
Allow at least 4 weeks for delivery